D1068317

Prince Undercover

To my favorite journalist,
Fareed Zakaria, with
best wishes for a happy
and fulfilled life
Ashraf
1-27-2022

Prince Undercover

ASHRAF HABBAK

This is a work of fiction. All of the characters, names, incidents, organizations, and dialogue in this novel are either the products of the author's imagination or are used fictitiously.

Archway Publishing books may be ordered through booksellers or by contacting:

Archway Publishing
1663 Liberty Drive
Bloomington, IN 47403
www.archwaypublishing.com
844-669-3957

ISBN: 978-1-6657-1239-2 (sc)
ISBN: 978-1-6657-1240-8 (hc)
ISBN: 978-1-6657-1241-5 (e)

Library of Congress Control Number: 2021919147

Print information available on the last page.

Archway Publishing rev. date: 12/06/2021

Contents

Prologue

Zomorod, Terra Qurayshia
2 months ago

Crown Prince Sultan Qurayshi adjusted the neck of his thawb. He had to keep the flowing headdress away from his face for when he stepped into the room.

One of his security retinue announced his presence. "All rise for his majesty, beloved of the nation, Prince Qurayshi."

All those seated at the conference-room table rose and stood at attention. Qurayshi walked in and sat at the head of the table, and then the others resumed their seats.

"Gentlemen," he said, "let us begin this meeting of the Royal Strategic Committee. Welcome Faisal, Abdulaziz, Bandar, Abdulkareem, and Morgan." Qurayshi faced and nodded at each of them as he said their name. "His Royal Highness, King Farhan, is quite concerned." The prince paused and let his gaze wander over them. It held both power and menace. "This should go without saying, but it is not good for anyone when the king is concerned."

A small rumble of anxious whispers rolled across the table. Faisal put up his hand, and all eyes turned to him. Some fixated on his salt-and-pepper beard, too timid to meet his powerful gaze, but others, equal players in the game of realpolitik, met his eyes straight on with power of their own.

"What is it in our wonderful kingdom that would so trouble His Royal Majesty, my prince?"

The prince frowned. "Resistance to change. Every now and again, a nation gets a king who dreams about more than himself and wishes to better everything for the people and for the future generations to come. Those kings are rarely relaxed."

He cleared his throat. "In fact, I might suggest that there are those within this room who might oppose at least some of what our king is doing." His eyes wandered over each of them, searching.

A wave of protestations arose from the table. The prince held up a hand and waited for them to dissipate.

"What changes are being opposed?" Faisal asked. "My sources among the people say that King Farhan's reforms have been met with open arms. Free quality education? An overall and modernization of our nation's infrastructure? An opening of the private sector to foreign investment? These have all been lauded by the people. Even now, I expect some are busily hanging the king's portrait up on their bedroom walls."

Qurayshi nodded. "So it is. And even the new focus on creating an advanced chemical sector and opening up academies of science, alongside vast scientific research grants. Our king is a dreamer and he is doing many things. But his political reforms; let's just say that there are a lot of powerful people in the kingdom who might not agree with putting the reins of government into the hands of the peasants." Qurayshi spat the last word.

Faisal frowned while the rest of the men shifted awkwardly in their seats. "Are you unhappy?" he asked.

Qurayshi shrugged. "It is the right move. Just unfortunate timing. I would have liked to have enjoyed my own period of absolute rule before letting it go to everyone else."

The rest of the committee chuckled along with him, tension splitting like the frayed strings of an ancient violin.

"Our agents have done well in tracking the resistance. We know who believes what, and we have our fingers on the pulse of every organization that opposes the king. A somewhat ironic solution to our efforts to give free speech and power to the people."

A lesser chuckling pattered through the room.

"It is what it must be," Faisal said. "The operation has been a complete success, with none of our agents found out or exposed to the public. I assume the king has been reading our reports?"

"He has," the prince affirmed.

"Then I don't understand what is troubling him. Everything is going just as planned."

"The royal family wants him, or else his power, removed. Not all of them, of course. But most."

"They want to clip his wings?" Morgan asked. He uncharacteristically took off his sunglasses to reveal ice-blue Gallacian eyes deep set in the lined, deep tan of someone who spent far too much time in the sun.

"Didn't we predict this would happen, though?" Bandar asked at about the same time. His own pale skin ran opposite to Morgan's deep rich copper. He looked almost like a ghost. "We monitor them, clip their wings, and use the taken feathers to strengthen the king's. Not a hard thing to do, making the king's wings bigger."

Abdulkareem, a man with hard brown eyes and a small mouth, simply nodded and kept his peace. Next to him, Abdulaziz drummed long fingers on the tabletop before him. "What do you think, Your Royal Highness?"

Sultan Qurayshi stood up but held his hand up when the others started to do the same. "Please stay seated. I just wish to make it clear that I fully support His Royal Highness King Farhan in his views and plans. I share his thinking that the best course of action is to move our country to a more democratic society and achieve technological advances while following Islamic principles. But I do also feel that we have to respect the natural order of things if we wish to continue our financial prosperity. Also, I should add that I do not appreciate having my loyalty questioned."

Abdulaziz's eyes widened. "Of course, I understand. What

I meant was, what is the opinion of those opposing His Royal Highness King Farhan's views?"

"Well, they see that the world around us is changing and swinging back toward a more autocratic society, a society like the one we had before the king's reforms. And they question why we would change a good system for one that even the countries that tried it do not favor. They say that this proves that it is best to have an autocratic society to flourish economically and technologically. They argue that Arlandica, the current superpower of the world and most democratic, has proven that their system is ineffective, economically and politically. They see that giving employees protection through unions and labor laws has only made their system inefficient and slower to respond to crises and fast world changes and threats. They argue that you cannot have an agile, rapidly advancing, and democratic society at the same time. You have to sacrifice one of them. Their views are shared by many others from all over the world. They say that we must turn back before it is too late, that we must return to who we were to become great again. All through the world, nations are struggling—this truly is a worldwide political movement. Not just one of our own nation."

Sultan Qurayshi paused, both of his palms on the table, his gaze locked on somewhere unseen. Faisal traded nervous eye contact with the other men in the room and whispered into Morgan's ear, "That is not the look of a man who opposes such ideology."

Morgan regarded him with frightened, glassy eyes.

Sultan Qurayshi shook his head as if to rid himself of an errant fly, then lifted his hands from the table. "We have to be strong and determined. We must strengthen the mandate and powers of the king so we can deal swiftly and harshly with those opposing our views. I have submitted an emergency clause to our legislature that, in a time of crisis, will give back to the king all of the newly founded powers of legislature and presidency. I expect your support in passing it. There are too many powerful enemies without, and too many within, for us to trust in the fledgling powers of the new republic."

"So for the sake of democracy, we must allow democracy to be suspended?" Faisal asked, his voice an almost whisper.

"It is the way of the world," the prince said with an apologetic shrug.

Silence dominated the room.

Chapter 1

Zomorod, Terra Qurayshia
Now

Forty minutes before dawn on a cold and windy morning, Faisal Qurayshi snored softly despite the ruckus outside his window. Gusts blew strong and the palm trees swayed as blasts of cool, dewy air swept the streets of Zomorod.

His phone rattled and buzzed on the dresser near his bed and his snores softened to a sigh. He reached out and felt around, his eyes gummy with sleep, he grabbed the device and accepted the call.

"Hello?"

"*Abou,* Mansour, meet me at the airport in half an hour," the voice on the other end of the line said.

Faisal knew that voice. More than knew it, he realized. Urgency struck through the cobwebs in his head. That voice was family–Bandar Qurayshi, his cousin. And if Bandar was calling, things were urgent indeed.

"My helicopter will be ready," Bandar whispered.

"Have you confirmed the information you told me yesterday?" Faisal asked.

"Yes, I have. We have to leave immediately. We only have one hour at the most. After that, it will be too late," Bandar said.

Faisal frowned. "What about my son? I cannot leave him."

"Isn't he now in Jumairah?"

"Yes, he is. Can we pick him up?"

Bandar snorted. "There isn't time. He's in the opposite direction of where we're going. We are heading northeast, to Manara, Nactar. It's much better for him to drive to the Port of

Ziba and take a ferry to Port Zanobia in Keerypt. He can use his Arlandican passport."

Faisal wasn't happy, but he understood. There was no choice. He was probably already running late as it was. He had to leave his son and, all things considered, it might be better that way.

"Stay safe, cousin. I will be there shortly." Faisal ended the call without waiting for an answer, instead scrolling through his digital phone book directory until he found and selected Mansour.

The phone buzzed as he waited. Mansour soon picked up.

"Dad?" Mansour sounded newly awakened and a little confused, but Faisal heard the clarion ring of wakefulness. His son knew something was up.

"You need to leave now, my son. Get your Arlandican passport. I won't have time to meet up with you, so just drive to the Port of Ziba," Faisal said. "Take the ferry across, and I'll see you there."

There was a pause on the line, and Faisal strained to listen. Was the connection broken?

At last Mansour answered, his voice cracking fearfully. "I'm worried about you Dad, please be careful. I love you."

"I love you too, Mansour. Stay safe. We'll be in touch *in shaa Allah*," Faisal said.

"God willing," Mansour repeated.

Faisal grabbed his large rucksack, already packed for just this occasion, and ran outside to meet his fate.

Mansour held the phone to his ear even though the call had ended. The time was here, now, and he wasn't ready. Not at all. Would they all be safe? Would they all make it out alive? A hundred questions boiled in his head, but he didn't bother to ask them out loud. God willing, there would be time for such later. He sighed.

So what now? They'd rehearsed this scenario several times. It was time to call Sheikh Hassan. He was the big man at Arlandica International Project Management (AIPM), the consulting company where Mansour worked, and more importantly, he was the custodian of all of the expats' passports. Expats like Mansour himself. He needed to get his Arlandican passport, and Sheikh Hassan was the only one on duty with any access to them.

"Call Sheikh Hassan," he told the device.

"Dialing Sheikh Hassan," it answered.

The phone rang and rang but finally clicked on just before it would've gone to voicemail. A gruff voice coughed and muttered unintelligible words. Mansour covered the phone and chuckled despite the gravity of the situation. These were not the mutterings of a happy man.

"*Assalamu alaikum*, Sheikh Hassan. I'm sorry to have called you this early."

"Peace be upon you too," Hassan answered in Arabic. "Mansour, are you okay? What time is it? Shouldn't you be in bed?"

Mansour sighed into the phone. "I would never have called you so early if it wasn't so important. There's an emergency. My dad is very sick in Keerypt, and I need to go and see him now before it's too late. I understand he might not have long to live, so I need to leave within half an hour. I need to get my passport, please."

Hassan sounded shocked. "I will do this for you, my brother. Meet me at the office in twenty minutes. I'll get you your passport and things, and don't worry about missing work. I will explain everything."

"Thank you, Hassan. I owe you."

"Just hurry, Mansour. See you soon!"

Mansour set down the phone and grabbed two full suitcases from the floor. He'd been prepared to flee, but there was still time to be careful. He threw both open and quickly examined their contents. It was all there—his most important belongings, his inhaler, asthma and allergy medications, some clothes, and all his cash. Satisfied, he snapped them shut and then jogged over to the bathroom. While he had a little time now, it was more than likely that he soon wouldn't. He used the bathroom, then made his ablutions before glancing at his watch.

Time to hurry up. He was taking too long.

He cut off his morning rituals early and grabbed his luggage before flinging open the door into the windy gusts of the eventful day. It was just a short walk to his bulky red subcompact, and it wasn't long before he was on the road and heading to the office to meet Hassan. The dim morning light showed no traffic on the street, and he made it to his workplace in record time. Pulling into the parking lot of AIPM, he slammed the car into park but left it running as he sprinted into the lobby. Sheikh Hassan was waiting there for him, disheveled and with bleary eyes, but holding his passport.

"Mansour, you look very pale. I'm sorry for your situation. It is really bad. Do you need any help? Is there anything I can do for you?" Sheikh Hassan's words stumbled over themselves, but Mansour shook his head.

"Thank you for asking, Sheikh Hassan, but I only need my passport"—he hesitated—"and my visas. Then I'll be on my way to see my dad."

Hassan sighed. "Mansour, I have your passport here, but I didn't get you the exit and re-entry visas. I can't give you them because I can find no record of an approved vacation or emergency leave form in the system. Did this problem with your father come up just recently? Have you called the boss and requested it?"

Mansour reached for his passport and apologized for his lack of patience. "This is an emergency. It came up out of the blue, and there is just no time. I have to leave, no matter what."

Hassan nodded. "I'm not sure the passport will be useful without the visas. In any case, just take it for now, and when you get to the airport, if you have any problems, call me from there. We will see what we can do."

Mansour thanked Sheikh Hassan, got his passport, and ran back to his car. He plopped down into the seat and stomped on the accelerator. The local streets still had no traffic, but it wouldn't be long before that changed. He stuffed a hand into his pocket, grasped his phone, and yanked it out.

"Call Dad," he said. The phone complied. It took just two rings before his father answered.

"Mansour?"

"Dad, I'm on my way now. Where are you?" Mansour asked.

"We are in the helicopter now and getting ready to take off for Manara," Faisal said. "Things are looking good, my son. Hold on, there seems to be a problem." The measured three-round burst of military rifles crackled in the background.

"Dad, what's going on?" Mansour exclaimed. "I'm hearing some loud noises. Is that gunfire?"

"There's some sort of battle going on outside. Bandar's guards are taking fire. I can't see who they are fighting, but there's a lot of shooting!" Faisal yelled over the background noise. "Don't be alarmed, though. Bandar's guards have entered the chopper, and we're lifting off. We are in the air now."

Mansour sighed, relieved, and lifted up his head while clutching the phone to his right ear. "Listen. I will be—" A very loud noise cut him off. Was that an explosion?

"Dad, what was that? Are you okay?" Mansour asked.

No reply. The call had disconnected. Mansour tried calling his dad again. No answer. His father's phone was off. Mansour looked down, feeling both frozen and steaming. A chilly, burning sensation coursed through his spine and into his brain.

"Oh God! Oh God! Oh God!" he screamed.

Mansour took a deep, steadying breath and tried to keep the shock at bay. He had to control himself and get out of his own situation. There'd be time to find out what had actually happened later.

He sped toward the Port of Ziba, putting miles and nearly an hour behind him, his barely awake mind a fresh whirlwind. He made the exit onto the highway west and eased his foot back off the pedal when he realized he was well over the limit. Too much was at stake here to be pulled over for something stupid like speeding.

Five minutes down the road, however, things began to look rather shady. He spotted a police checkpoint up ahead, and they were stopping every vehicle as they came through. But what were they doing here? He definitely wasn't speeding. It didn't matter, though. As he got closer he could see that the police officers were not just stopping cars but also randomly searching them.

He couldn't risk going through. They couldn't stop and search him. Mansour breathed heavily, his body drenched in a sudden sweat. He instinctively clutched his phone before realizing that he had no one to call. At least, not right now. He was on his own now. Alone and terrified.

Mansour let go of the phone and pinched his arm. Was he dreaming? The sharp pain of twisted skin assured him that he was not.

"No," Mansour whined as the checkpoint came closer. "This is real. It's all real. I'm not imagining a thing. This is real; I am real, and I'm doomed. I wish I were de–" He paused on that last word. It wasn't unlikely that he might be very soon. Five-twenty in the morning, and everything was falling apart before his eyes. Ideas fluttered through his head at breakneck speed. Yet there was nothing he could think to do. Almost nothing.

"God, please help me. Please help me," Mansour begged out loud.

He tried to blink some brainpower into being.

The checkpoint drew closer and closer. He couldn't simply assume that the police here were sloppy, gullible, and corrupt.

Mansour groaned. He had no guarantee they were the kind of police that he could bluff or bribe his way past.

That was grief talking, though. His father might be dead, and the mission might be suddenly null and void, but he had to ensure his own safety. You cannot take shortcuts and expect things to work out, he remembered his grandmother saying. The words echoed from the dinner table, one that he'd never again share with his father. No shortcuts; just do what must be done, and let Allah decide the rest.

The metallic squawk of a speaker interrupted his reverie. "*Allahu Akbar!*" it proclaimed. "Allah is great! I bear witness . . ."

The *Azan*! The call to the dawn *Fajr* prayer! There was no better time. Mansour sent thanks above. Allah provides, he thought. It was up to the people to make use of the blessings at the time that He bestowed them. Mansour searched the sides of the roads. There!

A family had pulled their car over and was situating their mats, getting ready to pray. Mansour pulled out of the checkpoint line and parked his car behind theirs. He got out, pulled his own mat from the back seat, then held it up and nodded to the oldest man in the group. The grandfather tugged on his graying beard and nodded. Mansour's heart leaped, and he walked briskly over, joining them in their prescribed prayer.

When the prayer finished, he thanked the family, who began to pull up their mats and board their vehicle, but he stayed put, preparing for an even more special prayer, a *duaa* for his father, supplicating with his palms up to the heavens as taught by Prophet Muhammad (peace be upon Him).

"*Al-Rahman, Al-Raheem, Al-Khaliq,*" he began. "You are most merciful and exalted. Oh Allah, I beseech you. Please allow for my father to survive. He is a good man, and he has spent his life doing great things for all the people of the kingdom. He gives so much and never asks for anything in recompense. Bless all the people of the world, and help those who deserve such grace."

He finished and got ready to stand but felt the firm pressure of a hand grasp his right shoulder. He glanced up in shock. It belonged to one of the police officers! His hand curled, and he shifted his weight beneath him, then relaxed when he spied the friendly face beneath the cap—his neighbor Zohair.

"That was a beautiful prayer, Mansour. Allah will provide," the small man said. He helped him up and walked with him back to his car. As they walked, he whispered, "Mansour, why do you have a warrant out for your arrest? What is going on? What have you done?"

Mansour kept his face friendly, though his insides turned to ice. This had to be another opportunity. Allah would not give him to the authorities. He remembered again the conversation of long ago, the talk of the oppressive regimes and the ills that it caused. This must be a test!

"Zohair, why would I have a warrant? You know me. I always try to be a good man who does good things. I would never be a thief. I don't understand what this is all about."

"Allah frowns on spying, Mansour. The warrant is for espionage. Are you a spy?"

Fresh sweat erupted and he failed to suppress a shiver. He prayed Zohair wouldn't notice, or think anything of it. After all, it was a cool morning. Mansour had to think of a way through, and fast.

"Espionage?" he asked. "There must be a better explanation. Perhaps my father's connections in government have made me an enemy." He applauded within his mind. This was not a lie. That may well have happened!

They reached his vehicle, and Zohair peered into his eyes. Mansour kept his gaze straight forward. To look away now would be a sign of guilt.

Zohair sighed. "Yes, it is silly. The arrest warrant is local rather than national, which backs up your idea of an enemy above. Why would a spy be wanted only by a single province? And really, now that I'm here talking to you, I laugh to think about it. Who would you be spying on? Your business associates?" He laughed.

Mansour laughed as well, even as the icy chill of fear swept away from his body to be replaced by quaky relief. "Yeah, hey, don't laugh so hard," Mansour chided. "I could be James Bond, if I wanted to."

Zohair looked him up and down. "Maybe—but you'd have to be more soldier and less civilian. Double-oh-seven really isn't your thing, my friend. Anyways, I am glad I was able to talk with you here. What are you doing driving out this way, anyways?"

Mansour's face dropped. "My father is very sick, and I must leave the country to get to his side at the hospital. But I haven't had time to get my passport together. I don't know what to do, but I know I have to go to him."

Zohair nodded. "The paperwork wouldn't finish until after your father has passed, I expect. Arlandica has changed a lot in the last decade. And now that the president is declaring emergency powers—"

"What!" Mansour asked, surprised. If he'd been drinking anything, he certainly would've done a spit take and covered Zohair. Another tiny blessing.

"They had another terrorist attack, and now he's mobilizing Arlandican military inside the borders." He shook his head sadly. "Just like a dictator. Ah, yes, big things are happening in government now. The president's suspending the judiciary for the moment, and arresting anyone in Congress with connections to the Middle East. I wish you luck . . . though I doubt that anyone will wonder about your lack of an updated passport. I suspect Arlandicans all over will be waived through in deference to this chaos."

Mansour had no words to convey the perfect storm inside him. "This is . . . the timing . . ."

"With the overthrow at the palace here?" Zohair considered this. "Yes, very suspicious."

Dread swept over Mansour. The crown prince had overthrown the king. The attack on Bandar made a great deal more sense now.

"I heard your *duaa,* and I feel for your father. You have a lot of love for him. I will do what I can to help. The police checkpoint will only stay until the end of the hour. Turn back and park somewhere before anyone else sees you. There should be a rest stop a few miles from here. Then come back through in another"—he checked his watch—"forty minutes. We should all be gone by then."

Tears sprang to Mansour's eyes. "I appreciate this. Allah bless you, Zohair. I will do as you say."

"Allah's blessing be onto you as well, my friend. Good luck and safe travels. Oh, and one more thing—we did not discuss any of this, all right?"

"Discuss what?" Mansour asked.

Zohair smiled, turned on his well-polished heels, and walked back toward the checkpoint.

Mansour headed for that rest stop.

Chapter 2

Sunland, Arlandica
16 years ago

"I will not have my only son become a spy!"

Mansour froze in the midst of throwing the trash into the garbage can. He hadn't heard that right. His father, first of all, was a man well known for his kindness and gentle disposition. Mansour couldn't recall the last time he'd heard his father raise his voice. He was in the midst of this silent rumination when his father's voice drifted out over the large backyard again, and around the garage, where he was hidden from his father's view and this intimate conversation.

"You must have others who are better trained for such an assignment." A pause. "I understand Uncle is unwell, but you are not yet upon the throne."

So he hadn't misheard his father at all.

This time when Faisal Al-Qurayshi spoke, it was with a resigned chuckle. "You and your hundred-year plan. Yes, you know I approve. No, I have said, and I will say again, I don't think it foolish. Yes, of course, the plan on the whole seems just what the country needs. But . . ."

Mansour had already heard too much. A peek around the corner found his father near the driveway gate, which separated the sprawling front yard from the spacious backyard and four car garage. He had three choices, as he saw it. One, dart across the yard, onto the deck, and back into the house the way he'd come with the hope his father wouldn't notice him. Two, remain here and hope his father, who was a roving phone-talker, wouldn't come around the side of the garage to where the trash was kept.

Three, he could walk out in full view of his father and let him know he'd heard the unbelievable.

The Qur'an surely had a verse on eavesdropping and dozens on the truth, but the enormity and the alienness of the situation stole all the thoughts out of Mansour's mind. Indecision gripped him. If only he hadn't thoughtlessly jumped into the shower in the middle of cooking himself breakfast and nearly set his house on fire.

Then again . . . would ignorance have been better than this, whatever this situation now was?

"You do not think it dangerous?" his father asked. Mansour had seen and heard the softening tone a hundred times; Faisal was coming around to what the other man was saying.

The situation fell into place in Mansour's mind at last. A spy. A secret agent. His father was plainly talking with Mansour's great uncle, the next in line to inherit the Terra Qurayshian throne. The present king was, according to family gossip, not long for this world, and this clearly meant his great uncle was preparing to take the throne. This meant he was in the process of making plans and changes. And one of those plans . . . make Mansour a spy?

"I see." Mansour nearly hadn't heard his father reply. "You promise to ensure his safety?"

Great Allah, his father wasn't simply talking with Uncle about becoming a spy, he was capitulating.

"What must I do?" A long pause followed, the sort of pause which stretched out into a whole life set out like domino tiles, ready to fall and smash into the next, with Mansour somewhere in the middle, just another piece to fall and knock over the next. "I see."

A myriad of emotions surged into Mansour: resentment, for one, that his father would take his life out of his hands, and a thrill of fear with a hint of excitement. What would spy training be like? Would he learn martial arts and how to shoot various firearms, and be given spy gear? Surely it would not be so glamorous as spending time in casinos in a tuxedo with gorgeous women on an unlimited budget. Or would it?

"No, please listen, Uncle. No one can know." His father fell silent for a moment, listening. "Of course I will not tell Mansour! What if your planning committee scraps it? What if the king recovers? No, of course there will be no disclosure. Fatima will never understand . . . Perhaps after it's all done with, with my son home safe and sound. What you are planning is genius, but we must only reveal it when the time is right. Promise me now, or the whole deal is off."

Faisal fell silent again in the midst of pacing back toward the garage. Mansour ducked back against the siding, heart thundering his chest.

"Don't come back here," he muttered to himself over and over. "Please don't let him come back here now."

"We will discuss this further when I return. For now, I must attempt to have an enjoyable time together with my son, with this—this sword of Damocles hanging over our heads. *Assalamu alaikum,* Uncle. Until we meet again."

Mansour breathed a heavy sigh of relief as his father's footsteps receded into the distance. As soon as the driveway gate clattered closed, he sprinted for the house, over the deck, through the sliding door, and into the kitchen.

He was surprised his mom was still out but sure glad she was. Mansour took the time to compose himself and think of what he'd tell his mom. The revelation about his uncle and father could wait. He quickly cleaned up the kitchen, replaced the batteries in the smoke alarm, and wiped down the entire kitchen as best he could. Then he brought out the ionic air purifier from his bedroom. God willing, it would remove the eggy smoke odor from the kitchen and restore it to a reasonable facsimile of the pre-breakfast kitchen he knew and loved.

A few minutes later, Fatima opened the garage door and Mansour heard her car door slam.

She entered the kitchen holding two paper grocery bags. "What is that smell, Mansour?" Fatima exclaimed as her keen nose sensed minute traces of eggy smoke, burned plastic, and faux apple pie.

"Well, I just wanted to greet you with a pleasant fragrance upon your return, dear mother," Mansour replied.

Mothers are not so easily fooled. "It seems that something happened while I was gone," Fatima exclaimed. "You didn't *really* try to make breakfast, did you, son?"

"Oh, there was just a minor incident in the kitchen, Mom, nothing to worry about," her nervous son explained.

The twinkle in her eye told him she'd figured out what had happened. However, Fatima showed off her supreme wisdom and didn't press the issue further.

Besides, Mansour had done a very good job of cleaning up his little accident.

Faisal stood six foot four, and Mansour was now just shy of that. They came from a tall family, as did Fatima. Her father, Mansour's maternal grandfather, had been over six feet tall when he passed away. Mansour's blue eyes, blondish hair, and fair complexion also came from his mom's side of the family—the Keeryptian-Hellean side. He bent slightly to give her a hug, then helped put the groceries away.

"Your dad is leaving," she said later.

"Where is he going?" Mansour was still preoccupied with the enormity of what he'd heard. He asked the question before his mind could catch up with his mouth. After all, he knew the answer.

Fatima looked at her son. "Your dad's uncle, the king, is very sick and hospitalized at the Royal Qurayshi Hospital in Zomorod. Your dad is going to be with his extended family."

"Can I go with him?" Mansour asked.

"I'm sorry, my dear, but you can't. You still must go to school. Your father and I discussed this earlier this morning and have decided." Fatima said calmly, "This is your senior year of high school, and your dad will be gone for some time."

Afterward, he allowed the questions and speculation to wash over him. There were no answers to be found, at least not from his father, who was on a plane back to Terra Qurayshia before Mansour could find a chance to speak at length with him.

"I'm really going to miss you, Dad," Mansour said. He hoped the confusion and disquiet in his mind didn't show through, such that his father would magically see that he knew. He hoped, rather, to appear as if he missed his father already.

"I'll miss you too, my son. Don't worry. Everything will be all right. We can communicate every day by phone. Mansour, *habibi,* take care of your mom. You are a man now. I can rely on you," Faisal said.

"Yes, Dad, of course. I will take care of Mom," Mansour replied. *Habibi* meant "my love," and the word took on a strange meaning with the knowledge he now possessed.

Not twelve hours later, Mansour's phone beeped and buzzed. He pulled it out of his right pocket and took a look. A message from his father? He clicked on the notification and let it flash up on the screen.

I have just been informed that my uncle has slipped into a coma. The family is already talking succession, so I expect that he will be gone soon. This is a sad time, but the crown prince, my other uncle, is a forward-thinker with some tremendous ideas for the kingdom. I'll be gone a while to help him implement those changes. I'll call you when I can–study hard Mansour. I will see you in a few months!

Fatima and Mansour closely followed the daily events as they unfolded in the Terra Qurayshian kingdom. Blessedly, the king remained alive, staving off a growing unease Mansour felt every other day when his father called to keep them apprised of the situation. Many questions floated back and forth. Would they remain in Arlandica, or would they go to Terra Qurayshia . . .

or maybe even to Keerypt, where Mansour's mother's side of the family came from? Mansour's father wanted his family to stay in Arlandica until Mansour finished high school and college—which made sense. While Fatima and Mansour missed their beloved Faisal, they both agreed with him.

More questions slid beneath the surface: what had his father and his uncle really meant? What had his uncle said to his father? He'd only heard half the conversation but played it over in his mind dozens of times. It'd gotten bad enough that he was tempted to ask one of his three best Arlandican friends: Scott, Anthony, or Guillermo, but after meditation and consulting the Qur'an for guidance, he decided against it. His mother clearly didn't know about this bizarre plan to turn him into a spy.

For a time, Mansour hoped his father was correct. If the king's condition improved, perhaps this spy idea would never come to pass. But the call came less than a month later. The king was dead, and Mansour's great uncle had ascended to the throne. It happened on a gorgeous, sunny day like any other, a day in which you'd never guess history was being made.

About two months later, Faisal returned to West Beach, Sunland. The airport was busy and hectic as usual—filled with shops, food vendors, and a wide variety of cultural wear set against a background of business suits and shaved faces. But Mansour saw none of that; he could only see Faisal beaming a white-toothed smile as his eyes zeroed in on his family.

"Oh, Mansour, Fatima, I have missed you both so much. I am happy to unite with you again."

A week of rest and then a vacation for them all followed Faisal's return. He took the family to a resort in San Adelio, about two hours' drive south of West Beach. They took a four-day vacation, time for the family to be whole again and to enjoy each other without life's constant interruptions.

And what an amazing place the resort was! Parrots of every color chirped and chatted within a luscious garden of trees and flowers. They flitted free from branch to branch, unchained by the bars of cages. Another section of the garden boasted a magnificent stone-lined pond filled with fish and topped by ducks. The large, shiny fish glinted beneath the surface in the glory of daylight. And they were just big enough to keep hungry ducks from chomping them with their bills. Best of all, they were a few steps away from the beach, so they could swim and play in the sand during the day, then enjoy watching the sunset before trudging up to their rooms to sleep by the sound of waves lapping.

It was an instructional trip as well. Faisal had spent his time well with the new king and knew there were great things in the works. He gloried at night over the dinner table, gesturing wildly as he shared his optimism with Fatima and Mansour over the wonderful things that were about to take place in the kingdom. It was going to be a time of change, he told them. A time of modernization married with cultural conservatism. A time of better education all the way from kindergarten to college. A time of technological improvement and implementation. And a decline of monarchical rule. He explained to them that the new king saw the wonders of representative democracy and wished to slowly move the land to a constitutional monarchy.

And no hint of the ominous directive his father had discussed with the new king. No pensive stares or sudden looking away when Mansour tried to catch him. No clues among the things left on his desk. Mansour would never dream of going into his father's desk drawers, or God forbid, his computer, but he couldn't help but drift into the resort space his father used as an office from time to time and innocently wander around.

They were never apart, either. His father was tirelessly devoted to Fatima, which was admirable. Until now. Now it was bothersome. When he wasn't by his wife's side (or with Mansour also) he was taking calls late into the night, or working on whatever the king had him doing. Mansour decided that answers were in order. Two months of waiting were hard for an eighteen-year-old. Hard enough that it put enjoying the vacation in serious jeopardy.

At the end of the vacation they were all sorry to have to go. Mansour most of all, given the state he'd put himself in. But Faisal wanted Mansour to get back to school and to continue and complete his education in Arlandica. The mini vacation ended quickly, and the daily routine of life resumed afterward. Mansour got back to his high school homework. Fatima took care of the house and some rental property that she was managing. Faisal went back to answering his daily overseas phone calls to take care of his real estate and import/export businesses. Life went back to normal, praying the *Fajr* every day before sunrise, watching over his family, paying his wife compliments.

Not being open with his son.

That was, until the kingdom called again. And Mansour, after five wonderful and terrible months, had to say goodbye to his father once more.

Chapter 3

Sunland, Arlandica
16 years ago

Mansour graduated high school without a great deal of fanfare, although he attended several tame parties thrown by some of his closer friends. The day after his graduation, he returned home from one such party to find an envelope with his name on it. It was clearly his mother's handwriting. She'd left it at his bedside table where he wouldn't miss it.

"Hm," he mumbled to himself and flipped it open.

He slid out two first-class tickets to Keerypt, scheduled to leave the following day. They were wrapped in a note from his mother: *Habibi, pack your things! We're headed to see all your aunts, uncles, and cousins!*

He whooped at the surge of excitement–he hadn't been out to Keerypt since he was eleven or twelve. But even as he considered having a great time with his cousin Kareem, his excitement died in his throat as his thoughts turned once more to his father's phone call.

Suspicion took hold of him. Had his father arranged this trip to initiate his training? If it had been his idea, Mansour was sure to confront him over the lies and the secrecy. He imagined his first assignment in Keerypt, or disappearing to the Terra Qurayshian embassy to meet with his handlers who would show him the how-tos of his first mission. Or more probably, he'd meet with a host of different teachers who would instruct him in who-knew-what.

The conversation with his mother cleared up little.

"We're going for twelve days, then some time in Terra

Qurayshia, and then we head back here to begin your university." She seemed genuinely puzzled at his insistent questioning.

But of course she'd been kept in the dark. His father had already said as much! He'd spent months sulking and moping, wondering what his father had meant and when the spy talk would come, but now he went outside to the deck to bask in some late evening sunshine.

The spectacular sunsets this town had to offer always helped him center himself. He wondered why this resolve had taken so long to reach. If his father made a request of him, and it didn't align with the life Mansour had been building, he could always refuse.

"I won't let this dominate me," he told himself. "Whatever he was talking about might never happen." Just saying the words lifted his spirits. He promised himself he would enjoy the coming vacation, forget all about his father's furious tone, and resign himself to his agreement to make Mansour into a tool of the Terra Qurayshian government.

It would be a good chance to reacquaint himself with the Keeryptian dialect of Arabic, though he usually spoke it at home with his mother. In Keerypt, he could relax with family or strike out on his own, with no one knowing he was a foreigner raised in yet another foreign land.

Fatima's brother, Muhammad, was waiting for them at the airport terminal.

Uncle Muhammad was six years older than his mother, and stood eye level with Mansour. Those hazel eyes warmed at seeing them enter the immigration area.

"Uncle, have you shrunk?" Mansour teased.

Fatima joined in. "And where did all this white hair come from?"

"So glad to see you too!" Muhammad groused, but his smile betrayed him. "Your boy grows like a weed, sister. He's enormous!" He waved an arm back toward the VIP lounge. "My office manager will handle your passports."

They continued to make small talk while their passports were taken care of. After his office manager had stamped the passports, his pen failed to write as he was noting something down.

Muhammad calmly plucked it out of his hand and tossed it in the bin. "Any pen that does not write from the first stroke belongs in the trash," he told Mansour, as if this were an ancient parable of great wisdom.

Mansour grinned. Still, the pen reminded him of a prop out of James Bond. Whether the pen exploded or shot out a laser that would melt through a lock to open a door, the damage had been done. When his father asked him to kill someone for king and country, what would he say?

He shook himself and tried to live free of such thoughts.

Uncle Muhammad always wore a jacket, no matter how warm it was. He had scoliosis and so his back was not straight. The jackets made him look good. Muhammad was the chair of the Engineering Industries Holding Company, a very high position in the government. He liked dealing with smart, high-caliber people. He liked his things to be organized, kept in the same place, in good condition, and ready for use anytime. All this he told Mansour on the ride back to the family's residence.

The airport was situated outside the city in the sprawling desert of Keerypt, but soon enough they entered the lush river valley and the outskirts of the capital city. Massive sandy-colored buildings rose above the thick green. The desert fell away and seemed a distant memory by the time they arrived in the posh suburb of Almaza. Here the ancient trees grew together in places over the narrow streets and formed a green tunnel sparkling with gold sunlight.

They entered through an electric gate that slid smoothly back along its track and allowed them into Muhammad's estate. The circular driveway and the luxurious gardens were just as Mansour remembered them. His grandmother Amina and several other family members waited for them on the sprawling front porch.

He bent low and gave his much-shorter grandmother a big hug, then said, “Teta, I got you a backgammon set so we can continue our games.”

She often braided her hair, which was dyed with a hint of silver showing through at the roots. Her cheeks were fair and very soft. Mansour liked to kiss her on her cheeks.

“Oh, Mansour, you still remember!” Amina said.

“Yes, of course. I miss playing backgammon with you, Teta,” Mansour replied.

“Do you also miss molokhia with rabbit?” Grandmother inquired.

“I can smell it. Did you make it?” Mansour asked, while enjoying the smell of his grandma’s cooking. He remembered the days when he was young and would visit his grandma and eat molokhia with rabbit. He missed those days.

Mansour smelled the cooked garlic and could almost taste the finely cut green molokhia leaves with their salty viscous texture and savory aroma.

“I know you love it, so I made it myself,” Amina replied.

“I love you, Teta.”

Amina took him by the arm and led him into the house, which would be called a mansion in Arlandica. “Oh, Mansour, you have grown up so fast. Do you remember just a few years ago when you used to play pranks on me?”

“Of course, Teta. Which prank did you like the most?”

His teta chuckled. “Well, I remember when you used to play pranks on the phone.”

“My son is now more mature and will not pull pranks like that again, right, Mansour?” He and Teta both grinned at his mother’s admonishment from behind them.

“Mom, I miss those days. It was more fun. But you’re right, I won’t play pranks like that anymore.”

Although Mansour felt drained from the flight and had just eaten some fair airline food, the family all took their seats in the vast dining room.

Muhammad took his place at the head of the table, and as the oldest male, started the dinner by making a brief common supplication. This passage from the Qur'an was taught by Prophet Muhammad (peace be upon him), to recite before eating.

Our Lord, give us good in this world and good in the hereafter and save us from the torment of the fire.[1]

Muhammad spoke loud enough that he could be heard, but not too loud. The table was full of food. They had molokhia (green soup), poached rabbits, chicken, brown rice with mixed nuts, zucchini, okra with lamb, and salad. They all ate from every dish as it all smelled and looked delicious.

"I'm glad so many of you could come and see us on short notice," Fatima said. "Soraya?"

Samia, her oldest sister, had brought her children. "Soraya wasn't able to make it." Samia looked well, in spite of her late husband's absence. It seemed she had come a long way since four years ago, when Sherief had been taken from them in a head-on collision on the highway.

Samia's second child, Mansour's cousin Kareem, was his usual jubilant self. He was Mansour's best friend here and did a lot of the talking. Nour, Kareem's older sister, was clearly attempting to appear pleasant and welcoming, but Mansour caught several instances in which she appeared gloomy. Her husband was noticeably absent from the gathering.

During a moment of silence, Fatima asked, "Nour, it is very good to see you. Where is your kind husband, Nabil?"

Nour answered slowly and sadly, "I'm sorry, my dear aunt. He had to attend another event so he couldn't make it here today."

Mansour knew his mother to be smart. She'd clearly figured

---

[1] Qur'an 2:201.

something wrong was going on but didn't pursue it. Nour was clearly too uncomfortable to reveal the truth in this setting.

The spy he would never become called out to him from within—investigate this matter! Surely he could do his duty as an upstanding follower of Islam and pretend to be an undercover agent at the same time. Perhaps if he could play the part, he could pretend to do the work his father would eventually call upon him to fulfill. In addition, did the Qur'an not proclaim "Do good to parents, kinsfolk"?[2] Of course it did.

Mansour yawned despite himself.

He would do some good after he overcame his jetlag.

Mansour's grandmother began to reminisce about the past, when people had good manners, in general, and would not so lightly fail to attend family reunions that took place after many years apart. In fact, she went on, everything about the past in Keerypt felt much better than the present. In the time of King Fardoon, the streets were clean, the shops elegant and in good repair, the education at schools of good quality. People displayed good manners, and the cost of living was much lower than now.

Mansour felt his eyes drooping, so Muhammad and Teta Amina called a halt to the proceedings and wished them good night. Kareem followed him to the bedroom he'd been given.

Kareem asked, "When are you leaving for Terra Qurayshia?"

"In twelve days, so we still have some time. I'll go now and take a shower, change, pray, and get some sleep. I had a very long flight from Sunland," Mansour replied.

"I'll pick you up tomorrow. Just give me a call when you wake up," Kareem said.

"Yes, that sounds great! Thank you," Mansour said, then another yawn seized him.

He had a strange dream that first night back in Keerypt. He dreamed that he was climbing the largest pyramid, and the sphinx was at the pinnacle! The human head of the sphinx scowled down

---

[2] Qur'an 4:36.

at him, terrible to behold with its outstretched wings and swishing tail. The sphinx had the legs of a lion and the wings of a bird, which looked like huge eagle wings, and were flapping, getting ready to fly and attack. The sphinx's eyes glowed red with fire. Mansour felt fear pelt into him as a sandstorm might and wanted to run away. Instead, he ran toward it. There was nowhere else to run, and when he realized that, he had to gather his courage to be ready to attack the sphinx with all his physical, emotional, and spiritual strength. He had a very long way to go to get to the top of the pyramid, and though he tried to run and get to the top quickly, he moved slowly. The sphinx was fixed to the top of the pyramid and couldn't fly. Long before reaching the top of the pyramid and before the sphinx had the opportunity to attack, Mansour had a strong instinct that he would be victorious in the end, manifesting the meaning of his name—and then he woke up.

It was 4:30 am, and Mansour had only slept four hours, but he couldn't go back to sleep. The jetlag usually took about one week to get over. It was too early to call Kareem now. So Mansour washed up, prayed, and read some Qur'an. Part of the Islamic tradition as taught by Prophet Muhammad (peace be upon him) was to move the tongue when reading Qur'an. You didn't just read with the eye's movement. To get a reward by reading Qur'an, one needed to at least move the tongue as if reading aloud but not necessarily reading aloud. Mansour sometimes read out loud enough to hear himself when he was alone. When reading in a *masjid*, he didn't read aloud. He didn't like to bother the people around him. He disliked it when other people read aloud because he couldn't concentrate. Mansour liked to read the Qur'an in his favorite decorative green and gold colored hardcover book, which fitted comfortably in the palm of his hand. He liked the feel of it; the Arabic fonts were easy to read, and the pages were good quality and turned easily.

Mansour then continued reading one of his favorite Dale Carnegie books, *How to Stop Worrying and Start Living.*

Although he'd woken up, Mansour felt possessed of that powerful ability, which so many teenagers have, to will himself to sleep just a bit more.

He fell back asleep after reading a few pages, then woke up again a bit later and took a shower.

Aunt Samia, Kareem, and Nour had returned by the time Mansour went out to face the day, and they sat at the breakfast table on the veranda in the backyard. The feast this morning was only slightly smaller than the previous night, and just as delicious. The welcome to the table was just as warm as before as well, with a warm smile from his mother to top it off.

"We are happy to see your battle against jetlag has been won already," Teta said with a chuckle.

"Thank you!" He sat and was about to tuck in when he had a thought. "I feel as though I interrupted you last night, Teta. You were telling a story."

She waved this off, but he insisted. The others agreed–though Kareem didn't seem to be as keen. Perhaps his mother and cousin were hoping like he was to hear more about the shining beacon Keerypt had once been.

So, over tea, she took them on a nostalgic trip to the past and the good times when she'd been in her twenties. She talked about going to Trianon, which was very elegant at that time, for the best gâteaux with her parents, brother, and sister.

"The Keeryptian pound was more valued than the Arlandican dollar. People were freer to express their views and opinions on everything. There was so much more freedom and honesty," Amina said.

Muhammad couldn't resist adding a comment about that. "You are correct, Mother. One of the problems that contributed to the downturn of our economy is the increase in population without an equivalent increase in productivity. Military rule is not always the best way to manage a country and run a free economy. The increase in population should have been used as an asset and not become a liability. There are many more problems, of course, that would take a long time to list and discuss."

"In the old movies, we see the streets hardly had any traffic and people were much more courteous to each other," Nour said.

"And what of the corruption, and the nepotism?" Kareem asked. He raised his hands and kept his tone light. "Power was given only to the elite, and the rest of the population were poor and controlled. When the military took over, they gave opportunities to the poor and made education free. They gave farmland to the farmers and did a lot of good."

Teta set down her teacup. "It's obvious that some people liked what the military did. As you said, the situation wasn't perfect at the time of the king, and many people were eager for a change. However, change has to happen gradually–unless God Almighty Himself forces abrupt change on people.

"Islam was revealed over a period of twenty-three years. Of course, there is a big difference between God's guidance and a human's vision. My point, though, is that change needs time and needs to be done the right way. You need the support and buy-in from the majority of people. If you force the change on people based on the vision of one individual or very few individuals, eventually things will collapse. And collapse they did.

"Some of the ideas the military had were ideal, but they were not thought of or implemented properly. 'Free education' ended up as 'no quality education.' All the industries that were nationalized suffered greatly. The manufacturing industry went down; the farming industry didn't prosper as it had before. The rent control resulted in a huge shortage in housing. And later on house sale prices soared as they were not subjected to the rent control. Believe me, Kareem, poverty back then was very different from poverty now. There is a lot more poverty now, and their condition is a lot worse than at the time of the king.

"When you replace people with knowledge with people who have no knowledge, and their only qualification is loyalty to the leader, things for sure will go wrong eventually. That is a formula for disaster. The oppressive regime, the strict control of the population, and spying on people by the government created a culture of mistrust among people and generations of weaklings. It killed creativity, innovation, research, and development. It produced apathy and hopelessness. In general, keep in mind that what starts wrong will not last for very long. That goes for any system in government, or a company, or with individuals. You cannot take shortcuts and expect things will work out. In the long run, they will not," Amina concluded.

"I could not agree with you more, Teta," Mansour said.

After breakfast, Kareem took him by the arm and pulled him aside. After so long in Arlandica, the physicality made him uncomfortable, but he went along with it. "Tell me about high school in Arlandica! How is it? Do you have a girlfriend . . . or *girlfriends*? I want to hear everything, dear cousin!"

Girlfriend? *Girlfriends?* He wished. His mother would kill him. Mansour needed to work on his mission before he could go off and have any fun with Kareem.

"I need to go speak with my mother for a moment. Then we'll head out."

He steered his mother deeper into the backyard. "Mother, are you well?"

"Of course!"

"Before I go, I wanted to ask a favor of you." At her inquisitive expression, he went on: "Could you steer Nour aside and find out what's truly going on with her? I suspect it's her husband."

A quirk of smile appeared. "How thoughtful, *habibi.* I knew something wasn't right. You let your mother handle this."

"Thanks, Mom."

Chapter 4

Now
Terra Qurayshia

Mansour pulled into the rest area—given the shocking news about the end of his country's democratic tradition, he'd half assumed it wouldn't be there. But it was, and he found people milling through the lobby, grabbing drinks and snacks from vending machines on their way back from the bathroom facilities. The rest area hadn't declined either. It was a lush green oasis around an artificial pond filled with golden carp, one the size of a cat. Children giggled and threw bread crumbs to them. Mansour tried to relax. He watched it all for the rest of the hour, then returned to his car.

There was no news about his father; how could he possibly receive any? And he refused to grieve while he remained unsafe. After a third call hadn't connected, he turned his phone off and removed the SIM card. The new king's people didn't have the resources of the Arlandican intelligence agencies, but they weren't completely ignorant.

One thought gave him pause, though. What if Zohair's faith in him had been a ruse? What if, instead of a small checkpoint, he came back to find a full squadron of assault vehicles and soldiers? Perhaps with a few helicopters hovering overhead? Mansour felt out of breath as he examined the situation in which he'd been placed. His homeland had become an autocracy, and he had gone from a hero of the republic to an enemy of the crown. He opened his door a little too hard and banged it into the white sedan next to him. He admonished himself with quiet vehemence, peering about to make sure that no one had noticed. Then he slid into the driver's seat and started it up, sucking in as much breath as he could to let it out as a momentous sigh.

"The rest stop is still green and still full of happy people. The king needs time to consolidate power," he told his reflection in the rearview mirror. "Someone will resist. The process will take time." He shifted into reverse and backed up, jamming the brakes immediately as the horn of a tractor trailer bellowed in anger. He rolled down the window and threw the universal gesture for sorry, then gunned it out of there and back onto the highway. Army detachment or not, there was no other option left to him.

Thankfully the checkpoint was gone just as Zohair had promised. "Thanks be to Allah, who provides for those who are faithful," Mansour said. He drove just a little faster and reached the Port of Ziba before the next *Azan* called him to pray.

Ziba, Jewel of the Sea, famed port of the white sands, spread out before him on the horizon. It was a popular destination for tourists as evidenced by the line of tall and glimmering hotels and businesses stuck right to the edge of the umbrella-dotted beaches. For now, he felt tired. Nothing was certain, including his status as a free man.

What he wouldn't give to spend another day here, to forget his grief and worry under the rays of the sun with the cool lap of sea water at his toes, sipping juice from a frosted glass chock full of ice.

When he drew closer, the business district of the city's center towered up and over him, its skyscrapers blocking both his view of the beach and also the sun's glare. He drove through the suburbs of white-faced homes, past the worn-down hovels of the inner city, and made his way to the ferry port, pulling a ticket to the beep of a machine to get his vehicle into long-term parking.

Goodbye, my old friend, he thought as he pulled his things from the trunk and then grabbed envelopes of cash from the glove box. *It was a good run.*

The few months working here hadn't been the worst of his

life, certainly. Different, to be sure, but he was used to stepping between countries and living with culture shock.

He caught a couple staring at him, a man in white trousers and button-up shirt and a woman in the soft black fold of a burka, so he waved and made his way into the ticket lobby. A long queue stretched into rows of red lines that corralled people into a tight square of boredom. Mansour glanced at his watch. He had already taken too long. He looked about and saw no line for the first-class ticketing counter, so he made his way over there and walked up to the attendant.

"Passport please," the man asked, not even looking up from his computer terminal.

His blue uniform looked far too thick for this climate, and Mansour sympathized with him as he saw the heavy pools of sweat that had spread around his armpits. This guy didn't want to be here; he didn't want to deal with any trouble, and he was about the best thing that Mansour could have hoped for.

"I don't have one," Mansour said with a Terra Qurayshian accent. He certainly couldn't use his actual Arlandican passport, not with the warrant and whatever was actually happening halfway across the world.

The man looked up, his wet face filled with scorn. "You don't have one," he sneered. "Then why are you even here?"

"I contacted emergency services and have been expedited to leave the country. My father is very ill and will almost certainly die soon, so I must leave immediately. Check for Mansour emergency visa 5369631."

The attendant typed at his computer and then glared at Mansour. "Nothing here."

Mansour caught the man's eyes with his own. "What I say is true," he said. "And I understand that you can get in a lot of trouble for letting me out before that emergency expedite gets through. But we both know that might take weeks. Is there any way that I can skip the formalities? My father needs me." With his words he pushed a fat envelope full of bills across the counter.

The attendant looked down at it and, for the first time, smiled. "Next time you lose your passport just start with the money," he said, quietly so as not to be overheard. "The wife has been complaining about our broken air conditioner . . . and I'm late on rent."

Mansour nodded. "Thank you, my friend."

The scritch-scratch sound of a nine-point printer arose from behind the counter, and a moment later the attendant gave him a sheaf of papers. The envelope had already disappeared, Mansour noted, without him ever having seen the man pocket it.

"Would you like to check any of your luggage?" the man asked.

"No, I'm in a hurry. Thank you for all you've done."

In minutes, he was through and headed to the ferry that would take him across the strait and out of Terra Qurayshia. The country his father had called home his whole life was suddenly a place without safety.

Mansour moved up a carpeted and enclosed gangplank, vastly different from the sturdy board with rail that served the other passengers. A porter met him halfway and grabbed one of his heavy bags, dragging it up behind him. At the entryway to the first- class lounge stood the captain and his first mate, both clad in full white uniforms. Gleaming bits of brass and colorful ribbons festooned the fronts of their jackets.

"Welcome aboard." The captain showed the inside of the first- class lounge with a broad sweep of his arm. "Welcome to the *Turquoise Wave*."

"Thank you, Captain," Mansour said. The first mate gave him a curt bow, but was that a suspicious glint in his eye? Mansour's heart jumped and sped up. Even here, with the cushy comforts and tasty treat of first-class spread out before him, he couldn't relax.

He walked to an espresso machine, got himself a thick coffee, then walked out to the observation check to scan the heavy, roiling waves. Dolphins jumped and squeaked in the distance.

"So what do you think about Arlandica?" the first mate said from behind him.

Mansour jumped. He hadn't even noticed the man sidle up to him. He couldn't afford to be sloppy. "I have no real opinions on such things," he lied.

This close up, the first mate didn't look like a typical sailor at all. A scar scored his left cheek, and he held the bearing of a man constantly ready for a fight.

"Oh, come now. Everyone has opinions on the most powerful democracy on Earth. I'm a curious fellow. I like to talk about these things, and I don't have anything to do for the next half hour. Indulge me."

The ship shuddered and a low thrumming reverberated through the deck. The captain had started to idle the engines.

Mansour shrugged. "I haven't had time to catch the news this morning."

The first mate grinned. "I suspect not. Who would have the money and the nerve to bribe their way out of the country and get berth on a ferry back to their homeland? Certainly not a simple man."

Mansour frowned. "I have no idea what you're talking about. I'm Keeryptian." He certainly had a flawless Keeryptian accent.

The first mate shrugged and leaned back away from the railing. "I might be mistaken. The captain as well. But you sure look a lot like the updated all-points bulletin that we received after we docked at port. Perhaps we should call the police and have them look into it."

The hope inside Mansour's heart curdled, then fear boiled in its wake. He grabbed the first mate by the wrist.

"I don't for one minute think you know what you're talking about, and I will see to it that you and your captain are paraded through every court that it takes for me to get justice if you force me to miss this ship's departure. I am on a desperate bid to see my father who is, as we speak, dying in a hospital bed in Keerypt. You can call ahead to the next port, if you wish, but rest assured that if we do not leave as scheduled, you and your captain will live your lives out on the streets of the new kingdom, whatever that might look like, begging for food and ruing the day you ever thought of messing with me."

Mansour's eyes ran to the scar on the first mate's cheek. The man was a brawler, he decided, but he doubted that the man had the strength to deal with the courts. He might even have a few outstanding warrants himself under that tough exterior. Mansour locked his eyes with the first mate and glared. He could see that the other man was now very unsure of himself.

"Look, whatever your name is, and I don't care, so don't tell me," Mansour continued, "does this spy that you're looking for have a reward?"

The first mate gulped. "Yes, five thousand riyal."

Mansour jabbed his hand into his coat pocket and brought out an envelope. "Here are ten thousand riyal that say that you never saw me. Let's just get out of here and get to port, so I can see my father."

The first mate grabbed the envelope, but Mansour held on tight and brought his mouth close to his ear. "And know that, if I am a spy, you have just committed a federal crime by taking that money from me. No word about these suspicions."

The first mate nodded and fled from Mansour through the lounge and onto the bridge. Mansour expected he wouldn't see anything of either of them again.

Mansour had taken care of the captain and his mate, but the encounter disturbed him. He'd also spent a good chunk of his bug-out money and wouldn't have access to more until he contacted Kareem or Uncle Muhammad. Zohair had said that the warrant was just a local one, but the attempt to catch him here on this ferry showed that the warrant had gained in strength and scope. At this rate he wondered how long before he had his face plastered all over news reports. Mansour knew the new king would be eager to rid himself of anything or anyone that might challenge his supremacy, and it was only the weak beginnings of his centralization of his power that had gotten Mansour this far.

Neither the captain nor his mate was present when he disembarked in Zanobia, Keerypt, and that didn't surprise him. There was a lack of fanfare over his arrival, and that also didn't surprise him. The threats he'd made were top-notch, and when he had the time to do so, he would be sure to offer thanks to Allah for his protection.

Now that he was in Zanobia, he was just a long jump away from getting to home, his real home, in Arlandica. But this was a new set of problems. Arlandican flights were well protected and professional. He wouldn't be able to bribe his way onto a plane and then through Arlandican customs. They were so strict that they even made people remove their shoes when heading through airport security. He'd heard before that a carpenter had to leave all his tools behind when he moved to Arlandica, so strict were their standards. So he'd need something to show them.

He decided that Keerypt wasn't going to be a better place for him, nor would he be able to trust he'd be safe and anonymous traveling through it. The king undoubtedly had agents in Keerypt, and they were definitely looking for him. If he stayed away from his mother's side of the family, he could keep those agents away, keeping them safe, and saving time. He hoped.

Mansour figured out his money situation, counting out Keeryptian and Arlandican bills he might need before he stowed his bags at a coin-operated locker and left the harbor building. The cash went into his sock and the thin pouch wrapped around his waist.

He needed a cargo ship. They were notorious for smuggling, of course, and that was itself a gateway into the dark undercurrent of the criminal world. Maybe they could tell him a way to get himself out of here. It seemed like a long shot, but it felt possible.

He saw the ship *Kingswind* tied up at the very outer berths of the docking facility. Three men lounged by the boarding plank, smoking cigarettes and talking. This seemed like the perfect opportunity. He wandered over.

"Ho there, shipmen," he said, adopting the dialect of the sailing folk, "From where do you hail?"

"Dirty shores and unkempt spaces," one man snarled. He seemed to be the leader of this particular group. "What's it to you?"

Mansour was taken aback. Had he run the dialect wrong? This was going bad fast, and it had just begun. He decided he needed to cut to the chase.

"Listen, I lost my passport, and I need to see my father in Arlandica. He is dying, and I don't have time to get a new one. Do you guys know anything that I could possibly do to get on an airplane, today, and fly out to Arlandica, then get through security?"

The leader snorted and turned to his companions. "How much does a run like that cost? A thousand Keeryptian pounds?"

The man to his right nodded. "Double that for same day."

Though they looked incredulous, their talk was music to Mansour's ears. It could be done!

"What are you talking about? How is it done?" Mansour asked.

"Well, Kandia has resources if you go to the right people. A flight to Arlandica? Possible, but you need a lot of cash. If you have it, you can get a counterfeit passport, almost identical to the real thing. But hey, that's dreamland talk because no one has cash like that burning a hole in their pockets. Just forget it and call your pops like everyone else does."

Mansour pulled out his wallet and gave each of them nearly two thousand Keeryptian pounds, equivalent to three hundred

Arlandican dollars. "I have the money and the means. Bring me where I need to go to do this, and I will double what I just gave you."

The leader nodded and extended his hand. "Call me Ishmael. These are my friends. Let's call the tall one Ahab and the smaller, fatter one Moby."

"Hey!" his fat friend responded.

Ishmael shrugged.

"Greetings Ishmael, Ahab, and Moby. I shall assume the name Mansour. It's nice to meet you. Now, what next?"

"Next we talk to the captain, give him a cut, and get the time to drive you to where you need to go."

After spending half an hour cramped up in an old two-door Edison Sprint, Mansour noted their destination, a white plastic siding meant to look like white marble. The building reminded him of the vehicle in which he sat, his knees squished up to his chest next to the smelly aroma of Moby. Both were old and obviously faded. Both were small and quite unused to having large quantities of people within them. And both were obviously owned by illicit men. Mansour sent an apology to the heavens. Sometimes, as the Prophet Jesus had noted, matters of the terrestrial were very different from matters of the celestial. *Give unto Caesar,* Mansour thought, looking about himself. Just in case, though, he would give *duaa* at his next prayers.

The Sprint pulled into a paved driveway pocked with cracks and potholes, the tall grass sliding through wherever seeds had found purchase.

"We are here," Ishmael said over his shoulder, as if it wasn't obvious when he'd turned off the ignition. Mansour fiddled a little. Despite the quiet drive over, he liked these guys. He wondered if they'd live in the dark shadow of crime had they been given better opportunities growing up.

The four of them got out and headed to the door. A screen sat in front to keep out the bugs, but to their surprise, the actual door itself was wide open. Despite the hot day, one would expect such illicit trade to be more wary of unexpected visitors. Ishmael pushed the red doorbell, and they listened to nature sounds coupled with frustrated cursing and a struggle from within.

"Is he in trouble?" Mansour asked. Adrenaline rushed to his brain and he could feel his body loosening into a combat stance.

"Hey now," Ahab said, clapping a heavy hand on his shoulder. "That's just how he is. These brainy types, they don't treat life like the rest of us. This guy here, we like to call him Mad Salim. He never throws anything out, and it's basically one big landfill in there. You're just hearing him trying to get to the door."

Mansour wasn't sure if he should relax just yet. The guy sounded insane. But when he appeared at his screen door, his glasses askew with one lens completely spider webbed over in cracks, a sweater vest over a blue work shirt all drenched in sweat, he knew that Ahab was right. There would be no trouble from the man.

"M-m-may I help you?" Mad Salim stuttered.

"Yeah. Man here needs a passport to Arlandica. Fast," Ishmael said.

Mad Salim stared at Mansour as if he were some new and strange beast from some faraway land. Mansour waved.

"I-i-it w-w-will require lots of m-money. And a photo."

"Yeah, I told him. Hey, Mansour, give him the cash."

Mansour fished through his pockets and brought out an envelope, then counted the cash out in the daylight of the porch step. He also produced a smaller envelope with several leftover passport photos from his emergency go bag. Mad Salim licked his lip greedily.

"Yes yes, perfect. I-i-it will be done in the hour."

"Hey, Salim, you're not going to invite us in?" Moby asked. It was clearly an inside joke among the trio of sailors because they all elbowed and ribbed one another as they laughed heartily.

Salim's eyes bugged out of his head. "N-n-no, I n-n-never, t-t-too b-b-busy. W-w-way t-t-too b-b-busy."

"Suit yourself," Salim said. He pulled out a wrinkled soft pack of smokes and offered one to the rest of them. Ishmael and Moby took it, but Mansour declined.

"So what do we do now?" Mansour asked.

"We wait," Ishmael told him, popping his lips and letting a ring of smoke flutter slowly into the deep blue sky.

Chapter 5

16 years ago
Keerypt

"We can head to the sporting club," Kareem suggested. Mansour agreed but made sure to lock eyes with his mother and tip her a wink.

She responded with a barely noticeable nod and returned to where Muhammad, Amina, Samia, and Nour were finishing up their breakfast.

On their way to the club, they heard a loud screeching noise and gaped at a car speeding past in the opposite direction. Not a moment later, that car rear-ended the car in front of it.

"Unbelievable," Kareem muttered.

"We might have to stop."

The driver in the front car got out of his vehicle and yelled and cursed at the driver of the car behind him. The man was nearly Mansour's height and well built. The guy behind him, who'd hit him, reluctantly exited his car, clearly terrified. He was nowhere near the size of the first man. Clearly, the other guy would devour him.

Without hesitation, Kareem and Mansour parked their car, quickly got out, and ran toward the accident to prevent a worse accident from happening. They arrived just in time.

The bigger guy got a fistful of shirt and practically lifted the other guy off the ground. The one who'd rear-ended him drew back a fist.

Mansour grabbed his hand with the intention of pulling him away, but the man rounded on him and socked Mansour in the side. Luckily for him, the blow landed awkwardly, but still a bright flash of pain lit up Mansour's body. He staggered back and braced himself against the warm hood of the lightly damaged car to stay on his feet. He hadn't been in any serious scrapes in school—his parents had sent him to an expensive private school where any fight was a sure ticket to expulsion.

Luckily for everyone involved, his intervention had given Kareem time to interpose himself between the two parties. He wasn't as tall as either the furious man or Mansour, but he was also clearly no stranger to the gym. Mansour, bigger and more muscular from all the high school sports, soon joined him.

And while the big guy was clearly in the mood to fight, Mansour held his ground. "Sir, please, calm down. I'm certain—"

"He hit me!" the man shouted. "I'm the one who was wronged!"

"Violence isn't the answer here. It won't help at all and won't solve this problem."

The man seemed to realize he had no chance of fighting two strong guys along with the one who'd rear-ended him. The realization stole all the fury out of him, and he seemed to deflate, though some bitterness remained. "I'm the victim here!"

"Yes, we saw that. Let us discuss what happened in a calm, civilized way. I'm sure the guy behind you didn't hit you intentionally. We heard the screeching sound, so it's obvious he was trying to brake but was too late, unfortunately. Let us ask him and see what happened," Mansour said calmly and confidently.

There was no need. A moment later, the agonized shout of a woman came from the passenger seat of the smaller man's car. They all dashed over to find a very pregnant woman in the midst of straining against the beginnings of childbirth. She grabbed the smaller man's hand in a crushing grip.

"I need to—"

"Merciful Allah, give me your insurance card!" the larger man shouted. He'd already produced his phone and was ready to take a picture of the information so the smaller man could get back on his way to the hospital.

Everyone could see that the accident wasn't intentional. The guy in the front had braked hard and, of course, the one behind him was driving too fast and following too closely—a very common way of driving in Keerypt—and so he couldn't stop in time. The larger man stood silent for a moment, regarded Kareem and Mansour, then gave them the nod and drove away as well.

The ferocity of the larger man had come as a bit of a shock to Mansour. He could never become a spy—at least, not until he learned how to protect himself and the others around him. Mansour resolved, spy job or not, to spend some time on a mat practicing taekwondo, jiujitsu, or whatever was near his house in Sunland. He thought there was a jiujitsu school not a mile away. He could run or bike there and get into even better shape.

Now back behind the wheel, Kareem told Mansour, "This sort of thing happens all the time, but it's usually just aggressive driving and following too closely."

Mansour rubbed at his sore ribcage. "Well, I guess I'm not so eager to drive here at all."

For a while they drove on in silence, which gave Mansour some time to appreciate the beauty and difference of the Keeryptian capital as opposed to his home in Sunland. It also provided him a moment to collect his thoughts on the situation that left his side aching.

"You know, Kareem, I hope you don't take this the wrong way—my mom is Keeryptian after all. When an accident like this happens in Terra Qurayshia, people don't shout, yell, or fight. They just talk in a calm way and console each other. In Sunland, however, it depends on where exactly you are. There's a wide variety of people over there and their reactions differ just as much."

Kareem nodded. "I heard the same comment from someone else, and I think the reason is that people over here are too stressed out, and they use any opportunity to vent their stresses and frustrations."

Mansour replied, "Yes, you're right. People in Terra Qurayshia are more relaxed and have fewer worries. And in Sunland, it varies."

When they arrived at the club, Kareem ordered cold lemonade with mint for both of them and said, "You need this, my dear cousin, to calm you down after the shock you got."

The cold, refreshing drink had a sour taste with exactly the right amount of sugar–a very good choice.

A few minutes after they relaxed, Kareem inundated Mansour with a lot of questions. From "What do you do every day?" to "What are you studying and where do you want to go to college?"

Mansour was tempted to tell Kareem about the phone call from those months ago. Though it had remained on his mind, mundane existence was slowly taking the edge off the certainty that his father would suddenly appear and make him disappear from the life he'd always known.

The question of college was a good one, and he felt the familiar conflict bubble up: would his father allow him to choose, or "suggest" some career path Mansour should follow as part of his eventual induction into Terra Qurayshia's hundred-year plan?

Kareem laughed. "No need to be so serious. Tell me about the girls. You must be the most sought-after guy in high school or in all of Sunland. You are good looking, tall, muscular, well educated and sometimes funny. You play the piano very well and are a prince too."

Mansour laughed. "My mother wouldn't have it. I'm sure it would be nice to have one . . . Some of the Arlandican girls are much more aggressive than you would imagine. It was really tempting to succumb to a few of them, but thank God, I did not. This is the hardest test, my dear cousin, when you can and are able to do what you desire, but you resist, so you do not."

"I would think it the most difficult test of all, living in Arlandica."

Mansour said, "I'm convinced it isn't right to have a girlfriend but much better to only have a special relationship with a girl when I get married. I'm not bragging or claiming to be so strong in resisting temptation. I am sure God protected me through my *duaa* and my parents' *duaa* for me." Mansour explained that he learned from Dr. Hassan Hathout at the Islamic Center of Southern Sunland, "Be what you should be and not what you are."

The discussion continued for a while, then it was time for Mansour and Kareem to go and visit another cousin, and then go to late lunch. Mansour really enjoyed the social aspects of his visit to Keerypt. He looked forward to seeing many other relatives and old friends during his trip there.

Kareem took Mansour to visit their aunt Soraya, and their cousins Kamilia and Dina, whom Mansour had not seen for years. Even though their aunt's apartment was only about ten miles away, it took them forty-five minutes to arrive because of serious congestion on the roads.

Aunt Soraya's house was much smaller than Uncle Muhammad's, given she had much less money than his uncle, but it was tastefully decorated and spotless. Plush furniture made for a cozy place to converse, with a huge cabinet and bookshelf dominating one wall. Though it felt somewhat minimalistic and flat, the Persian rug beneath the coffee table swirled with colors and shapes. The blend of styles, as disjointed as they might be, gave it a homey feel.

Mansour felt happy to see his aunt and his cousins, and they were happy to see Mansour as well. After fifteen minutes, Mansour noticed that there was something bothering his aunt and his cousins. Was it because of him? Something he'd said or didn't say or do? Or what, exactly? When Soraya, Kamilia, and Dina stepped out of the room for a few minutes, Mansour asked Kareem if he'd noticed the same thing. Kareem told him that he had, and he'd ask them about it, as he thought they would open up to him.

"Let me see what I can do." Kareem stepped out of the room to ask what was going on.

The situation reminded Mansour of Nour, and the mission he'd given his mother. He decided now was as good a time as any to give her a call. Somehow, the terrible assignment his father had never given him had become like a game to him.

"Hello, Mother!"

"*Habibi*, I am glad to hear from you."

He breezed through the situation with the car crash, and downplayed the punch he'd received for the trouble of intervening. "I wonder if it'll be okay to ask about Nour. Did you have a chance to speak with her?"

He heard the joy in his mother's voice. "As it happens I did. But Mansour, you must understand, Nour confided in me. She was adamant that I not tell anyone."

Don't worry, he thought. *I'm the secret agent of the family.*

"I give you my word to keep everything you tell me a secret," he told her.

His mother wasn't a great storyteller, and he had to direct her back away from trivial details every so often, but over the course of several minutes the story came out.

Though Fatima was still jetlagged from the trip, she felt she had to do something about Nour and Nabil. She sat next to Nour and asked her directly how things were between her and her husband. Nour teared up and hugged her aunt and asked her if it would be all right to go to the family room to talk privately.

In the family room, Nour broke down in tears before she even began speaking. "Please keep everything confidential. I didn't even tell my mom all the details." Fatima hugged Nour again and kissed her on her forehead. Nour started crying more.

"Please tell me what is going on, *habibti*. It's a great pain to see you this way," Fatima said.

"I know. I love you Aunt Fatima, and I wouldn't tell you if I didn't know that you'll keep it confidential. I trust you, and I trust your judgment, so I want to know what you think," Nour whispered, her words tremulous, and she shook all over.

She told Fatima that her mother-in-law interfered too much in the life she shared with her husband. In the beginning, Nabil hadn't allowed her to interfere, but as time wore on, he just followed along any time his mother made a suggestion. It was getting to be too much. Nour could handle it no longer.

"*Habibi,* she asked him to divorce her," Fatima told Mansour.

Mansour breathed out a long, explosive sigh. It was worse than he had feared.

"I couldn't believe it either," Fatima said. "It was a great shock to me. I couldn't imagine her taking such a step without involving the family and her mother."

"How did he respond?" Mansour asked quietly.

"Nour said he didn't want to divorce her, and he left to stay with his mother. I counseled her not to ask him again to divorce her. As I understand, Nabil is a good man, and I'm sure these problems can be fixed. I told her that she needed to be very wise and think calmly about the best way to fix the situation."

Mansour agreed. "Have you suggested Uncle Muhammad talk with him, to discover a solution?" Nabil had previously showed that he liked Nour's side of the family, and he clearly thought highly of Mansour's uncle Muhammad.

"I will. She and Aunt Samia haven't left yet."

Muhammad would do the right thing and approach Nabil man-to-man. He was wise, very well educated, so he'd know how to handle the situation without making it worse.

Kareem reappeared not long after Mansour ended the call to his mother. "Well, you were right," he said. "I just found out that Kamilia was ripped off in a big way."

Mansour turned. "What happened?"

"Kamilia just told Aunt Soraya and me that her hairdresser

told her a long, elaborate story about her father being very sick and dying, and that he needed to have an expensive surgery. The hairdresser explained that their family didn't have the money to pay for the surgery. Kamilia has known her for many years, so she asked her how much money she was talking about. Apparently they needed a hundred thousand Keeryptian pounds–about twenty thousand Arlandican dollars."

This was no small matter.

Kamilia appeared, distraught, and stared daggers at her cousin. Then, when it looked like she might shriek and curse at Kareem, she instead buried her face in her hands and sobbed hopelessly.

Mansour rushed to her. "Cousin, please. I asked Kareem to inquire. If you should be angry, please turn your anger on me."

She shook her head. "I'm such a fool."

"Not at all. Come, I'm sure we can find a solution to this if we put our heads together. And over some tea, I will apologize for snooping in your business."

Aunt Soraya came in next, trailing eleven-year-old Dina behind. Mansour had only seen Dina as a chubby-cheeked toddler prior, and she looked as though a stiff wind might blow her away.

His aunt explained the remainder of the story while she served tea. Kamilia had gone to the bank, taken out a hundred thousand pounds–most of her savings and inheritance from her father–and given it to the hairdresser. "This happened a couple of weeks ago, and Kamilia didn't speak to anyone about the matter until now. Only yesterday, she found out from a friend that the hairdresser was lying. She used the money to get married and spend her honeymoon in Hellea."

Tea and the concern over her well-being seemed to calm Kamilia. Mansour couldn't hide his shock, though at the same time he felt relieved Kamilia wasn't really mad at him.

Dina simply peered around between the four older family members, seemingly unwilling to add to an already distressing situation.

Mansour advised, "You need to call the police, or . . . actually, you should tell Uncle Muhammad. He knows the right people to investigate this matter."

Soraya brightened. "Yes, of course. I will tell Muhammad. I just found out now, so I'm still in shock. I doubt they can get the money back, though, as Samira, the hairdresser, has already spent the money, and they are not rich, so we wouldn't be able to get it back from them."

"Well, at least we can stop them from doing that to other people," Mansour pointed out.

"Yes, my dear. I am sorry to bother you with this story," Soraya said. "Let us talk about something else. I want to know how you are doing."

"Yes," Kamilia blurted. "Please, anything else!"

They spent the next half hour trying to talk about other subjects, which was not so easy. They kept coming back to that horrible story.

After they left, Mansour told Kareem that he felt very bad about Kamilia's situation. He wasn't surprised, however, because—as Kareem informed him—Kamilia was very naive and kindhearted, and it was easy for people to take advantage of her. Mansour knew his aunt Soraya wasn't very wealthy, especially since her husband had passed away several years ago from lung cancer. He told Kareem that he wanted to help by giving some money to his aunt Soraya to help them recover from this terrible ordeal, but he wasn't sure of the best way to go about it.

Kareem told Mansour that he'd think about it and ask Aunt Samia. Mansour made a mental note to ask his mother as well.

Now it was time to tackle Nour's situation.

Chapter 6

16 years ago
Keerypt

Mansour asked his mother to let him listen in on her conversation with Nour from a nearby closet, but she gave him an expression that said, *if you don't tell me where this is coming from, we're going to have a serious talk.* So he dropped the whole idea. Even though he had brassy James Bond background music in his head, he explained that he was concerned for Nour's health and happiness, and he wanted all the best for everyone involved. That softened her up, and she agreed to explain how it went afterward. Though it wasn't what he hoped for, it was the deal he got.

So instead of practicing his secret agent skills, he had a great time in his uncle's pool, ate his grandmother's cooking, played some games, talked with Teta, and waited.

The seconds and minutes ticked on, and while it felt maddening at first, he eventually forget the very important mission he'd given himself and just relaxed.

That evening, though, after several days of partying, most of the relatives had gone home. They had a bit of normality to get back to before returning to their distant Keeryptian relatives. Fatima pulled him aside after the fourth prayer and sat him down.

"Are you sure you want to know all this, dear?" she asked.

He nodded. "Good or bad. I'm hoping if I work at it, we can clear things up with Nabil too."

She shook her head, astonished. "Something's gotten into you, *habibi.*"

He tried to pass this off with a shrug and a smile. "I guess you could say I'm a concerned cousin."

After a few more soft sighs and mild complaints about her son being a bit nosy, Fatima launched into the story.

Nour had met with her in one of the mansion's many bedrooms earlier. She'd brought a tray of aperitifs, tea and a steaming teapot, and had a box of tissues at the ready. Fatima began by explaining their honest concern for Nour's well-being, and their sincere hope for understanding that anything said would be held confidential.

Fatima paused, frowning a little.

"I know," Mansour said gently. "If you don't wish to tell me, I understand."

"It was your idea, after all," she replied before continuing the story. "Nour agreed that Uncle Muhammad was indeed wise and could probably speak with her husband. However, she didn't want to appear weak, or as if she was backing off. She also wasn't willing to continue with this new Nabil. She wanted the old one back, not the domineering puppet Nabil had become."

Domineering. That was a strong word. Mansour noted this down in his mind. He promised never to be a domineering husband.

"I took my time answering, you see," his mother told him. "I understood why she'd use the word domineering. I told her that in a marriage, any attempt at reconciliation should not be seen as weakness but rather as strength. In marriage, they were one unit: a team of husband and wife united against the difficulties of the world. If Nabil mistook her attempt to do what was best for the family as weakness in herself, then he was already gone from the good man he once was.

"Then I asked her if he'd been abusive, or if he'd cheated on her with other women," Fatima said quietly. "The answer was no. He didn't hit her. And if he cheated on her, it was only in his dreams. But it felt like abuse.

"She said, 'Every day he tells me what I should do and what I shouldn't do. And it hurts. I hide away and cry sometimes.

Honestly, if it was coming from him, I would understand, and we could discuss it. But I know for sure it isn't coming from him. It's coming from his mother.' She was filled with hurt, *habibi.* Hurt and bitterness. She was so sure.

"Nour told me this was her mother-in-law's revenge on Nour for marrying him. She never liked her. And now she tortured her through Nabil, and it was a dagger in her heart."

Mansour absorbed all this like a star pupil before a favorite teacher: nasty mother-in-law, family must work as a team, no hitting, no cheating.

"I asked her if Nabil called her names," Fatima continued, "or mocked her himself. I asked if she thought he still loved her."

Mansour's eyes widened at that last question. He wondered how that forwardness must have shocked the young wife. "What did she say?"

"She was sure he still loved her. Very sure. She told me everything he parroted wasn't what he was interested in. It was everything his mother had disapproved of in months past.

"They've been married for two years, and Nour hasn't been able to get pregnant. Before, she'd been able to rely on Nabil to be there for her, to hug and cry on, but now he was nothing more than a conduit for his mother's vile words. She blamed Nour, and now she was convincing her son to blame her too.

"She was crying by now, *habibi.* And sitting on the floor. I held her like her husband should have, and asked her whether she was taking birth control. She denied this, and confessed that she didn't know whether the problem was with her or Nabil."

Mansour nodded.

"She said that the matter was solidly in God's hands. I said that if she really wanted kids she should seek medical help and make a lot of *duaa* to God. The prayer and supplication will help steady her mind, and Allah will reveal His wisdom eventually. I told her that Muhammad would be willing to speak with Nabil about the issue, if she were okay with this. She jumped at the opportunity to have an experienced, successful elder speak with Nabil."

Mansour felt the warmth of love and hope in his chest. After all the harsh words and the tense situation, it was good to have a direction in which to move.

♛

"Life is about becoming a better person," Mansour proclaimed to Kareem as they splashed about in the spacious in-ground pool behind Aunt Soraya's apartment. Some families with young children were there as well, but they stayed in the shallower parts of the pool, giving Mansour and his cousin monopoly over its depths.

"Pffft," Kareem said, rolling his eyes. "If this is the lesson of life, life is an easy class indeed."

"Haha, yeah. That is just the introductory lesson though. How do you become a better person? If everyone knew the answer, then books about it wouldn't be a billion-dollar industry."

Kareem nodded. "This is true. So I suppose you've divined the wisdom of Allah. Have you become an esteemed scholar of the faith?"

It was Mansour's time to roll his eyes. "Don't make me out to be a blasphemer, Kareem. No, I study under such a scholar, Dr. Maher Hathout, but I still have questions, as does he. You seem to imply that I am saying how to become the best person. Only Allah knows that. No, I have an answer for you about how to become better, and it involves struggle."

A beach ball pounded over from the kids' side of the pool. Both eyed each other and then splashed into action, racing to be the first there. Mansour sliced smoothly through the pale blue leaving small ripples in his wake, and arrived there well before his cousin.

"Struggle," Kareem gasped when he got there. Mansour nodded and knocked the ball back over to its grateful owners.

"Yes, struggle. I struggled every chance I could to swim faster and now, as we saw, I am the better swimmer. Everything is like that. Of course, every person has their own unique style and character, and there is nothing wrong with that. I assume that if we both joined an eating contest, you would finish your plate before I even touched mine."

Kareem laughed. "I see you've become a comedian."

"Yes, I joke. But seriously, we must struggle against unhealthy habits. We must try. That's the key. Allah doesn't judge us for failing. He judges us for the attempt. We must try to quash our selfishness, arrogance, laziness, and immorality," Mansour explained.

Kareem looked skeptical. "That still sounds too easy."

Mansour punched him in the shoulder playfully. "It's harder than it might seem. I've accidentally just struck you a blow, quite selfishly. All in the space of a second. Eh?"

"Yeah, I guess. But what about the other faiths? Surely life is about something else for all of them."

"You'd think so, but it doesn't hold true. My very good friends Scott, Anthony, and Guillermo are very good Christians, and they believe the same thing," Mansour said. "I know they do, not just because of their words but also their actions. The girls at school swarm them like locusts on a plain of grain, but they stay celibate. They struggle with themselves, and they don't give in, and that makes them better people."

Mansour paused and then grinned up at the blazing sun. "You know what? The more you know, the more responsible you have become in front of God and toward the whole of society. So with knowledge and just by having resources in general—like health, time, and wealth—comes responsibility."

"Did you just rip off Spiderman?" Kareem teased.

Mansour splashed water in his face and they descended into playful chaos.

♛

Fatima called Mansour later, while he and Kareem sipped some ice-cold lemonade by the poolside—heavenly in the devastating heat of near a hundred degrees Fahrenheit.

"Nour told me there are no changes," his mother said. "They haven't talked to each other for more than a week now."

"Do you think we could arrange for him to talk with Uncle Muhammad soon?"

"Let me make a call, *habibi.* Keep your phone close."

Kareem just smiled. He'd overheard their conversation and chuckled ruefully. "Lucky you . . . You know if I get involved and mess things up, my sister hates my guts, and her in-laws think I'm nosing around where I have no business. But you'll only be here for a few days."

"Exactly what I was thinking," Mansour said. Exactly what you used a secret agent for.

His mother called back a few minutes later. "She doesn't want to bother anyone with her problems."

"And you immediately told her we're more than happy to be bothered with her problems?"

"Of course! Nabil has agreed to meet Muhammad at a restaurant. I'll send you the address."

"Let's hope he's open to speaking, *in shaa Allah.*" God willing. With luck, the situation would have something of a resolution, because it was nearly time for the Keeryptian side of the family to say goodbye to Faisal, Fatima, and Mansour.

Kareem dropped him off about forty-five minutes later in downtown Azima. Parking wasn't easy to find, and while Mansour waved goodbye, Kareem wasn't able to move for several infuriating minutes. Mansour laughed, strolled back over to the car, and leaned down.

"Road rage does not become you, cousin."

"Go save a marriage!" Kareem yelled in fake indignation. They shared a laugh, and Mansour headed into the restaurant.

This one was situated on a hill, which gave it an excellent

view down into the valley, especially as the sun set. Huge glass walls went with those trendy geometric pools that sluiced water in a strange illusory way that Mansour found hypnotic. The interior was top-notch as well, and if the food tasted anything like it smelled, it was going to be superb. He hoped he had the appetite for what was sure to be an expensive meal.

Mansour had been surrounded by family for so long it was nice to get a moment to himself, especially if it meant he could arrange his thoughts on Nour's marriage trouble.

Muhammad arrived half an hour later.

"Uncle," Mansour said, and pulled out a seat.

Muhammad stretched out his back, which popped several times, and he exhaled a strong sigh of relief.

"Shall I sit with you, or nearby?" Mansour and Nabil had never met, so it shouldn't be a problem to overhear the conversation, so long as he was cool about it.

Muhammad arched an eyebrow and grinned. "Mr. Bond, I presume?" They shared a chuckle. "It will be better if you're at the next table. Nabil won't take lightly to being told what to do, except by an elder of some repute. I'm impressed with your discretion and consideration, Mansour." He waved over a waiter to relay instructions.

Mansour positioned himself facing away from Muhammad's table. He'd be able to hear well enough, and could check out Nabil in the reflection of the restaurant's enormous windows.

Nabil soon arrived, and Muhammad waved him over, stood, and shook his hand. "I'm so glad you could make it," he said. "What would you like to drink?"

"Cold lemonade will be great," Nabil answered.

Muhammad got the chair for his nephew-in-law.

"Thank you for the offer to meet," Nabil said. "I admit to being puzzled though."

Mansour also felt thirsty and hot from his journey and

motioned to the server. "I'll have an iced lemonade please," he told the server quietly, making sure to use his Keeryptian dialect.

In a serious and concerned tone, Muhammad asked Nabil, "I hope you can be very open and candid with me. You know, of course, that Nour is from a very good and supportive family. It goes without saying that we want the best for her and for you as well. I will be very direct in my question. Do you want to continue in this marriage?"

This seemed less shocking to Nabil than Mansour expected. He pulled in a deep breath, seeming both resigned to how the conversation would go and ready to go there. "Yes, of course. I love Nour, and I want us to stay together forever."

Interesting. Mansour had wondered whether Nour's husband was simply tired of her defying him, or if it was something else. Apparently it was indeed another reason. Unfortunately, the server chose that moment to reappear and take their orders. After a few moments of awkward menu browsing, Muhammad ordered and offered to share with Nabil. Nabil agreed, and the server left.

Mansour's own server appeared, and he ordered the first item he saw. The dinner was far less important than this.

"I'm afraid Nour doesn't see your willingness to remain together. By not talking with her for over a week and staying out of the house, she's been receiving another message."

"I just wanted to give her some time to calm down. She gets really angry when I talk with her and advise her on certain things," Nabil explained.

A server appeared with their cold blender-mixed lemonade, so fresh that it had lemonade foam at the top. It was the quickest and best service Mansour had experienced so far in the city. And judging by the satisfied sound, the lemonade was the best Nabil had ever tasted. Hopefully it was so good that it would help calm him down.

Muhammad continued the discussion. "I don't want to get into a lot of details, but again, as I said earlier, I will be very open with you. My understanding, and with all due respect to your esteemed mother, is that you are allowing her to get involved in your personal life with your wife." Muhammad delivered this in a serious tone, and then continued before Nabil could become defensive, "I know you are a good Muslim, and you value your mother, which is really honorable and commendable. However, there's a big difference between being good to your mother and following everything she says, especially when it pertains to your wife. My dear brother, if you can consider me as a brother, you need to separate the two things. You can be good to your mother and good to your wife at the same time. In most situations, mothers-in-law don't think the same way as their daughters-in-law, and this creates a lot of friction, which leads to major family problems and many end up in divorce.

"All this could be avoided if the husband would separate his mother from his wife. Some characters cannot mix together easily. It doesn't mean one is good and the other is bad, or one is right and the other is wrong. It doesn't mean that at all. I'm not a professional counselor, and I would highly recommend seeing a family counselor who can help you fix the different problems and concerns. For the time being, though, since you indicated that you want the marriage to continue, I recommend that you call Nour and tell her that you love her and care about her. And you should both stay together in your home. I would avoid discussing problems or giving her any advice now. Just focus on the positive qualities she has and things you have in common, and tell her you want to fix the problems because you want to be together for the rest of your lives.

"You know, of course, that I went through a divorce. It was a very painful experience, and though I learned many lessons, I do not wish this to happen to anyone at all. That is why Prophet Muhammad (peace be upon Him) said that the most hated lawful thing to God is divorce."

Nabil took his time before replying. He had another sip of that refreshing lemonade, then said, "Thank you, Uncle Muhammad. I really appreciate your advice. You know how much I respect and admire you, and I will be very happy if Nour and I get together again. I just hope that she will be open-minded and accept me back into her life."

The food arrived, and in a testament to Fatima's planning, it was exactly what they needed at this moment: spiced, succulent, and fresh.

"Well, you won't know until you try. You cannot remain silent and stay away because you think she might reject you," Muhammad said.

Nabil seemed well disposed to listen. Plus, he raved over the food, and Mansour knew from experience that the best way to a person's heart was through his or her stomach. Afterward, in the taxi on the way home, he called his mother, who put him on speaker with Nour in the room.

"I hope you can forgive him, cousin," he said. "He seems a decent man, with a good heart. There's no shame in seeking help, from your family or from a counselor."

He heard some hushed words and possibly some crying as well. Finally, a tiny voice responded, "Thank you, Mansour."

He smiled. "I'm responsible for nothing, but if it works out, that will be all the thanks I need."

Chapter 7

Now
Port Zanobia, Keerypt

"Here you are," Ishmael said, pulling the dingy old Sprint up to the side of the airport. Mad Salim, true to his word, had created a passport that to Mansour's eyes was indeed indistinguishable from the real thing. He wondered what the government visa services would be like if they had a genius like that man at the helm. Then he remembered the state of his house and shivered.

The airport was all hustle and bustle, and this area was temporary parking only, so he thanked the men and grabbed his bags. He had a plane to book and then catch, if such a thing were possible. It had better be possible, considering all of the money he'd burned getting himself out of here.

A couple of police officers walked by and Mansour froze. They continued on their way, however, swinging by a concession stand selling salted dates for five pounds. Good. But their very presence made it clear to him that if there weren't any open seats, he'd have to think up something else. Staying here a day longer would have definite repercussions.

He rolled his bags through the terminal and went to the information kiosk at its center. A large gentleman in a light blue airport uniform saluted him. He looked like recent ex-military, his hair still growing out from the shaved high and tight it had sported before.

"Hi there. Could you tell me how to book a ticket to Arlandica? I've never flown before, and I'd like to get a ticket and leave today, if that's possible."

The big fellow barely glanced at Mansour before crushing his hopes. "Sir, what you are asking is almost impossible. Passengers are advised to book their flights well in advance. What is the nature of your flight?"

"My father is dying. I wish to be at his bedside before he passes on from our world."

The man's face changed not one iota. "I'm sorry to hear that, sir. I'll check the flight information now to see if there are any seats available for emergency services." His fingers tapped across the keyboard, clicking and clacking by instinct alone, Mansour supposed, since the keyboard's letters and numbers had worn to near illegibility. He wondered why the airport hadn't bothered to replace it.

"Ah, here we are, sir. There is a single seat on Arlandica flight 2457, Solitos Airlines, out of gate A57. Boarding ends in thirty minutes. I'm sorry to say that there's no way you will be able to get a ticket, check your bags, go through security, and board the plane in time."

Mansour stared at him. "You wanna bet?"

The ex-military man's neutral facade cracked for the first time, showing incredulous disbelief. "If I thought I would ever see you again to collect my winnings, I would."

"Put a hold on that seat, please, and just watch how quickly I can get through. I will make it."

Mansour saw the man salute him as he rushed off to find the Solitos ticket counter. He appreciated the gesture, saluted back, and fell over an empty luggage cart left by some lazy stranger. He hopped back up quickly. He was going to make it. He was going to make it because he had a plan.

Like with the ferry, Mansour took the first-class queue, avoiding the tired, long lines of coach, simply because only one person stood in front of him. A fat lady with a cutesy white fluffy dog sporting pink ribbons at the base of its ears stood making cutesy language at the pup. He waited patiently as she waddled to the desk, gave them her papers, and went off on her way. The woman at the counter gestured him ahead, and he put all of his documents and passport on her desk.

"Hi I'm Mansour and I need to book a seat today for a flight that is leaving in . . . twenty-eight minutes so there isn't any time to tell me anything but what I need to hear. There's an open seat, I'm assuming coach, on flight 2457, and you are going to book me it right now."

The woman opened her mouth to complain. Mansour slid five hundred pounds in bills onto the counter from his pocket. She shut up and started typing, pausing only to glance at his passport before typing a little more. The scritch-scratch of the ticket printer ran a moment later, and then he was off, bags banging off his back as he sprinted for security. The man at the information kiosk saluted him again as Mansour ran on by.

Mansour took a right at a bookstore, a left at a MacArnold's, then hit the end of an impossibly long queue. He stared ahead and sighed. This was going to take a bit more planning.

He spied a huge man just coming out of an area labeled Medical Escort Services and readied his envelopes full of cash again.

♛

The towering bald man stood behind him, looming over Mansour's wheelchair. He was a giant of a man, the sort of being who made people believe the Daeva might well have married into the human line and had unholy offspring. He was the perfect candidate for the next step in Mansour's plan, especially since there were just fifteen minutes left to get on the plane.

"Coming through!" the giant bellowed. Mansour kept his head covered, a mask affixed to his face and his shoulders slumped as if exhausted.

"Hey! What are you doing?" someone yelled as the giant unclipped a rope from the queue and pushed his passenger through.

"Medical pass, man needs to make his flight. Surgery in under twenty-four hours!" the giant yelled. It looked like the annoyed future passenger was going to make a bigger fuss, but he blanched when the giant raised a large, ham-sized fist.

They clattered through to the security station.

"What is going on here?" one of the security detail asked.

"We've got a medical. He got delayed in transit from Niero Hospital and now he's about to miss his flight!" the giant replied. Under his mask, Mansour smirked. He was going to make it.

"All right, hold up, buster. Let me scan you two with the wand before I let you through. We still have protocol here. We aren't savages, you know."

The white plastic wand whirred and beeped as the man waved it over Mansour and his quickly found and more quickly hired accomplice. Mansour had known as soon as he saw the medical escort service that the large man was used to getting his own way. In fact, he'd thrown another wad of money into betting that the man would get him to the gates right in time to miss their closure.

"All right, you are clear to pass. Get him to his surgery, would you, Bilal? You're scaring the children."

The giant, Bilal, laughed as he kicked up to a sprint. The blanket covering Mansour fluttered at the edges, threatening to catch in the chair's wheels. They took a hard right. The chair actually tipped just a little off the ground before settling again upon the thin carpet flooring of the walkway.

"Outta the way!" Bilal boomed.

A couple of children screamed and cowered while most everyone else froze. Everyone except for the people in front of him. They scattered like rabbits before a hungry and vicious wolf. "Coming through!" he added in case no one got the picture.

Mansour watched them whizz through and started to count the gates as they flew by. A52, A53, a restroom, A54, A55, a smoking lounge, A56, A57! Bilal ran him up to the counter and, in one motion, deposited the ticket and passport on the counter before him. "That's one sick passenger, with a seat, heading for Arlandica. With one minute to spare," he grinned, giving Mansour a wink. An airline attendant took his wheelchair even as the counter woman processed his ticket and passport.

"Have a safe flight," she told him as he wheeled away into the aircraft.

The flight to Sunland, Arlandica, would take a day, counting the layover in Aragonia. And that was fine by Mansour. He stretched, he picked out a magazine, and then he promptly fell asleep, waking only when his snoring became so unbearable that a flight attendant was called over to sort it out. He woke again after the flight had landed and a pretty, blond woman with clear blue eyes shook him gently.

"Sir, we are here. Are you ready to be wheeled out?"

He shook his head in confusion. Wheeled out? Then it all came back to him. The heady rush through the airport, the bribing of the health attendant services giant, the salute of the ex-military information services man–it was no wonder he'd conked out so hard and for so long. But he'd made it! He was here–his first stop, a four-hour layover in Aragonia. And he had plenty he needed to do.

"Yes. Thank you. If I could be rolled to the nearest terminal restroom, actually, that would be fantastic."

The attendant nodded knowingly. There was something about airplanes, their gentle vibrations and constant hum, that sent everyone running for the bathroom. Her eyes grew even more understanding when his stomach loudly rumbled, visibly shaking the green shirt that he wore.

"Oh, and could I have a sandwich?" he asked sheepishly.

Mansour was wheeled out, the airline version of a kebab sandwich in his hand and three more in his lap, to the outside of the nearest bathroom.

"Au revoir," the attendant said. "Until we meet again!"

Mansour smiled. "Goodbye and thank you. I will be sure to visit the company website and give you all an excellent review."

It took some doing, rolling to the bathroom, then changing some of his Keeryptian pounds into Aragonian notes before wheeling himself to the rows of old-fashioned payphones, each specially designed with international calls in mind. "Ten Pesetas, ten minutes!" a sign boldly proclaimed. Considering how much he had spent already, though, it was quite the deal.

He rolled to the nearest phone cubicle, lifted up the receiver, then scanned behind him. There was nobody out of the ordinary, nobody interested in him. He tapped in a number long memorized and close to his heart, and waited.

"Hello?" a voice asked. Nadia. Good. She was awake.

"Hello, Nadia. It is me, Mansour."

"Mansour! Oh, thank Allah. I have been worried sick about you. The news says there has been a coup and a seizure of power, and that a number of foreigners have been rounded up and imprisoned for espionage."

He couldn't have summed it up better. "Yes. That's all true." He lowered his voice. "And I'm on that list as well. I spent a lot of money to escape, and I'm not home yet, so I must be careful."

Nadia remained quiet for a long moment. "What can I do, my love?"

"My flight to Sunland is heading straight to West Beach Airport. I'm going to need a pickup at 7 p.m. I'm in disguise as a handicapped man now, but I'll try to change before we meet. So you won't have to act or do anything other than greet me like you would otherwise."

"Okay. I understand. Just be safe. Is your father with you?"

Now Mansour paused. The words didn't come out easily. "I don't think he made it." He looked away from the phone and out into the terminal, tears burning in his eyes. Through the wavy beginnings of tears, he saw them. Three men in black suits, black neck ties, and white buttoned shirts coming directly toward him.

"I'm so sorry–"

"Nadia, I have to go. Just make sure you're there on time. I can't wait to escape this nightmare and be done with this, and I won't be free until I'm back on Arlandican soil."

"Okay. Bye, Mansour. Be safe."

He clicked the phone closed and almost stood up before remembering himself and rolling out of the kiosk, angling for a nearby Taco Bueno. The approaching men did a half-left facing movement and kept on his trail. Well, so much for the idea that it might be a coincidence.

Okay, okay. So there was no way they were here to make a public scene. As agents of Terra Qurayshia, they weren't supposed to be conducting such operations on foreign soil. That should be an operation of the Aragonian Police Agency and Interpol. However, he knew that the new king didn't care at all about protocol. That was to his advantage. He couldn't make a scene either, though. Otherwise he really would have to deal with Interpol.

He scanned for inspiration as he wheeled, with the agents power walking behind him. He came to an intersection and paused for just a second before recognizing his objective. At the end of the long hallway to his left, past all of the shops and boutiques, was a dimly lit maintenance section with a hallway branching off and out of sight. It was almost certainly empty. And would make a great place to store some bound undercover agents for the couple of hours he'd need before he could fly on out of here.

He spun his wheels and turned, going down the hallway at a nice clip. Behind him, the agents began a light jog. A few spectators stopped to watch, and the agents seemed to change their minds. They broke off pursuit and headed to a clothing boutique, presumably to make it look like they were investigating a security concern. It was a bit annoying, but Mansour knew they'd be back. He continued to the maintenance cutaway and rolled through the red-lit corridor past sinks and drains. Then he left his wheelchair.

A series of lockers stood at the far end. These, he opened one by one, marveling at the incredible array of chemicals they contained. As he picked out a large monkey wrench, a formula popped into his head: $C_2HBrClF_3$. Fluothane, better known as sleeping gas—and quite doable with the proper household supplies.

Amazing what all the late-night study sessions with his dearest Nadia had put in his head. Her medical degree might just save his life.

He ran back to the first locker. There, trichloroethylene—grease solvent! He grabbed a jug of the stuff, then checked through the second and third locker before coming upon some hydrogen fluoride, a.k.a. spot remover. Double-check. In the fifth locker, he found cables sheathed in antimony as well as a cable stripper on the bottom shelf. He threw them all in a yellow-wheeled mop bucket and wondered where he could find some heat. Mansour flung open lockers six and seven, peered into eight, and was about out of hope when he found propane and a welder in locker nine. This maintenance section was a treasure trove. He paused. It was also incredibly dangerous.

Mansour grabbed the cables and stripped and peeled the antimony-laced rubber from them, making sure to bare as much of the metal as possible before dumping them all back into the mop bucket. Then he poured in his chemical concoctions, ran back to the lockers, made himself a chemical mask by soaking a rag in ammonia, and sparked up the blowtorch. It wouldn't be long now. He hovered the flame over the surface of his witch's brew to keep it heating evenly. Soon visible noxious vapors rose from the surface. It was time. But would his pursuers be joining him?

He heard the clatter of their boots moments later. He would have preferred a thicker fog, but hopefully this would do. He set the device in the slot generally reserved for the mop head to allow the flame to keep doing its work and he sent the bucket rolling toward the entrance as evenly as he could. It soared smoothly, bumping into an agent's legs. The man tripped over it and, as the fuming liquid boiled over the edge, he promptly passed out. The two others moved to grab their friend and then they too crumpled to the floor, off to dreamland.

Mansour checked his watch. Just an hour left 'til the plane took off. Boarding in thirty minutes. The tying up, gagging, and sliding of unconscious bodies took some doing, but he was up to the task. A few minutes later, he settled into his wheelchair and rolled on out, stripping off his mask and tossing it at the last second. He headed out into the hallway and then to his gate, watching the whole way through. Once near the entrance, he settled back in his chair and let himself sleep. They'd come close, and had probably reported his whereabouts, but for now he was as good as back home.

Chapter 8

16 years ago
Keerypt

"I'm not sure you could survive here, my soft cousin," Kareem said. "Here it's the modern world, all noise, exhaust, and nights that never darken."

They'd played in the gleaming waters of the pool until the sun turned orange, hanging low like ripened fruit on the horizon. Now they nestled within the burgundy-purple confines of Kareem's Matsumoto Aria, swerving from gap to gap in what looked to be the traffic jam of the century. The cars honked and beeped so frequently that they might well be mechanical cousins to the crickets of his own country estate in Arlandica. It was incessant, and he found himself wishing that he had brought along earplugs, or at least a USB key with some good tunes.

"You're right, Kareem. I'm not used to any of this," Mansour sighed. "Is it always this way?"

"It is this way everywhere, Mansour! This is how humans live now. Welcome to our world."

Mansour looked out the window as Kareem cut off a dirty yellow sedan, taking over the space in front of him. The driver saw Mansour and rolled down his window to yell something unpleasant. Mansour kept his window closed and looked away.

"Life is very different in Arlandica, Kareem. But not primitive different. People think differently and have different priorities. Different vehicles too," he said, pointing at the dirty yellow sedan, whose driver was still yelling from the driver's side window.

Kareem shot a glance over his shoulder to take it in. "He's a poor man with a poor car. Are you saying that Arlandica doesn't have poor people?"

Mansour chuckled. "Wouldn't that be something? What a wonderful dream. But no, I'm saying that life and how people think is very different. Especially in my state of Sunland where I live. In Arlandica, you have more freedom to choose how you want to live and what to pursue for your education and your dreams. You have more flexibility, but it puts more responsibility on the individual. You can make it big or you can waste your time and lose big. And people know it–in Arlandica that man with the yellow car wouldn't have a car at all. He'd be wise and patient. He would take the bus."

Kareem's eyes widened. He turned to regard Mansour, then hit his dashboard with an angry fist when a light blue Sprint tore into a sudden gap in front of him.

"We also don't punch the dashboard in Arlandica," Mansour said, grinning. "But not all use this freedom wisely. There are people who don't or can't plan their lives properly. But that is fine too, because certain basics in life are taken for granted in Arlandica, and you don't need to think or worry about them. Food, water, electricity, places to live–these are all things that the government supplies to its citizens, and so the people there can focus on living their lives as best as they can live them."

Kareem smiled. "It sounds like a grand place to live, cousin. Keerypt gives little but takes much, and getting anything done with them is a nightmare. There are so many papers and such long wait times. I don't understand why things have to be this way."

"I think my point is that they don't." A sudden thought flashed into Mansour's head. Is that what being an agent was for? To protect such a wonderful way of life from becoming, well, this? A cherry red four-door almost plowed into them from behind and laid on the horn. The man screamed through his windshield with murderous rage in his eyes. Mansour shivered.

He imagined himself chasing a villain through the streets

on a motorbike, or perhaps hopping from car top to car top. The fellow had stolen some state secrets belonging to his uncle, and he was desperate to get them back. Would there be gunfire exchanged? Had they just tried to assassinate his uncle, and he was hot on their trail?

Kareem had a few moments of standstill traffic to regard his cousin. "The people here have to pay fees for everything. And they don't get paid a lot, most of them. They spend fortunes on licenses, registrations, and passports. Forms after forms that take weeks to process, and then they get married and try to find an apartment in which to raise a family and find themselves mired in debt from the day they step across the threshold. And all that hurts, all the hopelessness; that's who we are when we go out on the streets. But it isn't the real us. I hope you don't forget that, Mansour. In between tears and struggle, the Keeryptian people are kind and gentle souls."

Mansour looked guilty and felt chastened. "I'm sorry. Yes, I think I know that, but it's good to hear it anyways." He peered out the window again, at the smog-ridden city. Its wealthy towers drew all eyes away from the many slums that surrounded them.

Kareem nodded. "You are a very smart man, cousin. Your whole family is. So why have you come to such a dark pit as this? You don't belong here. It's a dirty place, filled with sadness and sin."

"Because we wanted to visit all of you sad saps," Mansour said and laughed.

Kareem joined him.

"There is our exit, finally!" Kareem exclaimed. "Let's get out of this mess and go find a good place to eat."

They ended up getting takeout Nipponese noodles and stir-fry, enough for four, and hiking up to a friend's house. The last time Mansour had been in Keerypt, he'd been a preteen, shuttled around wherever his parents wanted to go. He couldn't remember ever meeting his friends at their own houses. Yasser lived in a flat as part of a boxy brown high-rise. It wasn't cramped like Mansour assumed it would be, and Yasser's parents were gracious in retreating to a back room to watch television while Mansour, Kareem, Yasser, and their other friend Sameer ate and played video games and talked.

"You guys are lifesavers." Yasser brought over all the plates and forks, while Mansour separated his wooden chopsticks and grabbed himself some food.

"Tell me all about the girls," Sameer asked with a mouthful of noodles. "How many girlfriends you got, eh?"

"Gotta be at least one," Yasser mumbled around a mouthful of food.

"The girls on the shows are fit . . . They're not all like that in real life, right?"

Mansour chuckled and wondered just how many times he would be asked these sorts of questions. Perhaps if he recorded some voice notes onto his phone, he could send them to his friends ahead of time, so they could just have fun without going on and on about females. They kept at it though, which brought to mind some of the girls who'd come onto him at school, sporting events, and the rare occasion he attended a party. And now, with this secret agent situation rattling around in his poor head, with his simmering anger at his father, he wondered if maybe he should've indulged a bit and let some of those strong Arlandican girls take advantage of him a time or two.

And yet, he was also glad he hadn't. Their beliefs and lifestyle would've always come crashing against his own sooner or later, and a moment's worth of pleasure was not worth months of pain, drama, and disappointment. This was an idea that soothed him every time.

He explained this without much care for Yasser or Sameer judging him. He'd remain true to himself without bothering with their idea of what he should be. "By staying away from the temporary pleasure and controlling my cravings, I feel liberated.

I am not a slave to my desires; I am a free man. I free myself to do productive things such as reading, learning new hobbies and new skills, volunteering my time to help others, and focusing on building myself academically, intellectually, physically, and spiritually."

Sameer and Yasser gave him odd looks, which allowed Kareem to mash the controller buttons and knock out Sameer in the game.

"I don't want to sound preachy, but I really think that if we follow the teaching of the Qur'an and stay away from doing the wrong things, we will be much more successful in this life and the next. And that, for the moment, means success in kicking your butt. I'll fight the winner."

They played on for a time, and finished up the remainder of the late lunch—or was it early dinner? The conversation hopped around to different topics: the Sunland sports teams, girls again, Mansour's uncle, the new king over in Terra Qurayshia, upcoming video games, which character had the easiest special attacks and which were the cheesiest, easiest to win with, back to girls, and then to what university life would inevitably be like. This naturally included another topical dive back into the mysterious world of girls.

Mansour made clear his intention to stay away from any relationship until he married. Saying it out loud affirmed his resolve, made the truth of it easier to swallow, and Kareem regarded him with an expression of respect and admiration he rather enjoyed.

Mansour thought of Nour and Nabil, and considered even marriage to be a potential challenge. And now that he was focused on it . . . would his father allow his beloved to be in on the secretive nature of his future profession? Would he instead be forced to live a series of lies about where he was going and what he'd be doing? This idea rankled him because he had followed the Qur'an so closely. It was clear on the topic of lying. Worse still was the notion that he wouldn't be allowed to marry, and the profession would rise above all else. No, he was adamant about marriage; his father wouldn't dream of forbidding him from it.

He had so many questions and no way to ask about them.

"But . . . it's just guys all the time?"

"Not at all. I spend time with guys, girls, couples. We go bowling, watch movies in the theater or at someone's house, head to the park, head to the beach."

"The beach . . ." Sameer said wistfully.

"The bikinis . . ." Yasser followed.

"Do you two think of nothing else?"

Kareem laughed. "You cannot blame them, cousin."

"My friends are a mixture of nationalities and religions. I have friends who are Arlandicans of Hellean and Zhouan ancestry, Middle Easterners, and South Zhouans. They have different beliefs: some of them are Christian, some are Jews, some are Muslims, and some are Hindu or Buddhist, and one is an atheist."

Sameer said, "I actually respect you for taking this position. I agree with everything you said. That is the smart thing to do, but of course, very difficult."

"The struggle is real," Yasser agreed in a sage tone.

"How do you work on resisting the temptation and staying out of trouble?" Sameer asked.

"Well, what I found to work for me was to develop a list of things to do whenever the thought comes to me of wanting to have a girlfriend. In other words, it's a way of deflecting my thoughts to something else that's positive and productive. For example, instead of dwelling more on the idea, I would force myself to go and finish any homework I have, or I'd wash up and make ablution and then pray and make supplication to God—asking God to give me strength and keep me out of trouble—or I would play the piano, or I would call my friends or read the newspaper, a book, or a magazine. The activity would depend on the situation, my mood, the time of the day, where I am at the moment, and how much time I have."

At last, after Yasser had tidied up the dishes and they sat around talking even more, the discussion turned in a direction Mansour hadn't anticipated: politics. It started with a story about Sameer's good friend Akram.

A few months ago, Akram's dad had been taken into custody for several days of questioning before he was released. He'd been in a high-level government position and was arrested soon after he retired. Akram also told him that the government took all their family's money before releasing his dad. Apparently, someone had notified the authorities that Akram's dad had a lot of wealth without justification.

Mansour was confused about what in the world "wealth without justification" could possibly mean, and asked if they'd found any evidence of wrongdoing.

Sameer explained they hadn't found anything wrong. Here in Keerypt, the burden of proof was on the accused. So they could accuse someone of becoming wealthy illegally, and the person had to prove that the government was wrong. And of course, if the government wanted someone to be guilty, they would be found guilty. There was no rule of law over here.

"So if the government suspects someone," Mansour asked, "they arrest them until that person proves they are innocent? Even if the authorities didn't find anything wrong?"

Sameer nodded.

"Are you saying that in Keerypt, you're guilty until you prove you're innocent?"

"Yes, again, you are correct. It sounds really strange and unfair, doesn't it?"

Of course it was unfair. It was probably against most, if not all, constitutions in the world.

Sameer said, "Well, this is one of the ways to keep people under control and afraid of the government and unable to ever think of going against the big power. The system of corruption, where government employees are given very low salaries, seems to have been created on purpose and built into the system. They force people to think of other means to support themselves and their families. When the time is convenient for the people in power, they catch those who are no longer within their circle and charge them with disobeying the law."

Of course, he'd never learned such things on his last trip; he'd been barely a teenager by that point. His mind swirled almost as it had when he'd overheard his father's phone call. The world was rapidly expanding and darkening, and he didn't like it much.

"The unfortunate thing is that most people stayed away from Akram's family, including some from his own extended family members. They were afraid to get caught up in these problems. It would be an understatement if I said that Akram and his family were devastated. The court's verdict was against Akram's dad and mom, as well as Akram and his siblings. It was obviously unfair. The government just wanted to destroy the whole family."

Kareem said, "Do you think it could be a test for Akram's family? And I guess their friends also."

"What do you mean, Kareem?" Yasser asked.

"Well, life is full of tests. God said in the Qur'an that He will test us in different ways. God says He will test us with some fear, hunger, loss of wealth, loss of lives, and loss of the fruits of our labor. But the verse ends by saying, give glad tidings to those who are patient,[3]" Kareem answered.

"Injustice at the highest levels doesn't feel much like a test. More like a swift ticket to prison yourself," Yasser said.

Kareem went on, "Those who were close to them, will they stand by them in this tough time or run away? That is the test: to differentiate genuine people from fake superficial people who are only attracted to wealth, position, and status."

Yasser commented, "Would you blame people for trying to

---

[3] Qur'an 2:155.

protect themselves from danger?" When they all gave him the eye, he continued, "Oh, sure, it sounds simple. You just rise up against the government and their police and soldiers and prisons and courts."

"I don't think anyone would blame you for keeping yourself out of harm's way," Kareem said. "What I'm saying is, it's a choice and it's a clear path laid out in the Qur'an. I don't think there's a harder test in any of the Suras, but it's still a test. This is the time when you need your family and friends the most."

Mansour nodded. "As Dr. Maher Hathout says, this is what differentiates men from boys."

Yasser eyed them a bit defensively. "I'm not disagreeing with you, but I think it's easy for you to criticize other people if you're not in that situation yourself."

They became silent for a minute. Yasser clearly felt he was being judged, though Mansour hadn't intended that.

Sameer said, "I don't know the situation of other people, but my dad contacted Akram's dad, and I didn't stop talking with Akram. I'm not saying we're better than other people. We just felt that we needed to stand by them at this time, and they really appreciated it."

Mansour added, "I'm very sad to hear this story. I don't know Akram, and I think I would've reached out to him if I knew him."

And what would Mansour 007 do in this situation, had he been Akram's friend and ally? He would love to pretend he'd sneak into some Keeryptian government office—probably under heavy guard—and get some evidence of malfeasance by the people who had torn away everything Akram's father had worked so hard for. Perhaps schmooze some of the perpetrators at a black tie event, swipe their identification, and turn the tables on those who would perpetuate such injustice.

"I'm also sad about what happened to Akram's family . . ." Yasser trailed off before collecting himself and going on. "I know, for example, that my dad feels sorry for what happened to Akram's dad. But my dad's position is very sensitive, and I know for a fact that my dad's phone is wiretapped and he is being watched."

"That's very scary and creepy and should be illegal," Mansour said.

"Unfortunately, this is reality, Mansour. I'm sure that your home here in Keerypt and probably in Terra Qurayshia as well is wiretapped," Yasser replied.

Mansour stared and nodded. "Thank you for letting me know. It has been a long day, and I can barely keep my eyes open. Jetlag has me ready to sleep at all hours of the day, I fear. I must go. Take care, Yasser."

"*Tusbah ala khair.* Good night, Mansour. And remember to speak lightly."

Chapter 9

16 years ago
Keerypt

Though Mansour had awoken in the dead predawn hours to curse jetlag, make ablutions, pray, and recite a few more verses, he made an effort to get a bit more sleep. And again, as his luck—and teenage habit—would have it, he succeeded. Sometime after eight, he awoke to the mechanical whir of an industrial blender accentuated by the chop-chop-swish of a cutting board in full operation.

Mmm, breakfast. He blinked away the sleep dust and took in the morning light. He'd slept well, and his stiff body demanded recompense, so he spent a moment popping, cracking, and stretching before exiting to the kitchen.

His mother Fatima stood poised over a large, fat tomato, her blade arced for battle. "Hello, my dear," she called without looking. "How was your sleep?"

Mansour looked at the things she'd already chopped. White cheese, olives, mint leaves—with her addition of sliced tomatoes to the mix, this was going to be a breakfast to remember.

"I slept well, Mom. Maybe too well," he said as he stretched a sore tendon in his shoulder. Then his jaw dropped as he spied the contents of the house blender. Banana. Dates. Smoothies. "You are the best, Mom!" Mansour wrapped her up in a hug from behind.

"I am. And I'm happy that my brilliant son has finally realized this. Go call everyone else to the table. Breakfast is officially done."

Mansour left the room and called the family together. "Food's done, and if you don't come quickly, I guarantee there'll be nothing left!" he yelled.

The pitter-patter of hungry feet followed. Everyone knew that to leave a growing boy like Mansour alone with a platter of Fatima's phenomenal cooking was an invitation to go hungry.

It was a busy morning, though, and conversation was hushed as they hurried through their food. Mansour's father, Faisal, would be arriving today, and he, his mother, and Uncle Muhammad were slated to pick him up from the airport. Mansour couldn't wait—it'd been a while since he'd seen his old man, and he was also curious if his mission might not come up soon, now that they were in Keerypt.

His suspicion that such a thing might be coming heightened when they arrived at the airport. Muhammad passed by the sign for visitor parking, veered off onto a side road marked VIP Only, and drove to a security booth staffed by armed officers. He slowed at the booth, and without a word, one of the officers waved a wand over and under their sedan while the other scanned an ID wedged into Muhammad's wallet. Then, with a nod, he allowed the car to pass, not a word spoken. Mansour couldn't imagine what else this could be. He was about to be inducted into whatever secret agent organization his father had spoken of!

And then they arrived at a white and gray building covered in lights. VIP Monarchy Class Guests Only read a large band of letters across its front. His excitement dampened, but only by a little. He'd never gotten to experience the luxuries of an elite class lounge. Such things didn't really exist back in Arlandica. Not like this, anyway. He'd heard tales and, stepping through the rotating door into the cool mist of the lobby, he knew they were true. He felt like a boy who'd just won a golden ticket.

Comfort rooms, each with their own specialty, circled the lobby: a place for beverages, a place for fast food and snacks, a more upstanding buffet filled with meats and veggies, a library in which to read, a row of private cinemas where one could select a video off a playlist and spend their time immersed in the glory of movie magic. A friend of his had told him long before that anything you want, you can have at the Monarchy VIP Lounge in Keerypt. Mansour now knew it to be true.

He made a line for a massage chair and flinched when an attendant rushed over to him. He was not chastised, though. Instead the man asked him if he would like something to drink, and soon the chair was pounding his back while he sipped iced orange soda through a straw.

Muhammad laughed at the sight of it all. "I sometimes forget what a vacation the VIP lounge can be. Enjoy it, nephew, because it will be a while again before we return."

Mansour relaxed, and then his eyes fell upon a man with a chiseled jaw and proud mustache. Famed actor Omar Narif! His eyes widened as he realized that the place was full of notables. Singers, actresses, actors—a cornucopia of who's who in Keerypt, and he was smack dab in the middle of them.

Muhammad interrupted his starstruck reverie with a chuckle. "Yes, take it all in. One day, if you are successful like your father, this will be your life as well. Enjoy yourself. I must go get your father. His gate is a particularly high security one, and I fear I'm the only one with the clearance to meet him."

The clearance to meet him? Was Muhammad part of the same organization? Mansour's mind, already reeling, began to free-fall into creative thought. He pictured his uncle, in a white suit with a rose in its lapel, dodging bullets and riding jet-powered skis away from pursuing snowmobiles through the alps of Stotterland.

The image was at once appealing and difficult to digest. Such people weren't real. The secret agents of the real world couldn't possibly live such glamorous lives. His father had made it sound dangerous and unappealing. Allah had specifically forbidden spying: God says, do not spy on one another.[4] Mansour resolved

[4] Qur'an 49:12.

to get the truth out of his father before this trip was over, one way or another.

Muhammad smiled, patted his shoulder, and walked out of the building.

♛

Faisal swept Fatima and Mansour up in a grand hug, and soon they were on the way back home from the airport. It was a long drive from the airport—even wealthy and important VIP passengers didn't get a special secret route around the constant traffic jams that marked Keeryptian life. Faisal and Muhammad talked politics while Fatima hummed happily to herself next to him. Mansour felt a bit left out, and bored besides, so he seized on this chance to talk about Kamilia.

"Kamilia got swindled," Mansour said as nonchalantly as he could.

Muhammad grunted. "Too often it happens here. There are bad people who do not respect the rules. I heard all about it."

"So what do you think, Uncle Muhammad? Can anyone help catch this crook woman and make her return the money?"

Faisal regarded Muhammad and then his son with eyes that spoke pride. Mansour suddenly felt all grown-up.

"Well, we can catch her," Muhammad replied, "but I doubt the money can be returned. If they spent it already, and they don't have enough money to pay it back, nothing can be done. But that doesn't mean I'm not doing anything about it! I called up one of my contacts, and he has asked the local news media to cover this story and expose it to the public."

"That's a clever idea, Muhammad. Well done," Faisal said. "Also, on the TV program, they should mention steps to be taken when facing such a situation; for example, people in need should be referred to the Ministry of *Awqaf* (Endowment). Donors have placed a lot of money in endowment funds to help people in need. That way, you'll have professional people checking into the situation, making sure it's a real need and not a scam."

"But would Aunt Soraya be all right with being put in the media spotlight over getting conned?" Mansour asked. "Don't get me wrong, those are great ideas. I'm just not sure she'll be okay with it."

Muhammad rubbed his chin. "That's a good head on your shoulders. Yes, it could be a problem. But what if we interview Kamilia or Soraya without showing their faces? We could also obscure their faces and voices."

"And don't worry, my son, about the money," Fatima added. "I am already preparing to send them a large sum of money to replace that which was lost."

Mansour smiled and nodded. While he hadn't had much involvement in the situation, it was good to have helped in some little way. It would all be taken care of.

Mansour's father soon disappeared on day trips out with Fatima, and when he was at Muhammad's estate, relatives swarmed him: Aunt Samia with her children Kareem and Nour, Aunt Soraya with Kamilia and Dina, and of course, Teta—always around to help keep his mind off the secret agent situation—and Uncle Muhammad with his graceful, easy wisdom and ability to solve problems.

Father hadn't spoken to him privately, as he had the ability to do. Mansour found it frustrating the first day, angering the second day, and infuriating the third. He hadn't imagined the discussion, nor had he imagined his father's responses to whatever the king was planning. Now he made it impossible to breach the subject.

He saw two possible reasons. First, that the spy notion had been scrapped by his uncle, the king. In this case, there was nothing to speak to his father about because the program no longer existed. The second reason was simply that this was a test.

He figured the first was unlikely, given the reforms the king of Terra Qurayshia had put into motion in the first few months of his reign. Not impossible, but unlikely. So more likely a test.

Luckily, his mother took the fourth day off to relax in bed, complaining she wasn't feeling well. The whole family was at Uncle Muhammad's house, and while his father was in the office speaking with Terra Qurayshian officials about some official matter, Mansour took in some of that uncle wisdom. Aunt Soraya had asked her older brother to dispense nuggets of wisdom about schoolwork to her youngest daughter.

Mansour caught the tail end of her request to Muhammad. "She's doing poorly and lounges about the house entirely too much. I just can't convince her to do her best . . . I know she's capable!"

"As you wish," Muhammad said. "Take some time with Samia, and see if Nour is feeling any better, would you? Fatima had a word with her, I believe, and I've had a talk with Nabil, but I'd love an update, if you would be so kind."

Just like that, Muhammad had isolated the likely source of stress from Dina's life—her mother—and advanced the other family project on which he worked: Nour's qualms about her husband. Mansour took notes while he waited for his father to reappear.

"So, my dear Dina, what have you been up to lately?"

She put away her phone. At least that lesson had sunk in. "Not much, just going to school and working on my homework." This was clearly the answer she knew Muhammad wished to hear, though it was much more likely she was spending time chattering with her friends over the phone.

"How are your grades?" Muhammad asked calmly. He had a gentle tone and a calm smile, but also a knowing twinkle in his eyes.

"I think I've covered the letters of the alphabet up to D. I have A, B, C, and D. I'm an equal-opportunity student." Dina laughed.

Muhammad threw back his head and gave a great belly laugh.

"That's funny, you little rascal; it's a smart and honest answer too. Well, you know how much I love you, my dear, so may I give you some advice?"

"I love you too, Uncle Muhammad. Yes, of course, I like to learn from you," Dina replied.

"You are a smart young lady, but it's not enough just to be smart; you have to still work hard to achieve a lot in life and be successful. Part of being smart or becoming smarter is to distinguish between the different levels of good and the different levels of bad. Efficient or less efficient. Worthwhile or filler."

Dina nodded, caught up in Muhammad's calm presentation and gentle speech. Mansour wondered how much such guidance Aunt Soraya provided.

"The smart person will know which choice is better than the other, and the wise person will take action on the better choice. For example, you need to figure out how best to spend your time. Will you watch your favorite TV show or finish your homework? Decisions like that will have a major impact on your life because they accumulate over time. If you have too much homework, then you need to decide on which one to start with and which one is more important. These are small examples, and as you grow, you will need to make tougher decisions."

Mansour thought that no teenage girl in Arlandica would take this advice so well. They'd most likely excuse themselves to get out of this long lecture. Dina impressed him. She might have some lazy habits, but her mind was sharp.

"Everyone, young and old, needs to develop the skill to figure out the different nuances of good and bad. Most things are not clearly black or white, and it would be wrong to assume they are. The smarter you are, the more you can see all the different colors and shades of people, things, and situations. You develop this skill by reading a lot, by learning from people and previous events that happened to you, as well as other people around the world. The world is becoming more and more competitive and sophisticated.

The earlier you realize that and act on it, the better off you will be." Muhammad paused to give Dina a chance to digest and come to terms with this advice.

This felt like advice for Mansour's ears as well. He'd had opportunities to confront his father about the conversation back in his house. But he'd lost those opportunities. Likely because he hadn't had the guts to stride forward, seize his father's attention, and get the answers he felt he deserved.

"Thank you, Uncle Muhammad, for this valuable advice," Dina said. Then she spoke very softly, almost whispering so only her Uncle Muhammad would hear her. "My friends, though, tell me that I am pretty and don't need to work hard because I'll just marry a rich man and he will take care of me for the rest of my life."

Muhammad answered her, also with a soft voice, "Thank you, my love, for being honest and sharing with me your friends' and apparently also your thoughts. First of all, you are pretty, but that doesn't mean that you don't need to work hard. I am afraid your friends are misleading you. Also, keep in mind, my dear, that being pretty helps you only for a very short time. Having a beautiful and pleasant character is far more important, will take you much farther, and will last a lot longer and help you for the rest of your life.

"You need to work hard no matter what you look like. What you do today will determine what you become tomorrow. You need to be able to reach your maximum potential to be able to benefit yourself the most and also provide the best contribution to your family, your society, and the whole world. Our looks and body are only temporary and are a test from God. What will remain for us is our good deeds."

Mansour took the words to heart and retreated back to where his mother rested while his father kept busy. As he approached, he heard his father's voice raised. They hadn't shut the bedroom door all the way, and their voices emerged clearly.

"Well, what is it? Don't fly, or fly sooner than we'd hoped?"

"*Habibi,* please, someone will hear," his mother said.

So his father wasn't in the office on official business.

Mansour knocked and slid open the door in the same motion. Eavesdropping wouldn't give him the answers he needed. "What's going on?"

His mother sat at the vanity holding her head as if it pained her. She appeared pale, more so than usual, and the circles beneath her eyes weren't normal either.

Faisal whirled with an expression that melted away so fast Mansour wasn't even sure what he'd seen. Had that been anger or worry? Either way, it was a troubling development.

"Your father's scheduling an appointment for me in Terra Qurayshia," his mother said. "There's some difficulty in fitting me in."

"Even though there should be no such difficulty! It's a regular check up, nothing more!" To his wife, he said, "We may be forced to cut the trip short, my dear. Will the family be upset?"

He was used to hearing his mom play the piano on Saturday morning, mostly Keeryptian music, and she'd skipped doing that for about two weeks. He'd thought it might be the stress and fatigue of traveling. Now he was pretty sure his parents were lying to him.

"Of course not," his mother responded, though with a detectable hint of disappointment.

"Mother, what's really going on?"

She smiled, but it was full of emotions that shouldn't be there, and he couldn't sort them out: sadness, perhaps, or worry; probably compassion, for her eyes showed her love for him whenever they met his; also . . . exhaustion? Pain?

"Oh, Mansour, do I look like a doctor?" She chuckled, but the joke fell flat. "We'll know soon enough. Now, try to enjoy your time here."

Chapter 10

Now

As tired as he was, Mansour didn't even remember getting wheeled onto the plane, and he barely remembered being put into his seat by the attendants. It was just a blur of movement and kind words, followed by a light blue blanket and dreams. They must've been good ones, because he couldn't remember them. The bad ones were the ones that hung about, he mused as he rustled in his spot and people filed by him. He looked out the window and saw that he was home.

He wondered if those agents felt as safe, having fallen asleep on the job. He imagined that the new king was not a forgiving man. Not his problem, though. He didn't even feel guilty as he stretched his arms out. If the three of them were smart, after the fumes dissipated and they woke up, they'd set out to start new lives as new people, leaving the king to tell their families that they'd died on a mission. The families would receive pensions, cry their tears, and no one had to die. Win-win for everyone.

He tried to imagine that the danger level was lower, but he remembered something about the president of Arlandica doing something that'd never been done before. He peered around, snatched up a newspaper from one of the nearby chairs, and marveled at the headline: TERROR REIGNS. This time the terrorists had blown up a senator from one of the conservative states, and the president had declared a state of emergency and suspended the judicial and legislative branches. Only, the "president" assured people, until the police, the national guard, and the Arlandican military could find, arrest, and execute the perpetrators of this grave injustice. And from where were those terrorists assumed to come? Why, Zamanistan, of course. Certainly not Terra Qurayshia.

The lines moved fast. People grunted as they pulled their belongings from the overhead bins or tried to heave a heavy pack over their shoulders, and everyone chattered basic nothings about finally arriving and being here. Some had formed short-term friendships and wished various newly met people safe travels. Mansour listened intently. None of it seemed utterly wrong, or like Arlandica had shifted into something else overnight. It should've been music to his ears. The sound of freedom. The sound of the Arlandican way.

After the passengers had all exited the plane, a middle-aged attendant came over to him and helped him into his wheelchair, then wheeled him down the ramp and out into the boarding area.

"Have a great day!" she called.

He waved and wheeled himself to the nearest bathroom. It was time to ditch the disguise and go back to being someone Nadia would recognize. He rolled himself into the men's bathroom—a complicated thing with an entryway that bent a full 180 degrees before letting you even glimpse the urinals—and made his way to the toilet section. One door was closed, a red semicircle showing that it was occupied, but with no one else around, Mansour decided to take his chances and change right there next to the sink.

He stood up, pulled off his mask and coverings, and stowed them away in his bag. A gasp behind him made him spin about, limbs in place ready for combat.

From the previously closed door of the toilet stall, a little boy watched him, open-mouthed. He pointed first at his wheelchair and then at him.

Mansour smirked. "Ta-da!"

The child grinned and clapped, then left the bathroom.

Good, that was all over with now. It was time to become Arlandican Mansour. He checked the mirror and ran his fingers through his greasy locks, recreating the semblance of civilization from the tired bedheaded figure of before. *Good, looking good,* he said to himself. He checked his watch. It was evening in Arlandica and about the same exact hour that he had left Terra Qurayshia. Long international flights were a mind bender, as he knew well. Ah well, he wouldn't besmirch having an extra day to do things in. He had important things to deal with.

He received a frown from the immigration officer, but he used his actual passport now, not the emergency Keeryptian forgery, so nothing could incriminate him. He'd torn the forgery to shreds and deposited it in the absolute bottom of a bathroom trashcan.

"Mr . . . al-Qurayshi?" the officer asked slowly. The officer who should otherwise appear bored and simply stamp his passport, but didn't.

"Yes, sir."

The pale-skinned officer with his reddish hair typed into his computer, peered back at Mansour, then typed a few more things. Oh, if only Mansour could jump over the plastic partition and get a look at whatever the officer had on his screen right at this moment.

"And you had visited . . . which countries?"

"Terra Qurayshia and a layover in Aragonia."

"Is that like Smith, then? Al-Qurayshi?"

Mansour chuckled, and hoped he didn't sound as fake as he felt. "That's right."

"And you're a citizen. Born here?"

Mansour nodded. "Yes, sir."

The officer stamped his passport with a blue-gloved hand and, with all the mirth gone from his voice, said, "Welcome home."

Mansour questioned the interaction on his way to baggage claim, and by the time he checked himself through customs, he was wondering whether he was overanalyzing it. If the officer had put something down in the computer, wouldn't they have arrested him at immigration? Yet he'd passed through, and through customs as well. Soon he was out into the airport proper.

"Mansour!" a woman yelled from the throngs of waiting relatives and loved ones. It took him a moment, but when he recognized her, a broad toothy smile lit up his face.

She was just as beautiful as he remembered, as was the *hijab* that covered her curtain of silken hair–this one a geometrically patterned masterpiece of delicate turquoise and yellow.

"Nadia! It is so good to see you again! Oh, I love you so much. You can't believe how much I've missed you."

He hopped the rope barrier to the disappointed shake of a security officer's head, then wrapped his arms around her and gave her a big wet kiss. He lifted her up and she squealed happily.

"I was so worried, Mansour. I thought, with all of the news on the television and then our talking on the phone–"

"No worries, Nadia. The world is my oyster."

She stared at him, bemused, then punched him in the shoulder. "You really shouldn't be so cavalier. This is serious business. You could have been hurt or even killed."

He thought about telling her about the agents, to let her know that he could defend himself, but it would just worry her more. And, to be honest, this homecoming felt too good to be allowed to spoil with the real world facts of violence and authoritarian mayhem. He'd just live in this moment and let it cleanse him of the past. He felt cool and newly alive, like a snake must feel after it sheds its skin.

"Let's go home, Nadia. I can't wait to take a shower and feel like myself again."

Nadia talked and talked on the way home. It felt strange to hear all of the ways lives had changed in his absence. When he'd been gone, they just kinda paused for him. He felt like they should've waited and felt a little sad that they'd gone on without him. That was foolish, of course, but it didn't stop him from feeling like he'd missed out.

When they arrived at their home, hung up their coats and took off their shoes, then settled around the coffee table, it was his turn to talk.

"Nadia, things aren't good. All of the hopes and dreams that we had, all of the stuff we used to talk about–I think those days are over. There's no place for such conversations in Terra Qurayshia anymore. They were after me for espionage, but it won't be long before they'll be after people simply for talking about the old king, or mentioning democracy in a positive light. I feel that the country is heading back to an era of secret police, gangsters, and self-appointed vigilantes."

Nadia nodded. "I spoke with your father long ago, and he said that it seemed the direction the country would be headed. Prince Qurayshi was always quite closed to the idea of his uncle's reforms. He mocked them openly under the guise of sarcasm, even in public."

"But things are worse than that. The prince is now king because he had his uncle assassinated."

Nadia stared. "Murdering one's uncle for power. What a cruel joke of a man he is. He claims to want the nation to be great again, to go back to its roots and to follow the Qur'an to its most strictest interpretations. And he does this by killing his uncle? Even if he had a point, which he doesn't, he curses his whole enterprise by breaking the most important tenet even as he promises to enforce it."

Mansour put his face in his hands. He felt exhausted all over again. "That's the trouble with a lot of kings. They feel they're above the laws of Allah. We're all men, but they think they're angels. And I don't think it's just the king he has killed. My father called me to tell me to flee. And I fled. Then when I talked to him in the car, there was gunfire, helicopter blades and . . . and then silence. A dropped call. I think King Qurayshi killed my father."

Nadia grabbed his hands. "Oh, Mansour. I am so sorry. Faisal was a good man, and he will be missed. These are dark times. But I'm thankful you're back in Arlandica, where such things don't happen. Here we are powerful and free."

About that.

Mansour looked at the TV. When he'd left, the set in Nadia's home had played the news twenty-four seven. He was pleased to see that this hadn't changed in his absence. He wasn't at all pleased to see what it was reporting, though: the suicide bomber with the senator, an attempt to kidnap a governor, absolutist groups attempting to seize power, riots, and mayhem. What was going on?

Nadia followed his gaze and watched alongside him, quiet for a moment. Then, for the first time in all of the years he'd known her, she turned it off.

"Don't worry about that, Mansour. There are crazies in every country. Arlandica is still the land of the free and the home of the brave. We'll never bend our knee to kings."

He nodded, then asked, "Can I use your phone?" I haven't lost hope yet that my father might be alive and well. You know how faulty the networks in Terra Qurayshia are. Plus, I think I've been sitting long enough. I feel like it might do me some good to pace about the house with a phone to my ear."

"What if you can't reach him?" she asked.

"Then I shall pace and use your phone to check all the latest news. Maybe, just maybe, I'll see him mentioned there."

Nadia handed him her phone, and he wandered off with it, clicking through her contacts and clicking on Faisal. He heard a click, and then a robotic woman's voice began chewing his ear off.

"The number you have dialed is not receiving calls at this time. To leave a callback number, please press 5. To leave a voicemail message, press 0. If you believe you have received this message in error, hang up and try the call again. Message 01432."

Mansour pressed 0.

"At the tone, please record your message. When you have completed your message you may hang up or press 2 to delete and record again."

The phone beeped. "Dad, hey. It's me, Mansour. I'm safe for the time being. Call me when you get this message. Love you!" he said. "Oh, and I'm using a proxy, so my location is scattered. I'll tell you where I am when you get in touch," he lied, just in case someone dangerous listened to the message.

Right. Okay. Now it was time to check the mainstream news. He tapped on In-Finite and typed just his father's first name, Faisal. A number of articles popped up—his father was an important man. But none of them were dated recently.

Next he checked through the side sites, the often partisan tabloids that ran as much fiction as fact, but were much more likely to stumble on an odd article of truth from an authoritarian hotspot than the regular sites. With their journalistic standards, they'd never publish something without concrete verification. But there was nothing new there either, not even an article talking about how Faisal was a member of the Shadow Government or was a secret lizardman spy from Neptune. His eyes moistened. Faisal had loved to read such articles, usually from sites like Freedom Forever or MESIS. He'd always joke about it, holding up the article at breakfast time and joking that there needed to be an investigation.

"How are you doing in here?" Nadia asked, entering the kitchen where he'd unknowingly plopped himself down on a counter. His face turned red, and he stood up.

"I'm sorry about that. There's just . . . there's nothing. Nothing at all."

"Why don't you call everyone you know back in Terra Qurayshia?" she asked. "Someone has got to know something."

Mansour looked down at the floor and pinched the bridge of his nose. It was supposed to be a relaxing move, something to make him feel better and calm down. But at this place and at this time it did nothing but make him feel silly.

"If I call anybody at all, the government will imprison them, I'm sure. The king will torture them and ask them questions about things they know nothing about, then ask them about me and where I am, and then he'll cut off their hands and maybe even their heads. No, I can't call them."

Nadia sighed. "All right, so what do we do now?"

"There is nothing we can do, Nadia. Not yet, anyway. I'm going to pray for answers. Then I'm going to sleep. And maybe in the morning, things will be better than they have been."

She bid him good night, and Mansour fell asleep almost as soon as his head hit the pillow.

There was a reason the state was called Sunland. The birds chirped and leaves rustled outside the open bedroom window, sighing as if to say, "Get up, you sleepyhead. I made you a beautiful day, extra breeze, and you'd be a fool to miss out on it."

Mansour smiled. It was good to be back. Then the previous night swam back into his head, and he grabbed his phone from its charger at the side of the bed.

No new calls. He froze. Wait, he needed a new SIM card anyway because he was in Arlandica! He dressed quickly in freshly laundered clothes from his closet, which felt amazing, and ran out to the living room. There sat Nadia, holding a delicate steaming cup of what smelled like jasmine tea. The eager and desperate pinch of his face as he entered the room had her on her feet at once, and she rushed to his side.

"What's wrong, Mansour?"

"Nadia, quick, may I check your phone? Also, I need to go

get a new SIM card so I can use my phone. I need to see if my father has tried to contact me."

Nadia took her phone from her pocket and checked it, but there was nothing. "Let's go to the phone shop and see what they can do."

He nodded and they left. A short while later, they pulled into a vacant-looking strip mall, right up to a shop where a man in a company vest unlocked the door.

Nadia wasted no time. "We need a new SIM card now," she said.

The man finished opening the door, then, looking red and flustered, he rushed about the place, his eyes still bleary from the early hour.

Mansour was surprised. He'd gotten used to the almost lazy atmosphere of Terra Qurayshian sales culture, with their late openings and early closing, filled with more gossip than pushes to buy. Back there, people would see Nadia as an evil and crazy person for treating the shopkeeper the way she was here. It was the Arlandican way, and he appreciated it since he couldn't wait any longer for his new SIM. What if his father was hurt and trapped somewhere. What if he needed his help?

Mansour got his SIM card, paid for it, and zipped out the door to try it out. His voicemail box beeped.

"You have one new message."

He pressed one and listened in eagerly.

"Hey, Mansour, listen; I don't know where you went off to, but there's something you need to hear." It was his dad's cousin, Abdulaziz, and he was crying. "Mansour, Faisal and Bandar were in a helicopter heading to some official function and, apparently, terrorists attacked and shot the helicopter out of the air with a rocket. The officials are saying there are bodies and signs of a heavy battle between rebels and security personnel on the ground. A group called 'Fighters for Western Liberty' has claimed responsibility. I've left the country for Arlandica, and you can reach me at 876-555-7347. Please call me when you get this and let me know that you're all right."

Mansour clicked out of the message and looked up at Nadia, who stood beside him.

"What is it? Did you hear something?"

"Yes. Abdulaziz has left a message. My father is dead. So is Bandar. He says that he himself has come to Arlandica, and he left me a number at which to reach him."

"Call him!" Nadia exclaimed.

Mansour brought up his number pad and entered the code, then waited for Abdulaziz. He picked up on the third ring.

"Hello?"

"Abdulaziz, it's Mansour. So it is true. My father is dead."

There was silence, and then a weak yes.

"Do you really think it was terrorists?"

"No. I'm in Arlandica now, so I can talk freely. I think the king was behind it. And I think I would be dead now as well, if Faisal hadn't called me and told me to not return to Terra Qurayshia. Very bad things are happening, Mansour, and the fact that the media is reporting what Qurayshi tells them to, without question, is a sign that already the country has gone back fifty years from where it had come to be."

Mansour balled his left hand into a fist.

Nadia grabbed it. "It is okay," she murmured, and began to massage the taut muscles in his shoulders.

Unable to stay upset with her, he relaxed. "So what can we do now? Have we lost? Can there be no . . . justice?" He wanted to say revenge, but he lived by the Qur'an.

Abdulaziz remained again. When he next spoke, his voice was soft, like a long and drawn-out sigh. "Mansour, we had our suspicions, but we never expected the crown prince to so brazenly seize power. If we had, we would've prepared something. A counter-insurgency, perhaps. A more powerful security force. We never expected that he would kill his uncle, and then try to kill all of us as well. All over the news, I keep seeing the names of the king's men, his closest confidantes. A slurry of terror attacks, if they are to be believed. We have nothing left. No power, no connections to anyone in power. We are lost."

A tear escaped Mansour's eye and trickled down his cheek. "So it is all done then. Truly."

Abdulaziz coughed. "Well, maybe not. I might have an idea. I will get into my car and drive to you in Sunland. Tell no one I am coming, Mansour. The crown pr—the king has agents all over, even in Arlandica."

Mansour was beginning to believe one of them might be the president. He looked over at Nadia. "I appreciate the kind words, Abdulaziz. Yes, I will make funeral preparations at once. Goodbye." He clicked off his phone.

They weren't safe here. More importantly, Nadia wasn't safe with the situation as it was, and that was completely unacceptable.

He must've been standing there for some time, just holding the phone and staring at the refrigerator, while she rubbed at his muscles. Eventually he folded to the floor and pressed his forehead against the tile, much as he would if he were praying. A soft sob came from Nadia.

So his father was dead.

More time passed before she gently removed the phone from his hand and laced her fingers together with his. For a time, she said nothing. Minutes passed.

"I'm so sorry, Mansour. Is there anything I can do?" Nadia whispered at last, still holding his hand.

He roused himself off the floor and faced her. "No . . . thank you, my dearest. I believe it might be time for me to take things into my own hands."

Chapter 11

16 years ago
Terra Qurayshia

Mansour could barely contain his anger. His mother's condition had steadily worsened the day before the flight, which had been both blessedly and infuriatingly short, and so full of activities he couldn't get a word in edgewise. It was becoming an unacceptable theme.

They all flew first-class and were pampered on the plane as Faisal knew the captain in addition to being from the royal family. The flight attendant served a nice meal and delicious expensive dates like Anbara, Barhi, Sukkari, and Safawi. Anbara were a bit larger than most dates, brown, with a particularly sweet taste. Barhi were yellow and crunchy, and luckily these ones were ripe, so they tasted like caramel or brown sugar. Sukkari, which was one of Mansour's favorites, were cultivated in Al Zefan area. Sweet and crisp, they were known to fight fatigue, prevent tooth decay, and lower cholesterol. And last but definitely not least, Safawi: soft, black, with a lot of vitamins and minerals, mainly cultivated in Manara, and known to kill any existing stomach worms if eaten on an empty stomach. With the dates, the custom was to serve Anadulian coffee in very small and special cups. Though black on the outside, they gleamed gold within.

The flight passed quickly; the short distance combined with first-class care from the gracious flight attendants. He tried not to enjoy it, and failed. Now his father was keeping two secrets from him, one of which directly connected to his mother's health, the other with the potential to steer the course of his life.

A few moments after the plane arrived, Faisal's limousine

appeared on the airport tarmac. Police officers greeted them and stamped their diplomatic passports. They didn't even need to go to the VIP Royal Lounge. His uncle, the new crown prince, met them in the limo and chattered away during the drive, oblivious to the tension. Mansour attempted to keep his eruption from burning anyone other than his father. His absent father, who couldn't be bothered to confide in his only son.

Police cars escorted them to their residence in Zomorod, so they didn't see the very long lines at the airport. Faisal's royal family welcomed them outside. Mansour's cousins and many family members were there waiting for them. Many of Mansour's cousins hadn't seen him for a long time. Though they used to play together when they were very young, they'd all grown quite a lot. Mansour wished he could enjoy seeing his dad's side of the family. They all gathered in a very large room in the huge house with a lot of food, kabsa, mandi, maqluba, lamb, fish, rice with mixed nuts, different kinds of dates, a lot of fruits, and Mansour's favorite dessert, *umm ali.* They ate a lot.

Well, they did. Mansour hardly touched anything. Instead he locked eyes with his father, politely excused himself, then tried to restrain himself from slamming the door once his father finally appeared.

"What is going on, Dad?"

His father peered around the gigantic estate room like someone might be listening, and held up his hands in defeat. "Son—"

"I want the truth. Either you've been avoiding me, or avoiding talking to me. That's over. Now . . . what's going on with Mom?"

"She needs to see a doctor for us to be sure. She's been feeling nauseated and low on energy. Truly I say it. I haven't covered—"

"I know about your plan to turn me into a spy."

His father stared as if he had been punched in the guts. "You . . . what?"

"I heard everything." Not everything, but he wouldn't let that stop him. "I was around the garage, throwing away the . . . You know what? It doesn't matter. Now, I want to know what's going on. If it affects me, and my life, then I deserve to know."

His father blinked, processing a lot at once. Gears and wheels turned behind his eyes as his son's words sank in. Calculations were going on, and Mansour couldn't have that. He had his father off balance and needed to keep it that way.

"Now, Dad!"

His head fell. "It's . . . true."

"What's true?"

"I . . . Your uncle has this plan, you see. It's complicated."

Mansour's hands opened and closed. "Uncomplicate it."

"The final decision hadn't been made, you see. That's why I decided against telling you. I cannot say if the king will call upon you or not. Some members of his council have pushed hard for this plan, and I've done the opposite. I didn't want this for you. In point of fact, it may not happen."

"And . . . what? There's no way for me to refuse? My destiny is etched in stone, if the king wills it?"

"Of course not! You have a choice, as you have always had a choice. You write your destiny, my son." Faisal got back into the rhythm. "Mansour, you know me to be a direct person, so I'm just going to be straight with you.

"While I was back in the kingdom, I had several discussions with the king and other members of our royal family. Important discussions. Our country and our region must make serious changes if it is to thrive in the coming years. We all realize that nothing ever stays the same. If we ignore the changes happening around us, we will become marginalized. We will become a mere footnote in history."

All of this sounded well and good, but Mansour was curious as to how he would fit in. Faisal took a sip of his Anadulian coffee and continued, "His Royal Highness, the king, has set up a committee to study and formulate a detailed, multistage hundred-year plan. This committee will carefully analyze our current situation with respect to the general economy, the business climate, the education system, and even the political system and introducing democracy in our kingdom.

"Only the most influential members of the royal family are on the committee—your dad included."

Mansour listened intently. Finally, after so long, answers.

"To fully understand where to go in the future, we must determine exactly where we are now."

Mansour responded with his eyes, and let his father continue.

"My son, we plan to gather as much information as humanly possible, so with God's help, we might fully understand the present situation—the positives and the negatives—from as many angles as possible.

"I don't believe you're ready for such an assignment. I've advised the king to monitor your progress through college, and then perhaps entry-level work in Arlandica. The sort of place Terra Qurayshia could learn from. With this perspective and knowledge, you could help us get into the cracks of society, and see where and how to fill them."

Mansour's mouth dropped open. "After . . . college?" At least four years from now.

His father nodded. "More than that, most likely. The king mentioned possibly taking you in after a few years on the job."

At least seven or eight years from now.

"Son, I'm so sorry you overheard that phone call. It was surely not fair to occupy your head. And even further, it wasn't fair to go so long without answers."

Now it was Mansour's turn to gape like a fish. He thought he'd been prepared for this, but it wasn't the case. All he had readied before now fled from his mind while a storm of new information broke everything apart. Like the great tornado in the Wizard of Oz, his entire situation had gone flying, and he now sat in the midst of a new and alien landscape.

He had years to prepare.

"Will I need to . . . kill anyone?" he asked.

"Great God, no!" his father exclaimed.

"How about spy training?"

Faisal seemed confused by this for a moment, then waved his hands as if he were shooting the idea down. "Son, the plan is for you to live and work under an assumed Keeryptian name, taking notes about the systemic problems you encounter, so that the king might address them with reforms. No car chases, no piloting a helicopter, no explosions, no James Bond stuff."

It was both a relief and a slight disappointment to learn there would be no evil masterminds, no chase scenes, no gadgets or sleek women he'd have to seduce. In all honesty, he didn't think himself capable. Not only was it an affront to Allah, but he had zero practice.

On the other hand, a small part of him had enjoyed the idea of going to martial arts training. Perhaps Mother would consent to setting up martial arts lessons anyhow. The situation with the car crash had shown him that although he wasn't a small man, he also wasn't a fighter. He would eventually be wed, and a husband ought to be able to protect his wife, if—God forbid—such a situation ever arose. It was possible to take this secret agent revelation, the safe and blessedly boring version he was going to engage in, and use it to better himself.

His father clapped a companionable hand on his shoulder and peered into his eyes. "I wish you had come to me with this straight away, my son. Such a burden must have been painful to bear. But that's over, understand? You're safe both now and in the future. I would never agree to put you on that path if I thought it might endanger your life."

"I understand."

"And you must also understand this, before we make our way back to your relatives. First, this will be a choice for you to make . . . or not. It remains possible King Farhan will cancel or shelve the plan until even later, so it might pass you by. But when that day comes, you are free to say no."

Mansour nodded. It was like his whole body was unwinding, the pressure lightening, the stress melting off.

"Second, your mother is not to know. She would never understand, and given that it may not happen, I don't want to add to what she has to deal with." There was the gentle and kind father he'd grown up with. "This you must promise, my son."

"I promise, Father."

"Good. Now, I hope you won't mind if we go spend some time with your cousins, aunts, and uncles. Our time here is limited."

"You must also promise me something, Father."

Faisal had started to turn but seemed to hunch down to ready himself for some difficult revelation. He regarded Mansour with some wariness, the first time Mansour could ever recall seeing that expression turned his way.

"I can handle the truth. Promise me if there's anything else, you will tell me. And if I have questions."

"Of course. Consider that promise made."

Late the next morning, the housekeeper in charge of the Sunland house called. They'd hired a darling Nueva Aragonian woman named Juanita, who had great references, to live and work in the house and keep intruders away while they were on vacation.

Mansour jumped out of the crystalline waters of the pool, saw Juanita's name on the screen, and answered his buzzing phone with an equally buzzing heart. This had to mean what he thought it meant.

"I wouldn't have called ordinarily, but you did say if a letter came from the college, to call you," she said.

"Mother! Father!" Mansour turned back to Juanita on his cell phone screen. "Go ahead and open it."

His parents got up off the couch and met him near the back door. He dripped on the carpet, but at the words *we are pleased to inform you* he and his father began hopping around the den and exulting, while his mother—who was looking and feeling a bit better—smiled and joined him for a wet hug.

"What's the commotion?" one of his cousins asked.

"Mansour will be studying civil engineering this fall at the University of Sunland West Beach. He just received his acceptance."

And even though his mother and father had had talks with him about his choice of a major, and they'd steered him toward it—before the great revelation—Mansour didn't mind. Civil Engineering would be a great asset to Arlandica, to Keerypt, to Terra Qurayshia . . . whether it was in an official capacity or not. Now with at least four years of studying and a few years of entry-level work to come, he had plenty of time to decide: secret agent or not? He could learn self-defense, consult the Qur'an and Dr. Hathout about how to proceed, and make a much more informed decision later.

Now was the time for enjoying life.

Without the sword of Damocles hanging over him, he could finally start enjoying his time abroad. None of his royal cousins, aunts or uncles had the sort of drama he'd seen in Keerypt from his mother's side—or they hid it well enough that it slipped by his secret agent senses—so he wasn't able to engage in any more life-saving family espionage. That meant sleeping in late, sightseeing, praying at the largest *masjid* on the planet, and eating some of the best food known to man. And although he enjoyed his time in Terra Qurayshia immensely, the trip ended after only a few days, and then it was back to Arlandica to prepare for university.

He'd had enough fun with his relatives that he completely failed to notice what was going on with his mother. It wasn't until he'd arrived back in Sunland and had over a week of fighting off jetlag—again—that the lightbulb came on over his head. Which, to be fair, was because he was researching campus life, looking at different clubs and fraternities, and taking an early look at the textbooks his professors had provided on the online course syllabi.

Soon after they arrived at their home in West Beach, Mansour noticed that his mother was acting a bit differently; she looked very concerned and quieter than usual. Mansour asked his mother if she was okay.

"Yes, my dear, I am all right. Why?"

Mansour couldn't let go of the stone that had dropped into the pit of his stomach. She'd gone to the doctor back in Terra Qurayshia, and with the confrontation he'd had with his father, it had totally slipped his mind.

"You seem awfully quiet and worried. Is there something you are not telling me?"

"No, my son, I'm just tired from our trip. It was a long journey, and I'm getting old."

He laughed, despite the unease that grew steadily within him. "Oh no, Mom, you're not! You're still young."

The next morning, Mansour heard his mom calling and getting an appointment with her doctor. "Mom, are you feeling sick?"

"Why do you ask?"

Yes, she was being evasive. His level of concern grew another notch. "Because I heard you calling to get an appointment with your doctor."

"Yes, my dear, I'm just calling for a general checkup."

"Can you please tell me if you're feeling all right? I'm really worried about you, Mom. I love you. Please be honest with me."

Fatima moved through the kitchen with practiced ease and the same grace she had always done. This allowed her to avoid eye contact with Mansour, a fact not lost on him. "I love you also, my son. Please don't worry. If there is anything wrong, I promise I will tell you. Now, let's prepare some breakfast. I'm quite hungry."

"Okay. I'll join you in the kitchen in a minute."

Fatima and Mansour prepared a very delicious breakfast for just the two of them, as there was no one else at home.

He couldn't force anything out of her, and didn't try. She was stubborn at times, and implacable, and this was one of those times. He fell back into his new post-vacation routine: jiujitsu training each morning from ten to eleven, out with his friends for lunch some days, home for lunch others, praying throughout the day, meeting once or twice a week with Dr. Hathout, and studying up on the studying he'd be doing at the university. Plus, with summer vacation still on, he was rarely home.

Almost two weeks later, Mansour was at home enjoying a bit of television when his mother came home and sat down nearby. The whole air of the house changed. She seemed to sit up stiffer than usual, and stared at him as though she'd never really seen him before.

"Mom."

"Mansour, my son, I have something very serious to tell you. I met with several oncologists and they suspect that I might have breast cancer."

Mansour's face froze for a moment. In the scramble of his thoughts, he felt and thought that he was sleeping and must be having a nightmare. His ears stopped working correctly, and whatever his mother said next was a wonky, muddled mess that didn't penetrate. The words *breast cancer* ricocheted around and threw him to the floor like his jiujitsu master had done earlier this morning. After a time, the words sank in, and it didn't appear at all that he was sleeping. He really wished he was.

"What?" he asked.

Chapter 12

"I must have misheard you," Mansour said very slowly, heavy with disbelief.

Fatima took a deep breath and said, "Mansour, you are not a baby; you are an adult, and that's why I'm telling you the news as I heard it. Please be strong and accept whatever God wills for us." Fatima spoke with authority to show strength, though how could she? Mansour could scarcely believe she possessed the power not to break down then and there.

"Does Dad know?"

"Not yet. I just got the news. I will tell him later tonight. It's very late at night for him now. I'll wait till it's morning for him. He'll need to come here soon, as I'll be going through surgery."

"What kind of surgery?" Mansour asked while trying to catch his breath. Mansour had mild asthma and the terrible news aggravated it.

"It would be a mastectomy. They'll remove my left breast."

"How can they be sure?" Mansour asked with a glimpse of hope in his question.

"They did a biopsy and the results show that it was malignant. They will send it to another lab to double-check. I should know by tomorrow, *in shaa Allah*." She sounded resigned, as though she'd given up hoping for a different result.

"God willing," he repeated, numb. "You're not sounding hopeful. They might be wrong. Don't you need a second or third opinion?"

"Yes, of course, I got two opinions already from very good doctors and will be getting a third one in a couple of days. But we have to be realistic. The evidence has been pointing to the same diagnosis."

This was too much for him, too heavy on him. "I don't want anything bad to happen to you." Mansour looked down, head in hands. It seemed that at any moment he'd take a dive off the carpet, crash into the floor, and then possibly even further.

"Mansour, you are a good believer, and as a good believer, you must accept the tests given to us by God. It's a test for me, for you, your dad, and our family." She shouldn't have had to reassure him, yet here she was, doing just that.

"I just wasn't ready at all to hear this," Mansour said to himself out loud.

"No one is ever ready for this kind of thing. The test is really measured in the first reaction we have when we face such a situation."

"You make it sound so easy, or like it's not a big deal."

"I'm not saying it's easy. It's just, we have to think deeply about it and realize that we are all here temporarily and we have to return to God sooner or later by one way or another. I guess we always have to be ready to accept such a test when we least expect it. It's similar to training for a marathon, but you're not sure when you will be asked to run the marathon. You just have to be ready to respond on very short notice. We think of physical fitness and mental fitness, but we don't think too much of spiritual fitness. It's a wake-up call for all of us."

"I am going to pray to God to heal you and make things better for all of us." It was the only thing he could think to say that meant anything. Every other word that came to mind seemed wrong, or insignificant.

"Thank you, Mansour, that's very good. This is the right way to approach this difficulty, in addition, of course, to doing everything we can within our capability, which we are doing and will continue to do, *in shaa Allah*."

♛

Five days later, two days shy of Mansour starting college, Teta arrived in West Beach, followed a day later by his father. Fatima had her surgery. It was a very difficult time for the whole family given that the doctors had little good news to share. His mother had stage four cancer, and they were cautioned about being too optimistic about Fatima's recovery. Summer vacation had taken a sudden back seat to rearranging Mansour's view of the world.

Fatima stayed in the hospital for three days, after which she returned home to continue her recovery. If there was one upshot to all this, it was that Mansour was able to see and converse with his father much more than before. The devoted and gentle man with great love for his mother was back, and he spent a great deal of time attempting to move worlds to save his wife. He vowed to do everything he could to try to save Fatima's life and get her the best medical care anywhere in the world. That meant a lot to Mansour, and he knew that his dad meant it and had the ability to do that.

Late at night, though, after his mother and Teta had fallen asleep and quiet had stolen over the house, that resolve faltered. His father stood in the living room staring about, as if the solution to their problems might be under the sofa or lie with one of the magazines on the end table. Mansour, who had stopped trying—and failing—to focus on one of his school textbooks, stood up.

"Dad, hey."

Faisal blinked, and like his mother had just a few months prior, seemed to see his son for the first time.

"You're doing your best. I know that. Mother knows that."

Faisal closed his eyes and nodded. "Ultimately, it's in God's hands. Allah alone knows what the outcome will be, and . . . and we have to accept that.

"Of course. But we keep fighting."

"We fight. Of course we will do everything we can."

Fatima's reports were sent all over the country, as well as overseas to Welton and Gustave Roussy in Aquitaine to get several opinions. It was a very difficult time for everyone. Mansour's grandmother now planned to stay in Sunland for a while to be with her daughter. They spent much time going to doctors and hospitals for chemotherapy and radiation.

Fatima grew weak and started losing her luxurious light brown hair. The chemotherapy and radiation sometimes made her feel sicker than the cancer itself.

Mansour's freshman year of college was off to a terrible start. It wasn't easy to focus on his studies, but he did his best to keep up with both his education and following up on his mom's health situation.

Luckily for Mansour, Scott and Anthony, two of his best friends, also joined his college, though they had different majors. Scott was studying computer science and Anthony political science. They shared some of the common general education classes. It was good for Mansour not to be alone, especially going through this difficult time with his mom's health. Mansour also met another Terra Qurayshian. His name was Sufian. The chubby new friend was very friendly and excited to meet a fellow countryman at the same school.

Mansour tried to spend time with Sufian and soak up the exuberance, but when he visited his home, he was dismayed to find alcohol in Sufian's house. After dinner, his friend headed straight to the freezer, produced a fifth of whiskey, and mixed up a Jack and Coke.

He arched an eyebrow Mansour's way and nodded when Mansour declined. "It's not as bad as you'd think."

Mansour's spirits sank. He spent the remainder of the night watching Sufian sully himself, not really listening to his new friend talk about the Terra Qurayshian royalty he knew.

"I tell you what." Sufian drained the remainder of his drink. "My girlfriend has this sister . . . hot. It was hard to choose between them."

Mansour's spirits sank further, but he couldn't just storm

out. This wasn't what he'd come to Sufian's home to experience. Music, movies, video games, maybe reminiscing about life back in Terra Qurayshia, sure.

He managed a neutral, "Oh yeah?"

Sufian laughed. "Not as nuts as my last girlfriend either. She doesn't even take my phone and go through it to see who I've been calling. No, this new girl is Zhouan. She's about five foot nothing. Really athletic, really fun. You'd like her. Name's Jia."

Mansour nodded along and made a bit of small talk, then gave Sufian a sketchy account of his mother's illness as an excuse for having lost his good mood, and headed home.

Mansour shared his disappointment with his parents. Fatima sat down and gave Mansour her opinion, while Faisal made them some tea.

"My son, this is not new. Unfortunately, I've heard of many stories of Terra Qurayshians who come here to Arlandica and lose balance completely. They were brought up in Terra Qurayshia, a very closed society, and are not used to living in total freedom. Most Terra Qurayshians have no interaction with girls or women, other than their moms and sisters. So when they come over here with no one to tell them *do* or *don't,* they rebel and do the opposite of what they are supposed to do."

"But that's not . . . I've never . . ."

His mother chuckled.

Faisal entered with piping hot tea and a compassionate smile. "You were raised differently. You lived in Keerypt and in Arlandica at a younger age. Also, your mom and I did not impose heavy restrictions on you. So you were raised to think and decide for yourself on what to do and what not to do, with guidance from us, of course."

His mother picked up where his father left off. "Yes, my dear son. It's not so easy to raise kids these days. We worked hard and thank God it paid off."

His pride in hearing these words was coupled with his

mother's improving condition. He resolved to be the best son and the best follower of Allah he could be. He threw himself headlong into his studies while his mother's health stabilized, and he brought home A after A.

And for a long while, everything went as well as could be hoped for. The semesters rolled in and out. Mansour went to school, studied at home, built his body and self-defense skills at the gym, and helped his mother in any way he could. This included making her tea, listening to her play piano, and explaining literally every aspect of both jiujitsu training and university life. Freshman year whizzed by, a slow lazy summer of beach walks and movie nights at home, followed by his sophomore year. Coursework intensified, now a clear departure in difficulty level from his high school studies. His parents remained solid in their support for his studies and pushed him to excel. This he did.

It was almost enough. So much time passed that he nearly forgot the doctors' projections of doom and gloom for his mother. And just around the time that he was taking it for granted that she would be there to cheer him on at graduation, it happened.

Mansour was in his junior year of college when Fatima became really sick and had to be hospitalized for over a week. She was very weak and needed good and continuous care. Later she came back home, and Mansour entered his house to find a nurse hooking up an oxygen tank and IV. The familiar fiction he'd built up in his mind, the one to block out reality, turned out to be made of glass. The plastic tubes running into his mother's nose smashed his fiction to pieces, and he fell back into that pit of fear.

A few days later, Mansour returned from school and heard his mom and dad filling out paperwork and discussing inheritance and details about burial. He burst into tears and could not hold himself. Fatima and Faisal heard him, and Faisal left the room and hugged Mansour.

"Mansour, we did not hear you come in. I'm sorry you heard

all that. Your mom is very practical and she wanted to go over these things. I didn't want to, but she insisted. She is very down to earth, as you know, and she wanted to be ready."

Fatima drifted into the room.

He turned to her. "I can't imagine living without you."

His mom couldn't speak but instead shared his grief with silent tears. Eventually she had to go sit down. Faisal led his son back to his bedroom and talked while Mansour flopped on the bed.

"Dad . . . I can't . . ."

"I understand, and I know what you mean. We just have to hope for the best and prepare for the worst. I love your mom very much, and I'm doing everything I can to provide her with the best treatment available in the world, but no matter what we do and how much money we spend, there are limitations on what doctors can do."

Mansour knew this. His mother had been to a host of doctors and hospitals in the last three years, and she'd gotten the best treatments available anywhere. He was just hoping a miracle would happen, that the slow crushing despair would disappear and leave her the person he'd always known.

His father nodded, as if hearing his thoughts. "Yes, of course, I'm always praying for her, and I'm not going to lose hope, but I just want her to be comfortable and do what she wants to do."

"I understand, Dad," he choked out. "I love you."

"I love you, my son."

Chapter 13

Now
Sunland, Arlandica

Abdulaziz called three days later. Mansour had spent the time productively, putting the depressingly small leftovers of his undercover bug-out cash into a new bank account, getting his suits dry-cleaned, and going out to obtain a Glock-19 9mm semiautomatic handgun. This last one had required a trip to a gun show to avoid the waiting period, but having the weapon immediately added a feeling of security that he hadn't known he'd been missing.

And now, next to Nadia in the living room, armed and looking professional once again, he was ready to get back to work. He'd never felt the twitchy, jumpy legs he now had, and nearly had a heart attack when the phone rang.

"Hello, Mansour," Abdulaziz greeted him with a heavy sigh.

"Hello, Abdulaziz. How are you today?"

"Fine, but let us cut to the chase. I am in Sunland as we speak, and I believe the time is right for us to meet and discuss all that has happened and what we can do about it."

Mansour gulped. He felt a fire in his heart and eyes that cried out for vengeance, but his brain knew they were again entering very dangerous territory. He was a good Muslim.

"Where do you want to meet?" he asked, hoping that Abdulaziz couldn't hear the quiver in his voice.

"Let us meet at Beans Unlimited. Your father mentioned the donuts and the quality of their iced coffee on more than one occasion."

"Agreed," Mansour said. "I'll be there within the hour."

Mansour clicked off the call and put his phone in his pocket. Nadia watched him with wide eyes.

"This is about the kingdom, isn't it? Are you really going to—"

"I don't think it can be avoided." He didn't want to worry her, not with his unsubstantiated worries about the president. He knew from the news that members of Congress were being held by the military "for their own safety" along with the members of the supreme court, and that a lot of cities had already seen riots as a result. Mosques had been set on fire, but also local government buildings and in one case, a police precinct. Buildings were burning and people were dying.

He couldn't look at her directly. He knew that if he did, he'd see wet eyes and an anguished face. Instead he grabbed a duffel bag and focused on filling it with gadgets and items for a what-if scenario.

"You're meeting Abdul. But he's a bigwig, a very important person! He might be followed! He might be a spy working for the new king! Mansour, you don't need to do this. You've done what you could."

He paused. Had he? Was there anything he could've done to save his father? Finally he turned and looked into her eyes.

"Nadia, my love, I will be as careful as I can be. But I must do something. All that evil requires to win is the inaction of good men."

She nodded and sighed. "That sounds right. It also sounds like something you copied from someone else."

He put up his hands and tried for a reassuring smile. "Guilty, I'm sure. But does that make it any less true?"

She didn't hesitate but walked into his welcoming arms and wrapped him up in the biggest and most aggressive hug she could muster.

"Come back safe," she whispered.

"I'm going to be as safe as I can possibly be," he said. "I have planned for a lot of contingencies, and I will also call my friend Mike and have him bring his patrol car around to the area as backup. And if he goes out on a call, I'll cut my meeting short. Nadia, I'm well prepared and protected. Don't worry. Everything is going to be all right."

Nadia nodded and Mansour took out his phone and called Mike. It rang only once before the burly police officer answered it.

"Yeah?"

"Hey, Mike, I need a favor."

Mike chuckled ruefully. "You really picked the worst time, you know that?"

"Oh, trust me, I know. I have an important meeting that involves that political stuff I was off doing, so it might be dangerous. Is there any way you can swing by and keep an eye on things while I'm in the meeting?"

Mike's shrug was audible through the phone. "Sure . . . I'm off duty today, but I'll grab the squad car and get in uniform. But if I get a call I'm gonna have to respond."

"Yeah, I understand."

"And, hey, you know what? Why don't we wire you up before the meeting so my partner and I can hear what's happening? You ain't doing nothing illegal, are you?"

"Not at all!" Mansour exclaimed. "The plan is to talk about the Terra Qurayshian coup and what we might be able to do about it."

"Yeah, we'll wire you, and then we can get a jump on saving you if there's any trouble. But Mansour, let me ask you something personal. You just spent some months doing stuff for that country. It's not even your country. Are you sure you want to jump back into all of this? Nadia doesn't deserve to be left alone like that. And you don't owe them anything."

Mansour scowled. "Mike, the new king killed my father. This isn't for Terra Qurayshia. This is for me."

"Oh, man. I'm sorry to hear that. All right, I'll swing by and get you set up, and then let's get this meeting rolling."

♛

Beans Unlimited couldn't be a stranger place to have a secret, super-important meeting. It was spacious and inviting, with huge plate-glass windows and an open floor plan. Young people lounged at booths or in one of the many love seats that faced each other around cozy tables. Other young people hunched over their computers, while older folks talked loudly in groups of all sizes. The bright green interior didn't help the strange sensation that came over Mansour on entering, nor did the heady aroma of coffee everywhere, or the donut case, which immediately brought his father to mind.

Mansour played with the napkin, then took another sip of his peppermint milk tea. It was good, very good, but it couldn't distract him from the fact that Abdul was late.

Come on, come on. He drummed his fingers and pulled out his phone, then put it back away. He could force himself to be patient. So many innocent things might've happened and, to be honest, Adbul wasn't a man known for his punctuality anyway.

A bell rang, and a tall, tan man in a gray suit entered. Mansour glanced over hopefully, took in the man with a glimpse, then sank back in disappointment. It was not Abdul. The man scanned the room, locked his eyes on Mansour, and walked over.

"Are you Mansour?" he asked.

Mansour sat back up in his chair. "Yes, I am. And you are?"

"I am an associate of Abdulaziz. I understand that he was to meet you here at this hour. Unfortunately there has been an accident."

Mansour started to speak, but the man held up his hand.

"It is nothing major. He was parking in the alley and something snagged his tire. He sent me here to let you know what happened and to ask that we all meet there instead, under the cover of car maintenance."

Mansour stared at the man, trying to gauge the situation, and his intentions. The story felt off. But then again, repairing a broken vehicle would be a great cover. He wondered if the wire would transmit from that location. Once decided, he stood.

"So," he said loudly enough to make sure Mike had gotten the details, "Abdulaziz had a blowout while parking in the alley and the two of us will go to help him? Yes, okay, just let me settle the bill here, and I'll go with you shortly."

Mansour went to the counter and paid while muttering to Mike, then he walked out behind the associate, wary of any strange moves or attacks. But true to his word, he turned at the alley and walked in. Mansour followed closely. He could see the car and the snagged and torn tire. But he couldn't see Abdul.

"Where is he?" Mansour asked. "And where's the new tire? The car jack? What's going on here?"

"The king would like to have a meeting; that is what's going on here. Just come with me. Abdul is fine. He is inside the car, tied up under the protection of one of my men."

Mansour peered hard at the tinted car windows. He could make out the silhouettes of three figures, and, yes, one of them seemed to be tied up.

"If the king wishes to talk to me, he'd better be inside that car," Mansour said.

"I am sorry to hear that," the man said, and then he threw a wild swing at Mansour's face.

Mansour felt the hours and years of jiujitsu take over. He ducked, rolled to the ground, and locked his body around the man's leg, then clenched hard. He heard a pop in the man's knee, and he dropped to the dirty asphalt beside Mansour, bellowing in pain.

The car door flew open with a clunk, and another large suited man exited and headed straight for him. Behind him followed a third, both heavies, definitely bruisers used to a good tussle.

"Allah oh merciful, bless me in this fight," he prayed. Mansour hopped back to his feet and turned his body sideways to them to minimize his silhouette. A few good body blows from guys this tough would have him wheezing for sure, and so he had to play defense.

Luckily the two men seemed impatient. The first swung a hard straight, and Mansour dodged aside, grabbed his arm, and pulled him through, bashing the straightened elbow with his own and cracking his forearm into an unnatural angle.

"Gah!" the heavy screamed, falling to his posterior and cradling his broken arm.

The second paused, assessed Mansour, then charged him in a full-on bull rush. Mansour dropped back and leveled a kick at the man's chest, but it bounced off and sent electric shivers through his leg. This guy seemed built of solid concrete.

The man roared and slammed Mansour into the wall, pinning his arms to his side. Mansour stomped his foot and then kneed him in the groin.

"Ugh," the man moaned, loosening his grip. Mansour tore his arms free and slugged the man, then spun him around and threw him to the ground. The heavy wheezed and rolled over.

"I think the king is going to have to explain why Terra Qurayshian agents are trying to kidnap Arlandican citizens," Mansour panted down to the broken agents on the ground.

The sound of a police siren and red and blue lights filled the alleyway. "Freeze! Put your hands in the air!" a police officer yelled.

Mike and his partner stepped out of the police cruiser and, to Mansour's surprise, a backup cruiser skidded to a halt behind them.

Mansour grinned. "I didn't realize you cared so much about my safety."

Mike shook his head and laughed. "I let the captain know what was up, and he insisted. I suspect he got in touch with the FBI as well. This is some big stuff happening here, Mansour. That king might be the big poobah across the ocean, but here in Arlandica we have our own rules, and he needs to learn to respect that."

The police officers grabbed the injured men and arrested them, clamping cuffs on them to pained moans and curses. It was nice to see the country still functioning as it should.

"It looks like you did a hell of a job, Mansour. Maybe when you're done with all of this, you can settle down and get a job at the department."

"Hang on." Mansour peered through the open door of the car and saw Abdulaziz peering back, well trussed up and quite red in the face. He yanked the man out and undid the ropes.

"Oh, thank Allah you have come," Abdul said. "This was a trap! These thugs were sent here to interrogate and kill us, Mansour! The king feels threatened that he didn't get all of us in his purge, and now I fear we have prices on our heads. Thank you for the rescue, Mansour. I owe you and your late father a great debt."

Mansour took his hands. "There is no debt in war, Abdul. Now we must figure out why he feels so threatened by us."

"I think, with you, he simply fears the wrath of the vengeful son. It's not hard to imagine a king being afraid of the son of Faisal." Abdul pointed at the injured men being bundled into the police cruisers. "But with me, it is for the things I know. The king has expensive tastes and perversions. He has embezzled from the state and taken bribes for legislative favor. Hundreds of millions of dollars, all of it dirty money, have been funneled into the king's pockets. And do you want to know something funny, Mansour? If he had just left us all alone and let us go, I would have kept quiet."

Abdul popped the back of his car, and the trunk jumped open on jumbled springs. In it sat a number of hard gray plastic file cases.

"All of this, Mansour, is yours. You will find evidence for hundreds of high dollar bribes, bank account information for the king from before, when he was still just a prince, and even more than that. I have evidence that shows that the king has hundreds of politicians in his pocket as well. From Terra Qurayshia . . . and from Arlandica itself! Mansour, the president and much of the Senate is in King Qurayshi's pocket. And who knows just how much money he's funneled into the media to brainwash people with his lies."

Mansour gasped. This was top-level corruption. In a few sentences his mission had exploded from one of revenge to one of national security itself!

"So members of Congress were bought for the benefit of the new king in Terra Qurayshia?" Mansour asked.

"Yes, exactly."

"This makes sense of why the so-called "conservative" members act as if they don't see reality and follow the president blindly. I thought they were just being biased to their party." All of it fell into place neatly in his mind: the terror attacks, the aggressive moves by the president, martial law, suspending Congress and the supreme court; all these felt directly related to the new king. He felt strongly that Zamanistan wasn't behind any of this, or rather that the new king had bankrolled all of it. And these files might contain the proof.

"Yes, they don't care about the party or the country. They only care about themselves and their bank accounts. You see, Mansour, the king of Terra Qurayshia wants Arlandica to become a dictatorship. He wants the whole world to be a dictatorship, but he wants to start with Arlandica. He sees democratic ideals as weak and even harmful. And the current president, plus a lot of the party, agree. So they're in alliance, and if he is successful, then Arlandica will not be a republic for much longer."

Mansour frowned. If the king of Terra Qurayshia believed that republics made people weak, wouldn't he want Arlandica to stay one? And what better way to delegitimize democracy than to have the world's shining example fall first?

"Why is the king trying to make Arlandica stronger?" Mansour asked.

"Ah, well, he thinks that making the current president a dictator or even king over Arlandica would give him a powerful ally and would also legitimize his own rule."

"So the king is hiring Arlandica's president and his party to extend the military power of Arlandica to protect him personally and help him stay in power. If you'd told me all of this a month ago, I would've thought you'd gone mad."

Abdul nodded in agreement. "Yes, I thought I myself might be going mad when I first began to find details of this conspiracy. But these are the stakes, Mansour, and as you can see, we need to remove this king from power as soon as we can. We need to develop a plan."

Mansour thought back to the old days, when they all used to sit around the table and talk politics. He remembered all the back and forth about dictatorships and how they rot the country and the people's souls. He loved Arlandica. This was his home, a diverse place full of a thousand cultures and a thousand languages, a nation with a dream to be better. Arlandica acknowledged its mistakes and didn't cover them up. Instead, it tried to make amends. But Arlandica with a dictator or a king? It would not be Arlandica.

"I'll do anything necessary to protect this nation, Abdul. I was born here, I grew up here, I've lived most of my life here, and I'll die for it if I need to. Just tell me what I need to do, and I will do it."

Abdul's eyes shone with pride. "If only your father could see the hero he raised. Yes, for now we must hide the data in case something happens to either of us. I will try to find trustworthy contacts and allies in the Sunlandian government. And then, from there, maybe this cabal can be undermined and eventually overthrown. You, Mansour–you keep yourself and Nadia safe and wait for my call. I will tell you when I have need of you. Be safe and by the grace of God we will thwart the enslavement of our people and keep liberty alive in Arlandica."

Chapter 14

12 years ago
Arlandica

For a time his mother improved. Or seemed to. This cancer business was the worst kind of guessing game. Mansour hated it. Although his father liked to say "hope springs eternal," for Mansour, having his hopes dashed meant seeing the woman who loved him most in the world, the woman who cared for him, wasting away. Yet he was young, and that meant a month without any issues was enough to lift his spirits.

After the latest advanced chemotherapy course, things looked better. Mansour continued his college classes, thrilled that his mom was progressing back to something approaching normal.

And unbelievably, this held. A year passed, with Mansour cruising through his senior year of college, before Fatima got sick again. This time, the situation felt dire; she was hospitalized for days, which stretched into weeks. Surgeries were scheduled and his mother went under the knife, recovered, and underwent surgery yet again. According to the doctors, the cancer had spread throughout her body, fast.

Fatima was sent home with a nurse as they'd done previously, but this time it was different. Unlike before, where he'd felt she would weather the storm, the silence felt thick and ominous. She appeared to be deteriorating much faster. Her weight dropped along with her appetite, and she was thinner than he could ever remember.

Before she returned home this time, Uncle Muhammad flew in with Teta, to be with his sister. He stayed in constant contact with the rest of the family in Keerypt, updating them on the situation.

Fatima's morale went up and down. Sometimes she was very content and accepting of the situation; other times she would cry and wish she was back to her normal good health. Her love for Faisal and Mansour was heartbreaking, and it was clear she didn't want to leave them.

Mansour couldn't bear to go in and see her. It clutched at his chest too much. Sometimes he got as far as her bedroom door before stopping, unable to continue the last foot. One day while he stood outside her room, his mother's voice froze the blood in his veins.

"I want to see Mansour getting married to the best woman in the world. I wanted to be part of selecting his wife. I wanted to attend his wedding, but I'm not sure I will make it," Fatima said to Faisal.

"*In shaa Allah,* let us stay optimistic, my love. I am praying for you every day," Faisal replied in a voice heavy with emotion. He lumbered out a minute later, grabbed Mansour by the shoulder for a moment, then disappeared with silent tears running down his face.

Mansour's world unraveled. Just as he'd been wrong to think he'd be a secret agent soon, he'd duped himself into believing things would be all right. They wouldn't. He'd just begun to reach toward the doorknob to his mother's bedroom when she spoke in a wavering voice, thick with sadness and resignation.

"I put my trust in You. I entrust You with my husband and with my son. You alone can take care of them better than I or anyone else can. I ask You, Allah, to find Mansour the best wife for him and to bless them and bless their progeny. I ask You, Allah, to forgive me and forgive all of my shortcomings and to make my departure from this life easy and peaceful. I ask You, Allah, to grant me paradise in the company of the prophets and the righteous people and the company of my family."

Mansour retreated and sat alone with his shock and disbelief. He consulted the Qur'an after a fashion, but none of the words seemed to want to enter his mind. They all swam on the page, even after he wiped the tears away.

Some days later, Mansour heard his dad by himself in the living room. The telltale sounds of soft sobbing explained all they needed to. Mansour entered the living room and burst into tears. He couldn't recall ever seeing his father like this. A huge pain, indescribable and hot, swelled within him. Mansour had a lot of hope, but this time it seemed inevitable that he would lose his mom.

"We tried everything, Mansour, and the only way for your mom to get better is a miracle from God," Faisal croaked.

Mansour couldn't stop the tears. He hugged his father and let the sorrow overwhelm him.

Later, while Fatima slept in her bedroom, her mom, Mansour's grandmother, sat next to her, reading the Qur'an in a soft voice with tears in her eyes.

On Friday, Mansour, Faisal, and Muhammad went to pray the *Jummah* prayer as usual. Nothing about the *masjid* at midday was any different: not the mosaics, not the *Azan* that announced the call to worship, not the faces he saw each week before kneeling to pray. But all was not as it should be. He knew the *Azan* by heart but did not hear it, said the words but did not taste them, knelt to the ground but did not feel it.

When they returned, Teta and the doctor greeted them. Mansour knew.

"My Fatima is gone," Teta informed them quietly, then opened her arms to Mansour. He walked into her embrace, numb and cold.

A flood of tears followed. Time passed with nothing but tears to remember it. Mansour felt like the world had stopped and everything would just end. It was over. In the still of the house, this seemed doubly true.

Yet he was still alive. His father, his grandmother, his uncle, the doctor, still alive. He went out to look at the street, where cars passed by and the world kept turning. People walked by, oblivious to what had just happened. Some people laughed. Children jumped around and bothered their siblings. Nothing had stopped at all.

Faisal and Muhammad worked on the funeral arrangements. In the Islamic tradition, it was better to have the burial as soon as possible, so they arranged with the Islamic Center to have the burial the next day in West Beach, which was Fatima's wish. She had made it clear she didn't want to make it difficult for her family to travel and handle the travel arrangements for her body. She was very practical and considerate and had planned everything in detail, including her burial arrangements.

The family and friends gathered at the Islamic Center where they prayed over Fatima after she'd been washed in the special washroom there. The prayer was for those who'd passed away. For the first time he could remember, Mansour prayed standing up without bowing or prostrating. Then they headed to the burial site with special police escorting them to the Muslim cemetery. It was all happening so fast that Mansour couldn't comprehend the complete reality, and the only thought on which he could focus was that this wasn't the end. That he would see his mom again—in the next life, in paradise, God willing, where there is no disease and no death, only love and happiness.

After the burial, Mansour went back home full of emotions. Emptiness, grief, regret, and still others warred within him. Sadness that he wouldn't see his mother again in this life, anger that he couldn't change anything, hope in God that she was now in His good hands, and wondering where her soul was now. He wanted to be alone and found himself going to the piano, playing some music that he just made up to express his deep sorrow and sadness. It was customary in the Middle Eastern culture not to play music or listen to the radio or even watch TV for at least three days after the death of a family member. The only exception, of course, was to listen to the recitation of the Qur'an.

Mansour's dad, uncle, and grandmother were shocked and surprised to see Mansour play the piano. No one said a word. But they saw the depth of Mansour's emotions while, with tears rolling down his face, he played this new music that they'd never heard before. It made them all cry, and they retreated to their rooms.

After playing the piano for some time, Mansour didn't feel like staying at home without his mother. He wanted to get out of the house and be anywhere but here. He drove, heading west on York Boulevard, toward Santa Dominga, and found himself circling over toward the Islamic Center, unconsciously. He would later reflect on his need to be close to his mother, though it was no longer possible.

There was quite a bit of traffic, and Mansour had to stop at several signal lights. Just past the Islamic Center, at one intersection, he was distracted for a split second while looking at the skies and wondering where his mom was now. He rear-ended the car ahead of him. He'd barely touched the vehicle, and there was no damage, but it was all his fault.

The other car stopped and the driver, a young lady, got out of the car. Her face was a mask of annoyance, and she seemed ready to start a quarrel. Mansour exited his car, and as soon as she looked at him, her anger melted away. She gazed in silence at Mansour's blue eyes sparkling with reflections of the sunset, tears about to spill over.

"What happened?" she asked with no trace of her prior anger.

"I'm very sorry, ma'am," Mansour answered. Then there was silence for a few seconds, though it felt like much longer.

"Are you okay? Why are you crying?" the lady asked.

Mansour felt very strange. The same stew of emotions battled within him, now with an added element of embarrassment. At the same time, something about the woman's voice, her concern, and her beauty struck him.

"I'm very sorry, I-I'll take care of any damage . . . I did to your car," Mansour said.

"You're not crying because of that, are you?" the lady asked.

"No, no, I . . . I just came back from my mother's funeral," Mansour replied.

She paused and stared, searching his face for the truth perhaps, and she softened toward him further. "I'm very sorry to hear that," the lady said. "Do you mind if we get off the road at the next intersection and exchange information for insurance purposes? You can follow me."

Mansour agreed and did just that. They both drove out of the busy lanes to the shoulder, then turned down a side street.

By the look of her, the clothes she wore, she was likely also a Muslim. He wasn't far from the Islamic Center, after all. If he shared his information and showed her his driver license, she would notice his last name and know he was a Terra Qurayshian prince. It wasn't out of the question for her to get greedy and make a big deal out of this tiny bump. He wasn't sure what to do.

His insurance card had only his name and his father's middle name without the last name. He decided to only share the insurance card with her, and he removed his driver license from his wallet. She parked her car, and he stopped behind her. They got out again, and he tried to think while the lady looked again at the rear bumper of her car to see if there was any damage.

Mansour also inspected the situation again and finally got a chance to notice how beautiful she was. She had very straight, long, light brown hair and breathtakingly beautiful cat eyes—deep blue and clear like pristine pools. Her expressive eyebrows were shaped like little light brown comets headed toward each other. Slightly arched, they gave her a look of perpetual surprise and wonder. She had a fair complexion with a beauty mark on her right cheek, a small mole just above her rosy, slightly full lips. Her elongated high cheekbones curved with elegance and beauty. About five inches shorter than he, she dressed her slender figure elegantly and conservatively–a long, dark skirt, a light-colored blouse, a gold necklace with a small golden book-like ornament, and delicate little heart-shaped earrings. She was perhaps a couple of years younger than him.

"I'm sorry to hear about the loss of your mother," she said. "It must be very hard."

"Thank you. Yes, it's not easy. And again, I am very sorry for any trouble I've caused you."

She smiled, a welcome and rare sight these days. "There's no trouble at all . . . I don't see any damage to either car, so just for formality, if you don't mind, can we just exchange insurance information?"

"Yes, of course. My name is Mansour."

"My name is Nadia. Where are you from, if you don't mind me asking?"

Mansour paused for a couple of seconds and thought carefully before answering. That fun and ridiculous spy training popped back to mind, where he'd spent all that time obsessing over himself as Bond, Mansour Bond.

"I'm from Keerypt. How about you?"

"What a coincidence, I am also from Keerypt! I was born here. My dad is from Keerypt, and my mom is from Myria."

"It's a ni–an interesting coincidence," Mansour corrected himself. Why had he stopped himself from saying *nice* coincidence?

They exchanged insurance cards and spent a few quiet minutes taking down each other's information. If she thought it strange that he didn't share his driver's license, she didn't mention it. After all, there was no real damage to either car.

"So, do you go to school around here?" she asked.

"Yes, I'm at USWB (University of Sunland West Beach), and will be graduating this year, *in shaa Allah.* How about you?"

"*In shaa Allah.* I'm in my freshman year of college. I go to USSA (University of Sunland San Adelio)."

USSA was quite a good school. “You do speak Arabic, of course, don’t you?” he asked.

She nodded. “Yes, I understand it better than I speak it, though. How about you?”

“Yes, the same, although I was encouraged to practice it more at home, especially when I visit Keerypt.”

“That’s very nice. I visit Keerypt and Myria about once a year.”

He didn’t want to stop talking to her. She radiated life in a time of loss, and it drew him to her like a magnet. “Do you know your major yet?”

“Yes, I’ll be studying biology. How about you?”

“Civil engineering.”

“Well, that sounds interesting.” Her grin told him that wasn’t at all true, and also that she was joking with him.

He tried to laugh, but his body betrayed him. Instead, he lamely said, “Yes, it is. I enjoy it.”

The grin vanished, but her eyes remained mirthful. “That’s great. It’s good to get into a field that you enjoy. I also like science and biology.”

More. He needed to talk with her more. “Are you considering getting into medical school after your undergraduate?”

“Yes, that’s the plan.” She was hoping to leave, he could feel it.

“That’s great; it’s a very good field and, of course, a long one.” His words were so lame. Of course doctors studied for years and years. She would think him stupid. No, another part of him argued, she knew he’d just lost his mother. She would forgive him a plodding response.

Thankfully, unfortunately, she broke their conversation off. “Yes, I know. I hope things will go as planned, *in shaa Allah*. I’ll have to get going.”

“It was nice meeting you, although I would’ve preferred to meet you in a different way. But I enjoyed talking with you.”

“Same here. I wish you best of luck. Maybe our paths will cross again someday. I hope not this way.”

Nadia and Mansour shook hands and said their goodbyes. What had happened felt very strange to Mansour; it didn't feel real. It felt like a dream. He wasn't sure what to make of it. Destiny perhaps, or just a coincidence with no significance? Should he tell his dad what had happened? He wished his mom was there to get her opinion on the matter. He felt he needed to get home safely and rest for a while until the evening service at the Islamic Center. So, despite the whirling mass of emotions within him, one that Nadia had added to, he used his old Mansour self-control to drive himself home safely.

His father, Uncle Muhammad, and his grandmother were clearly relieved to see him arrive. Joy to see him again replaced worry, and they asked him where he'd been. He told them what had happened, even though he hadn't been planning to say anything. All three of them shared identical puzzled expressions. Faisal told Mansour to take it easy and rest for a bit, which was exactly what Mansour had planned.

He washed up, prayed, and listened to the recitation of *Surat Yusuf,* the twelfth sura of the Qur'an, the story of Joseph, on CD. This sura calmed him down and energized him to overcome difficulties. The *Surat Yusuf* was rich with meaning and wisdom and promoted patience and active acceptance of difficult situations, though not passive acceptance, by any means.

In the evening, Mansour and his family went to the Islamic Center to receive people's condolences. Though there were many friends and acquaintances who attended the service, he kept hoping to see Nadia arrive. It was a silly hope—they were strangers who'd just met that day. During the service, a good friend of the family, one of the most active community members, gave a recitation of the Qur'an. He had such a harmonic, peaceful, and loving voice that Mansour felt infused with serenity. Grieving was a process, but that process had begun in earnest.

Chapter 15

12 years ago
Arlandica

Uncle Muhammad and Teta left a week later and returned to Keerypt. They'd been in Arlandica for quite some time, and needed to return home. It was as understandable as it was difficult, since Mansour felt his home was empty. His father mentioned it on occasion, but Mansour in particular wished he had more family around. It wasn't long before Faisal returned to traveling around the world, as usual, taking care of his business, and leaving Mansour alone most of the time.

Before, anytime his mother had been at home, even if she slept or read quietly, the house had had an energy about it. It felt occupied. Now that was gone. The silence felt fuller, more invasive. Mansour sometimes found himself wandering into a room thinking she might be there, curled up with a book or watching the TV with the sound off, focusing instead on the subtitles. She never was, and Mansour chastised himself for not getting it. She was gone and wasn't coming back.

Something like a month later, he had his first ever shopping trip alone. Mansour wasn't fond of shopping for clothes, as his mom used to do it for him without him tagging along, but he needed . . . something. He didn't know what, exactly, but he seized on the idea that he had old clothes. This might've been true or not, but it was an excuse to get out of the house and accomplish something.

He located an upscale mall a half hour from his house and found a good shop close-by that had some nice clothes. He bought some pants, shirts with long sleeves and short sleeves, and sweaters. The salesman, a middle-aged Aragonian man, introduced himself.

"Can I help you, sir?"

"Yes, sure."

"My name is José."

"Mansour."

He found José friendly, knowledgeable, and unwilling to upsell for no good reason. It was encouraging to have a smiling face, even if he was paying for the experience. Mansour felt good dealing with José, and the shopping experience wasn't as bad as he'd thought it would be. The salesman made it easy by helping pick the right clothes for him, and they chatted quite a bit. A half hour later, he had a couple of new outfits that would do the trick.

When Mansour left the shop and went back to his car, he pawed through the bags for the receipt, then looked in his wallet, where he usually kept them.

He didn't find anything: not one of those credit card carbon papers old shops used to imprint his credit card, no receipt, or anything at all to show he had paid for the clothes. He'd been so distracted with his mother that he couldn't recall whether José had run his card or not. Mansour couldn't remember signing on the little touchscreen or one of those paper receipts. José had been talking . . . then he'd taken a phone call? The clothes Mansour had bought were worth something like $700. Had he forgotten to give Mansour a receipt? Had he forgotten to charge Mansour altogether?

Finally, he decided to head back to the shop. As soon as he entered, José beamed. You'd think he was just witnessing his prettiest daughter getting happily married.

"Thank God you came back! God sent you back to me."

"Yes, indeed, He did," Mansour replied.

"Thank you very much, I owe you." José chuckled ruefully. "My manager would've taken it out of my paycheck . . . I will take you out to lunch! I was going to be in real trouble, and you saved me."

"No problem at all. I had a duty before God to do what is right," Mansour said.

"You must be a very good Christian," José said.

"Muslim actually, and we are forbidden to cheat anyone. Otherwise we are not good Muslims."

"I'm afraid I don't know much about Islam, but I just learned something now," José said.

"Before we forget again, here is my credit card, and I'll not leave until I'm sure I signed the receipt." Mansour handed over the plastic, and the grateful José quickly ran it before he forgot again.

"Yes, of course, thank you very much," José said.

Mansour headed back home and frowned at the unwelcoming arms of the lonely silence that enfolded him. He couldn't even unload his new purchases without the sting of that unnatural quiet reaching into his mind. He put on the television just to have some sound, but even that wasn't enough. With the news on quietly, he sat down to study at the dining room table, and instead of putting information into his mind, found an hour had passed without him really noticing. Eventually dinner time came and went, and some food made its way into him. He prayed, then drifted back to his room and lay down.

In the midst of drowsing at only nine o'clock, his phone rang.

"My son," Faisal said.

"Dad? Are you well?"

"As well as can be expected. I had hoped to update you on the progress of the Royal Strategic Committee. I know I'm not supposed to divulge this information to anyone outside the committee, but"—here he chuckled—"someone happened to find out when he wasn't supposed to."

This woke Mansour up. "Where are you?"

As it happened, his father was back in Terra Qurayshia for a short trip.

Faisal explained that the day before, he'd had a discussion with his family back home about a grand plan to make major improvements to the kingdom in terms of productivity, significant improvements in education, introducing democracy for long-term stability, and improving technology in various industries.

Mansour hadn't thought of the secret agent situation in ages. And here it was again.

"This is all based on the vision of the new king. Son, he has a sincere and selfless concern about the country and the direction it is going. The committee is hoping to recruit key individuals from the royal family trusted by the king and his close advisors to play different, crucial roles in the king's plan."

Mansour tried to blink the sleepiness away and focus. Terra Qurayshia was technically his home. He had a TQ passport just below his Arlandican passport in his dresser. Plus, the old notions of spy work wormed their way back to his mind.

"The king is thinking of asking these individuals to work in the kingdom undercover without revealing their true identities."

"Under . . . cover." Yes, he'd heard that right.

These key individuals, Faisal explained, would collect a lot of data and submit it to the Royal Strategic Committee, the RSC, who would prepare detailed recommendations to the king for implementation at various phases: the short-term, intermediate, and long-term.

"The royal family is massive, you know. These mainly fall under three groups: those who agree with the king's vision and want a better life for the whole country, not just the top one percent; the second group we need to worry about . . . they're totally selfish and greedy, and want not only to keep the status quo but also, my son, they wish to grab the power from the current regime. We see this group as dangerous, and some believe they will stop at nothing to achieve their goals."

He paused. Mansour filled in for him. "What of the third group?"

Whatever had stopped his father from speaking was gone. "The third group does not care and will just follow the group who is in power. Some aren't political, just comfortable . . . others will try to back whoever they think will come out the winners. It's difficult to find where loyalties lie. Honestly, I can't wait to get out of the palace."

When his father returned a few days later, it was to inform Mansour that his name had come up a couple of times while Faisal was discussing the plan, as it had in his senior year of high school. It was apparent that he was a good candidate for recruitment but not ready yet due to lack of job experience. It was preferable for him to have experience outside the kingdom in one of the advanced countries, including Arlandica.

Mansour smiled and tried to make himself believe he was feeling anything other than awful. He was trying not to feel the grief any longer and unsure how long it would continue to gnaw at his heart. But despite repeated prayers, those prayers had yet to brighten his life back up to what it had been before the cancer diagnosis.

Mansour continued his senior year in college and graduated later that year with a bachelor of science in civil engineering. His father attended the ceremony and informed him that Fatima was presently watching over him, just as proud of her son as he was. This sentiment brightened Mansour's heart more than the cap, the gown, and the diploma case.

The summer found many of his fellow students and friends on beach trips to Nueva Aragonia, but his father advised he attempt to figure out his next steps while the rest were drinking their futures away.

He was still not sure what that should be. He'd discussed different future plans with his dad many times, such as returning to Terra Qurayshia and starting a construction company, going to Keerypt and starting a business as a developer, or staying in Arlandica for a few more years to gain some experience before starting any business. Going to Keerypt was his least favorite option: everyone he knew would remind him of his mother, and he recalled all the state surveillance and corruption Kareem, Yasser, and Sameer had warned him about.

"If you were me," he asked over *kafta* one night, "what would you do?"

"A life of luxury would be assured in Terra Qurayshia," his father replied. "But you would find it dull, unfulfilling, and possibly dangerous. So many in the royal family are clawing at each other to get the king's favor, just to get a glance their way. They'll do anything, which demeans them. They would ruin you without a second thought if they thought the king would like it."

"But I can find employment there," he said. "Honest work."

"Of course, but none of the employers would give you any responsibilities. You would be coddled and given nothing but ceremonial tasks. Or they might use you like a pole-vaulter would use the pole, to try to reach the king's notice."

Mansour smiled. "Don't sell it too hard."

"The reality is often much less wondrous than it first seems. Of course you have the power to determine your destiny, but if your choice were in my hands, I would find a place here in Arlandica."

Experience was what he needed, good, solid, respectable work for a company here to raise his level of professional skill, help people in the way a civil engineer could, and put some money in his pockets as well. The RSC would call on him in its own time. For now, he searched for work nearer to the place he considered home.

Mansour kept his eyes open for work opportunities in Southern Sunland. Not long after graduation, he spied an ad in the Sunland Times about a job fair at the Southern Sunland convention center. Armed with a few copies of his resume and the certainty his mother would approve, he followed the signs that said Job Fair through the massive complex.

Luckily for Mansour, many companies, consultants, and government agencies were looking for young engineers. He spent a couple of hours talking to recruiters and only felt a special calling to one, the Sunland Department of Transportation (SDOT). They seemed very interested in recruiting Mansour and told him that for sure he'd be selected.

He had his guard up but shoved aside the feeling that this was too good to be true, blaming that on his grief. He had nothing to lose by following up and submitting an application. If they seemed shady, he could always turn down the job.

A couple of weeks later, Mansour received a letter from SDOT asking him to choose where he wanted to go for an interview. He had the choice of Southern Sunland or Northern Sunland. Mansour chose Southern Sunland and two weeks later received a letter from SDOT with a date for the interview downtown.

The relatively quick response surprised him, given that it was a state agency. He went to the interview, located in a nondescript government building surrounded by Sunland's ubiquitous palm trees.

The interview panel consisted of three men and a lady. He recognized the man from the convention center who'd encouraged him to apply. Mansour felt very much at ease when he saw a familiar face. They asked him general questions about his education, his experience, and his plans for the next five years. Since he was fresh out of college, he had no experience to show, save for a handful of school projects. Still, they seemed delighted to view his meager portfolio.

At the end of what felt like a good interview, he treated himself to some ice cream. It occurred to Mansour, while he watched cars rush past in every direction, that his car insurance hadn't contacted him.

Nadia hadn't called the insurance company or tried to get

reimbursed for anything. In his mind, she slid over into the "honest" category. He thought of calling her to see her—he really liked her—but didn't want to come off as a stalker. He didn't know if she was seeing anyone. Plus, a nagging voice in the back of his mind said, James Bond didn't have a wife.

♛

A couple of weeks later, he received a letter from SDOT congratulating him on being selected to work for SDOT in Southern Sunland. The letter explained that they had a two-year rotation program for junior engineers where he'd spend six months in each of four selected divisions. It asked him to start work in three weeks or to call human resources to make other arrangements.

"This baby here is Bessy," the Arlandican manager told him, and patted the huge orange truck with the beacon lights. "Inside's your CB for talking with the office, other inspectors, and your TMC."

"TMC. Traffic . . . Management Center," Mansour said.

"That's the one. How's your CB lingo?"

"Good."

"Ten-four?"

"Message received. Ten-nine, repeat message; ten-twenty, what's your location?"

The big, bearded manager nodded. "There's a reference card in the glove compartment if you need it."

Mansour also carried a briefcase with his daily diary—amazingly still on paper—and other necessities. He'd be inspecting contractors' work to make sure they followed SDOT plans and specifications. All the relevant information would go in the daily diary. He'd also do a monthly estimate of payments to contractors based on his daily diary. The idea of doing this on paper was mystifying, but he wasn't yet ready to object that he had a laptop. Let him work there a few months.

"All right . . . We got you on night shifts, which you're gonna love. We're extending the 582 to link up with the 510, and you got to make sure everything's running smooth." The manager laughed, which strained his blue chambray shirt against his hefty gut. "Those people in Altafina hate this project, tell you the truth. Make sure nobody comes along and blows up any of the heavy equipment in the night." He stopped and stared at Mansour, flush with embarrassment, but Mansour only chuckled.

"I didn't mean . . ." the big guy said. "That just slipped out."

Mansour gave him a smile. "No idea what you're talking about."

Night shifts affected him strangely. On one hand, he had no time or energy to consider the loss of his mother. On the other hand, he barely had time to see any of his friends. Sleeping during the day was the worst, but he tried to put himself in Bond's shoes and say he was conditioning himself for the real dangerous secret agent stuff, though that would never come.

After Mansour's six-month rotation in the construction division, he worked in the design division and learned to use the Intergraph Computer Aided Design system. It wasn't nearly as lonely as tromping around the highway construction projects at three in the morning, and he very quickly made some friends in the new division.

They headed out to restaurants and movies together. In design, he met a special friend, Fareed from Zamanistan, who was very knowledgeable in all aspects of design and the process of project delivery. Fareed impressed Mansour, and they liked to attend the Sunday program at the Islamic Center together. Fareed was very active at work, and in volunteer work as well, and he always prayed on time. He had a very nice, pleasant character and was often optimistic and happy.

Not long after Mansour had started in the design division, a pretty girl appeared from another unit. She was short, about a foot shorter than Mansour, and had a permanent suntanned complexion that went strangely with the splashes of freckles on her cheeks and over her nose. Plus, she had startling green eyes that kept lighting back on Mansour, even though she'd come to see Fareed.

"Carmen."

"Hi, Fareed. I'm having an issue on my project," she told him. "Can you come take a look at it?"

Fareed nodded, clicked on his own ICAD design, and stood up to stretch. "Sure."

"You're new?" She'd already forgotten about her important project, it seemed. She also had an adorable accent. It really went with her compact form and upturned nose.

"That's right. I'm Mansour."

Fareed put a little bit of extra stretching in for no good reason. He headed over toward the window and torqued his neck back and forth so this Carmen could have time to speak with Mansour.

"Good to meet you! I like that tie. Where are you from, Mansour?"

"Keerypt, actually." His policy at this job had been to keep his blood relations a secret. Based on his dad's advice, it was better to keep his being a prince from becoming widely known.

"I've never met anyone from there. I told Fareed, people always think I'm Middle Eastern! I'm actually half Aragonian and half Stivalian."

What was going on here?

"I didn't have a chance to meet you before. If you are available for lunch, it would be great to get to know my new coworker," Carmen said.

Her looks and demeanor took Mansour by surprise. She was very friendly and very attractive, and he could hardly say no to that. "Yes, of course," Mansour replied. They agreed to meet at her cubicle and go to have lunch in an hour.

Fareed had watched the whole thing, and as soon as she headed off, he turned a concerned look Mansour's way. She'd left without getting Fareed's help on her project. Apparently meeting Mansour gave her the confidence she needed to deal with the real problem.

"A word of advice. Please be careful, my friend. I know she's very pretty, but she also has some problems, and I would not recommend getting too close. I can explain later."

Mansour's unexpected good mood at meeting the bubbly Carmen evaporated, comfortable lunch with an attractive girl or no. That night after work, he slunk back home to find the house empty again and a note from his father saying he'd flown overseas. Again. That gnawing feeling of wrongness flooded back into the house.

"Prayer," he told himself quietly. A pretty girl would not eradicate his recurring grief, but perhaps the Qur'an might.

Chapter 16

Now

The month after he rescued Abdulaziz was a blur of police and FBI, interrupted only by night and rest. They had so many questions, and though they made it clear that he was free to go at any time, Mansour felt like he himself had been arrested alongside those goons he'd fought in the alleyway.

It probably didn't help that after Mike had taken their statements and sent them away, he and Abdul had hidden the treasure trove of incriminating documents. The FBI agents seemed to smell it on him, a miasma of guilt and criminality that emanated from his very pores. But it didn't matter. He told them everything he knew, even the king's suspected involvement of the president, but he didn't furnish those documents. He'd hang onto those with his life if he needed to. He didn't know who he could trust.

Things got better after they hired him on as a consultant, though, and gave him a government salary. They made it clear that he wasn't to go anywhere, and it made him feel as though he'd never left Terra Qurayshia. He knew what it all meant. He was a suspect and a prisoner in the land of his birth. The days wore down on him.

But the nights were harder, and Mansour found himself jumping at shadows, or at creaks in the building as it settled about him. And in the mornings he found himself starting awake, thrashing from nightmares in which he was strapped to a chair, devious agents grinning bloody fangs at him as they cut his flesh and demanded to know where the papers were.

Each and every time, his lovely Nadia would grab him and

hold him, whispering sweet nothings into his ear. Until one morning he woke and she was gone, an empty tussle of sheet and blankets where she usually lay.

"Nadia? Nadia!" Mansour bellowed, getting out of bed hastily and knocking over a lamp in the process. He cursed. "Allah, forgive me," he followed, then he heard the liquid sounds of gagging coming from their bathroom. Was Nadia choking? He sprinted to the bathroom and threw open the door.

Inside, Nadia was on her knees before the toilet bowl, the lid and seat up, the contents of last night's mostly digested meal floating in the puddle therein. She turned her head and her watery eyes met his fearful ones, only to leave as she threw up again.

"Oh, Nadia, what is wrong?" Mansour asked. He rubbed her back and shoulders.

She spit and gasped. "Mansour, I think I'm pregnant." She stared at him, her eyes wide and open, her defenses never so fragile in her life as they were now.

"That's wonderful! So wonderful!" Mansour lied. It should have been the happiest day in his life, but all he could see was a son or daughter growing up without a father. He smiled and laughed, and Nadia seized him in a tremendous hug. But all the while, inside, he knew things were going to get harder.

Mansour helped Nadia up off the floor and led her out of the bathroom and to the bed.

Please, Allah, he prayed, *let me be here for my family. Let me be here for my child!*

"Lay down, Mommy, and let's see what breakfast Daddy can make for you."

She laughed. "You've regaled me enough about how well you burn eggs and ruin tea. But I love the thought. Do you think you could manage to cook up a bowl of cornflakes with milk?"

"Of course, my love."

"With, um, with sliced pickles?" she asked, her face going pink.

"Whatever you desire, my dearest. In fact, I think I'm going to take a sick day today. Why don't we relax and do something fun, hey? As a family."

Nadia beamed and her blush deepened, coasting down her face over her neck and chest. Mansour's heart pounded, struggling to fight his fear with the wonderful event that was occurring. He was going to be a daddy!

Mansour grabbed his phone. "The bureau," he told it. It dialed his FBI contact number immediately.

"Mansour," the gruff voice answered. It sounded more like a command than a salutation.

"Agent Pickering. Something has come up, and I'm afraid that I won't be able to come in today. I should be good for tomorrow, though."

"You aren't planning a vacation, are you?" Pickering asked immediately, giving no space between Mansour's words and his own.

"No, of course not. Just the wife is feeling a little ill, and I should give her a day to rest and get better." This wasn't good. Just like with the documents, Mansour thought, these guys could smell through the phone that he wasn't being forthright with his information. Still, there was nothing he could do. Who knew what they would do if they knew about the pregnancy?

"Yes, family is important. Very important. Take care of your wife, Mansour, and see to it that you stay in the county. I wouldn't want you to wear your sick wife out on a road trip."

"Of course, yes." Just listening to the man sent shivers through Mansour's body. Every word was innocent, yet each one of them felt like a threat. "TV and movies for us, Agent Pickering."

"Goodbye, Mansour. Call again if there is anything you need us to do for you. You can't imagine the lengths we'd go to for our most important consultant." The call ended and Mansour couldn't help but tremble. The message was clear: Do not try to run, little spy man. I'm onto your game, and there's no place on the planet that's beyond me. I'll catch you, and you'll pay.

"Is there anything wrong?" Nadia asked. She looked so happy and so innocent, a rose surrounded by thorns.

"Nothing, sweetheart. I was just thinking about my father and how much I wish he could be here now," Mansour said. Then he padded out to the kitchen to make the best cornflakes he could.

His doorbell rang sometime later. Mansour started awake and tried to blink the sleep out of his eyes.

It was three in the afternoon and Nadia had fallen asleep on the sofa. Mansour had nearly nodded off with her, not from the comfort of spooning his beautiful wife but rather from the absolutely dull romantic comedies she'd picked out for them to watch. Couldn't just one of them have an explosion or some sort of gun duel? But it was worth it, to make her happy.

Someone knocked on the door, breaking Mansour from his revelry. "Yeah, I'm coming," he said, hopefully loud enough to be heard but not loud enough to wake up his wife. The living room seemed dim and surreal as he padded through it. Too much TV and not enough outside, he admonished himself, almost tripping over an uneven rug on his way to the door.

"Who is it?" Mansour asked, and he peeked out the window. Two black suits stood on his porch, emotionless, and his heart spiked with fear. What was the FBI doing here?

"FBI, Mansour. Pickering sent us to check up on you two. Oh, and he told us to give you this." One of the agents held up a box, wrapped in blue paper and tied with a pink ribbon. Mansour unlocked the door and opened it, then took the present.

"Pickering says congratulations," the other agent said. The two of them tipped their hats and then walked off. Mansour brought the gift back inside and closed the door. What was that all about?

He put the gift on the table, feeling in his heart that his new joy had already become a liability. He gently eased the ribbon apart, unwrapped the paper from the box, and lifted off the cover.

Inside, nestled between soft and thin sheets of tissue paper, lay a cute light blue onesie. Daddy's Little Angel was printed on a white bib-like square on the front, surrounded by red hearts.

His house was wiretapped. Pickering was listening to everything that went on in his house, and the message couldn't be clearer: play ball or face the consequences. Mansour began to cry.

♛

The rest of the day trundled along wonderfully and soon Mansour could think of nothing but Nadia's starry eyes, her warm caresses and soft lips. They talked of baby names, what the child might grow up to be, and also of how large Nadia might become. She laughed and told him that she aimed to be the largest pregnant woman that had ever been, a record holder and someone to gawk at in public. It had been a brilliant time, but after she went to bed, all he could think of was Pickering and the FBI. Should he give them the documents? Could he? They weren't the enemy, right? That was the president, some senators, and representatives.

And the worry about the president had only grown. He'd seen stories about the national guard shooting rubber bullets at people who were on their porches and couldn't get inside fast enough. They went door to door asking neighbors if they'd seen anything suspicious . . . a.k.a. Muslims. The media sounded alarm bells, but some pundits countered that it was all down to public safety.

So assuming the new King Qurayshi had gotten to the president, how far did the rot reach? Surely he could trust these men in black. And even if he couldn't, was he willing to sacrifice a normal childhood for his unborn child to make sure that justice prevailed? Was this even about justice? Or was it just the bastard child of his previous thirst for revenge?

Mansour twiddled his thumbs, chewed at his nails, and found himself wishing he was a smoker. At least then he'd have something to do while he worried years off his life. Obviously the house was bugged. How else could Pickering have figured out what was up with him and his wife? Probably the phone was bugged too, otherwise he'd call Abdul and see if he could help him think of a way out of this mess. One thing was clear, he was going to have to do something and do it soon. The shadow of being locked up as a spy in the country of his birth haunted him, and it was draining him of his life.

His phone buzzed on the counter and he grabbed it, checking the name. Abdulaziz. He walked out to the kitchen and sat on the counter before answering. "What have you got, Abdul?"

"Wonderful news! I have the ear of the person I mentioned to you earlier, and she says that she can push ahead with this independently. But she needs something in return. There's a mole in the department. She said that everything you've told them has reached very influential ears. So she needs you to get what we talked about and bring them to the building immediately. She fears that improper agents might be coming for you soon."

Mansour closed his eyes. Was it Pickering? Was he telling the president and his goons? Were they now on a hit list and marked for death?

"Let me wake Nadia. I'll leave as soon as she's dressed."

Suddenly the air blew out past him, and his windows shattered from a powder bomb exploding with a boom. Flames licked at the front of his trousers. Men yelled commands, and something popped, then hissed. Thick smoke spiraled up through the living room.

"Nadia! Wake up! Get out of the house, now!" Mansour yelled. He turned out of instinct and launched a kick at the first shadowy figure to get near his position. Bone cracked, and the man fell to the ground screaming.

"He's over here!" the man yelled, furious. "I think the bastard broke my hip!"

A bullet whizzed by him, tearing a hole in the plaster of the kitchen wall. Mansour dropped low and grabbed at the M4 assault rifle the man was holding. He was dressed in black and dark green camo, Mansour noted. A mercenary from the Sagebrush Corporation! They'd been in the news before for their antics over in Farsia. The men had no morals and no honor. But they were stubborn, Mansour noticed, as the soldier clung tight to his weapon.

Mansour saw another dark shadow in the smoke and cursed. He kicked his leg out into an arc and felt the satisfying give of legs in motion. The soldier hit the ground hard next to him, and in his shock at being taken down so easily, he failed to grip his rifle tightly. Mansour seized it and disappeared into the smoke.

"Nadia! We have to go!" he yelled. Then he dived to the ground and rolled.

The sound of multiple rounds whizzed through the air where he'd been just a moment before.

"Mansour!" Nadia yelled.

She was near. He reached out and felt the soft skin of her hand clasp his. Coughing now and operating entirely upon the muscle memory of his home, he grabbed her up, offered a prayer to God, and jumped at where there should be a now blown-out window. If he was wrong, they were about to slam themselves into the wall. But thankfully, they breezed through into the biting chill of the Sunlandian night.

Almost before their feet touched the ground, more cries rose up, this time from a group of five men kneeling down with their rifles at the ready in a semicircle before the unmarked black vans.

One of them yelled into a radio mic. "Damn you, Henson! They're out of the house. I repeat, north-side backyard, they're out."

"Run, Nadia, run!" The two of them took off across the wet lawn under a black sky filled with silvery clouds. It was supposedly a full moon tonight, but the overcast sky did well to splay the light, making the night an eerie one. Mansour appreciated the help; a clear sky would've given them no chance to escape. As things stood, this was going to be difficult enough. He sent thanks to Allah.

Surprisingly, there were no more gunshots. They ran off across open lawns and increasingly large fallow fields of tall grass. They fled for hours, going at a nice jog instead of a terrified sprint, and finally they reached an area of the suburbs where they couldn't see any houses at all, just the thin outskirts of trees and thick, leafy forest litter that indicated the end of civilization and the beginning of the wilds.

The two of them stopped. The sky tinted the cool blue of predawn, indicating that they'd been running for most of the night.

"Mansour," Nadia panted. Then she started to weep. He took her into his arms and hugged her close, gazing out over the horizon and imagining what stories the president and his minions were going to plant about what had just gone down. He just knew that, going forward, they were going to have to disguise themselves, and at the first opportunity they were going to have to try to contact Abdul and also Governor Adele Schwarzenvalder.

Mansour released Nadia but held onto her shoulders, staring deep into her eyes. "We might be in serious trouble, my love. This has everything to do with King Qurayshi. I thought we were free of him once I returned to Arlandica, but . . . his ties with the Arlandican government run deeper than I imagined, and I fear we have just become public enemy number one. But there are people in the government who can help us. We just have to survive long enough to get to them."

"But, the baby!" Tears ran anew down her face. In the growing light of the morning she looked almost porcelain, a doll collector's dream come true.

"Yes, the baby. This is who we fight for now. We do this so that the baby can live in a country that doesn't treat her as a slave or a peasant, so that we all can live somewhere that treats us with respect and dignity. This is not what Arlandica is!" He surprised himself with the anger in his voice and he let go of

Nadia's shoulders. "Do you need to rest, Nadia? I can make a shelter with . . ." He gestured around at the woods. "It won't be the Hilton but it will be warm. And comfortable."

Nadia nodded and sat down with her back against a tree trunk, bringing her knees to her chest and hugging them tightly. She did that when she was in a bad way, Mansour reflected, and he vowed to himself that he'd give her the best breakfast money could buy when she came to . . . and when they had found proper disguises, of course.

He gathered up fallen branches and leaves and set about making her a den against the fat trunk of a black cottonwood. A hundred thousand years ago, he reflected, one of his ancestors might well have done this exact same thing. How much we regress under the violent overtures of authoritarianism, he imagined his father saying, and he almost laughed despite the gravity of the situation. But he managed to shorten the outburst to a curt snort.

Nadia looked up from her place. "Is something wrong, Mansour?"

He couldn't help it. Laughter broke past his lips and echoed through the air. "Has anything not gone wrong?" He smiled at her, true humor coloring his face for the first time in a long while.

She laughed as well. "It could be worse. Things could always be worse," she teased. "We could've been living in New Jameston and right now you might be fashioning us a shelter from cardboard boxes and old newspapers."

He finished laying the branches and began to plaster them with a mulch of dirt and leaves.

"You are absolutely right. And if we'd been living in New Jameston, you wouldn't ever have had the opportunity to live in such palatial accommodations such as these! Voila. Your castle awaits, my princess." He displayed the completed shelter with a flourish and a bow. She took his hand and pretended to lift up the long trail of a dress while ducking into the structure.

"Mansour?" Nadia asked, now lying in the soft dirt, her eyes already closed and her voice drifting. "We are going to be okay, right? In the end?"

He sat down at the entrance and stared off into the predawn distance for a time. "I don't know, Nadia," he responded, but she'd begun to snore softly. "I just don't know."

Chapter 17

Arlandica

Then

Astonishingly, years fell away in the rearview mirror, first one, then another. He did more rotations through the different divisions but kept in touch with the design people. Following his rotation in design, Mansour worked in traffic operations where he did traffic counting, traffic analysis, and many other miscellaneous tasks. He covered some nice areas such as the West Coast Highway (WCH). Mansour's last rotation was in contract and oversight, where he mainly checked the designs of and payments to consultants.

Some of the other rotations provided him with pleasant coworkers, but Fareed and Carmen had made the best impression on him, even if Carmen had made her interests uncomfortably clear.

Over time, he had learned more about the charming Carmen and her circumstances. Carmen revealed that she had a six-year-old daughter and an ex-husband, and a lot of nasty things to say about him. She snarled through one lunch—one where Fareed didn't tag along—that she'd thought Muslim men were supposed to be more self-controlled, more steadfast, and avoid liquor. Mansour agreed with her: they should. But it wasn't always the same for Muslims who made their way to Arlandica.

But he also had to be clear that he was in the relationship game for marriage only, and that wasn't a phase of her life she was ready to head back into. She eventually tried to convince him that "friends with benefits" was a thing he could maybe get into . . . with her. He politely declined.

On one of the days when Mansour was working the day

shift, he received a call from the SDOT downtown office. It was Carmen.

"I really need your help, right away. It's important." She certainly sounded frantic enough.

He agreed to meet her, and they went to a café in Bloomfield, not far from West Beach. She arrived with a darling little girl, who had huge eyes and wore a red ribbon that kept her hair well behaved.

"It's my ex. He threatened to kill me if I don't take him back. I need to stay away from my apartment today. I'm really scared and afraid for Tamara," Carmen explained.

Tamara had produced a coloring book, and Mansour wasn't sure if she was ignoring the two adults or listening intently.

Mansour hadn't expected to hear anything like this and was shocked by her request. He didn't know what to say.

"Please don't misunderstand me. I'm not trying to come on to you. You were the first person I thought of," she said, tearing up.

"Thank you for your trust. I want to help you, but I can't offer my house. I live alone right now, and it wouldn't be right. I just thought of something, though. One of my coworkers and friends at the office works as a reserve police officer. I'm sure he can help with suggestions on what to do. His name's Mike, and he's very nice and very helpful. I'll introduce you to him. I'll call him now and arrange for us to meet right after our lunch." Relief washed over Mansour for thinking of this solution.

"I just don't want anyone to know about this," Carmen said.

"He's a police officer. We'll ask him to keep it confidential. I'm sure he won't mention it to anyone in the office at all," Mansour replied.

Carmen wiped the tears from her face, and with smeared makeup beamed at him.

One Sunday morning, Mansour picked up Fareed at his house in the Silver Lake area to go to the Islamic Center to attend a special lecture.

Fareed took one look at Mansour and laughed. "Please tell me that you have more than one t-shirt the same color and style?"

Mansour grinned. "Who needs style? I'll be standing next to you anyway, so I automatically look amazing."

Fareed laughed again.

Mansour liked how laid-back he was, and how the jokes and jibes rolled off him so easily.

"If I didn't know you better," Fareed said, "I would've thought that you couldn't afford to buy any clothes. But I know for sure that this is not the case."

"Yes, my friend, but as you know by now, I'm not into clothes. I do that reluctantly–at the most, once a year. I prefer to shop for other things like electronics." Mansour replied with a chuckle.

"Six thousand dollars for surround-sound speakers. When's movie night at your house, again?"

By then they'd reached the Islamic Center. They parked and headed inside, leaving worldly concerns behind.

The prayer hall was on the left side of the main entrance. They removed their shoes before stepping onto the carpeted prayer area, and deposited them on the shoe rack just beside the doorway inside. The lights here were kept dim, the brightness level set to one conducive to calm, reflection, and peace. Sometimes the room smelled of the fragrance one finds in the shops of the holy cities, but for now he only detected the scent of the carpet-cleaning shampoo. The day was on the cool side, and the room nearly chilly since there weren't many people to warm up the space.

As greeting to the *masjid,* they prayed two *rakat.* Two bows would suffice.

The prayer area was nearly empty. Three young men scattered across the space, praying separately, with their backs to the entrance due to the *qibla.* He and Fareed faced the same direction for their two *rakat* and soaked in the quiet tranquility of the center and the meditative prayers.

Two men in their sixties sat on the carpet at each end of the prayer hall, reading the Qur'an quietly. Their faces and posture radiated the calm and languid joy Mansour began to feel. Their lips moved slightly. The one at the far corner, who had a longer untrimmed beard, read a bit louder than the one on the near corner, whose beard was trimmed short. Neither read loud enough to bother anyone.

"I forgot to eat," Mansour said quietly, following their prayer.

"You'd starve to death if the design team didn't drag you out to lunch every day," Fareed muttered in reply.

"I'll buy something in the social hall. You coming?"

But Fareed had produced his copy of the Qur'an. "I have a bit more reading to do."

Mansour nodded and left him to it, and headed by himself to the social hall, farther down the hallway from the main entrance of the *masjid.* The social hall had a small kitchen in the corner where they sold some food, tea, and coffee.

Nadia was there. Though she didn't attend regularly, and he hadn't seen her for years, he recognized her immediately. She had very distinctive features that were hard to forget: her eyes, her height, and her elegant, conservative clothes. She had her hair covered, and he wasn't sure if she typically wore the *hijab* or wore it just because she was at the *masjid.* Some ladies only wore *hijab* at the *masjid* out of respect for the place, like Christians wearing their Sunday best to church.

Floral patterning in light red and some blue decorated her beautiful, light green headscarf. The long, luxurious hair he'd remembered from before wasn't on display, sadly. She wore an elegant long, dark green dress with red and blue highlights that went perfectly with her scarf.

Avoiding her wasn't an option. "*Assalamu alaikum,* Nadia. Do you remember me?"

"Yes, of course, *wa Alaikum Assalam.* Mansour, right?"

A flare of pain shot through him. They'd met immediately after his mother had been laid to rest. He tried his best to conceal it. After all, he had very little female involvement in his life, and this chance meeting had all the feel of something ordained by Allah himself.

He tried to shove down the surge of loss he felt from missing Fatima, and instead tried out a smile. He hoped with all his might he didn't look the fool for her.

Wait, was she blushing?

"Yes, right, Mansour. I'm impressed you remembered my name."

"Well, you also remembered my name." She blushed.

"It was quite a day for me, hard to forget."

"I don't get rear-ended that often, and you left an impression on me with the passing away of your mother at that time. Are you feeling better?"

He nodded. "Of course, I miss her each day. She was an incredible woman. Are you still going to the same school?"

She also nodded. "I'll be starting my senior year now. When we met, I was just entering college. You've probably graduated already, right?"

"Yes, I have. I'm working now."

"Where do you work?"

"Since I graduated I've been working for SDOT."

Mansour took out his business card and gave it to her. His business card didn't have his last name, for obvious reasons. Nadia didn't look impressed, and he fought off panic. That look made him more determined than ever to see if he could get a date with her. Now the question was whether to try impressing her with his family name and title, which he was definitely against, or some other way. He decided to let it slide and try to convince her SDOT wasn't as bad as it sounded.

"Do you like it there?"

"Sure. I'm learning a lot and getting valuable experience. I know their salaries are not the greatest, but it's a good experience and fits into my plan."

"Are you here with your family?"

"I'm here with a friend of mine from work. His name is Fareed. My dad is overseas. How about you?"

"My mom is here. She's sitting at the table over there having breakfast, and my dad is at work."

She indicated a long table full of women talking and sipping tea. The one empty chair must have been Nadia's, before she went to grab tea and Mansour approached her. The women were a range of ages, with the older ones all in headscarves, and the youngest in longer dresses with their hair down. He hoped Nadia's own scarf didn't indicate she was spoken for.

He wondered why she was suddenly of such interest to him. All he had to do was ask his father, and the matchmaking would begin. His family in Keerypt or Terra Qurayshia would line him up a dozen girls all available to marry, possibly more. The answer was likely the providence he felt.

"Do you come here often?" Mansour accompanied this with a smile, even while inwardly he cringed. What a terrible line! Plus, he knew she didn't attend services here, or else he'd have seen her.

But Nadia smiled in return. And as an added bonus, he could tell she was definitely blushing. Her high cheekbones bloomed like roses and made Mansour's heart feel warm inside.

"Sometimes, not all the time. I haven't seen you here before."

"I usually attend Friday *khutbah* here most of the time and try to make it to the Sunday program when I can. We have some great speakers who give excellent lectures. I also play chess here on occasion."

"Chess? I've never played."

He grinned. "I could teach you sometime . . . but be warned, I won't go easy on you."

She smiled in return. "Perhaps I'll surprise you."

"How often are you here? I haven't seen you here either."

"Yes, I don't come here often. I usually go to the other Islamic Center across from the university. Do you know it?"

"Yes, I do. I've been there only a couple of times. It might be good to visit there more often." He found her smile and that rosy blush infectious. He grinned again, which set her smiling even wider. He couldn't recall the last time he'd felt like this, and he didn't want it to stop.

"Have you tried the falafel over here? It's really good."

That's what he'd been smelling from the kitchen this whole time. His stomach growled again at the fragrant spices wafting out. "I was going to have something here. I haven't had the falafel yet. I'll try it if I'm honored with your company. I'd rather not eat alone."

Come to think of it, he almost never ate alone anymore. He kept forgetting to make himself dinner at home . . . and this time it was this girl who caused his unintended fast.

Nadia swept her hand back toward the kitchen, and they made their way over to where the cooking scents nearly caused him to clutch at his stomach.

She ordered for them, and he carried the plates back toward the table full of women. "You're welcome to join me and my mom. You mentioned that working for SDOT fits your plans. What are your plans, if you don't mind me asking?"

Mansour thought about a response, but he didn't have a chance to explain. Nadia introduced all ten of the women sitting around the table, but the only one who stood out was her mother.

"My mother, Jamila." She bore a strong resemblance to her daughter. Jamila seemed young, with the same bright green eyes. She resembled a famous Keeryptian actress with whom he was familiar, Fareeda Zaman. Like Nadia, she wore a matching *hijab* and dress, which hid her hair but not her beauty.

"This is the man who bumped into me a few years back," Nadia explained.

"I recall." She turned to Mansour with a sparkle of mischief in her very green eyes. "You've been driving safely since then, I hope?"

It was almost exactly the type of thing his mother would say, and a bittersweet feeling welled up in his chest. He liked Nadia, and with two sentences, he liked her mother as well.

Mansour pulled a chair from another table. Four men sat at it, leaving three empty chairs. He knew three of the men and greeted them before returning to Nadia and Jamila.

"So tell us about your father, Mansour," Jamila asked.

He did, though he was careful not to mention his family being royalty. He was halfway through explaining his father's constant business trips around Terra Qurayshia, Keerypt, and Arlandica when the realization struck him: he would be asked, possibly any day now, to head to his 'homeland' and do the work of a spy.

Here he ran into two problems at once: one, any Muslim worth dating and later marrying would despise him for withholding the truth from her, and two, how could he possibly hope to live with the unspoken knowledge that he would one day put on a fake name and do a job forbidden by the Qur'an? How would Nadia react to such a revelation?

"Oh, I'm surprised to hear that. You mentioned you were Keeryptian."

He snapped back to the present. "That's correct, I felt more Keeryptian than Terra Qurayshian at that time as I lived more in Keerypt than Terra Qurayshia, and I was exposed more to the Keeryptian culture."

"So where does your dad live?"

"Between Arlandica, Terra Qurayshia, and Keerypt." Faisal had a house in Keerypt, the house where Mansour lived in

Sunland, and of course anywhere he wanted to live in Terra Qurayshia. He could stay in the palace or just have the king arrange a place in the capital where he might live while there. The king kept several such places for various reasons, whether personal or security.

"How about your dad, Nadia; what does he do?"

"He's a doctor, a neurosurgeon."

"Amazing! Is that why you want to be a doctor?"

"Partly. I also like the field and enjoy studying science and biology. So you were going to tell me about your plan for work and I interrupted you."

"Oh yes, I was going to say that my dad and I talked quite a bit about my future plans, and we decided that it was best for me to get some experience over here first before considering working in Keerypt or in Terra Qurayshia."

"So you're not planning on staying over here in Arlandica. How come?"

"Well, I'm used to traveling a lot, and my dad, as I mentioned, often travels between the three countries, so I'm considering working closer to my family."

Although Jamila and Nadia were impressed that his father was such an important man, and likely wealthy given that Faisal owned a house in each country he visited, they expressed displeasure at the thought of living on the move. Evidently, in their eyes, it was preferable to settle down eventually.

Mansour's emotions leaped in every conceivable direction throughout the lunchtime discussion: hope, elation, embarrassment, dread, and infatuation all had their time in the sun, sometimes two at a time.

"You don't like it here? Why are you thinking to go and work somewhere else?"

"I love it here. I've come to think of Sunland as my home." This was a revelation he hadn't considered privately. If he didn't think of Terra Qurayshia as his home, it wouldn't be as vital to do whatever his father and uncle were going to ask of him. "Well, it's all about opportunities and doing my best to maximize the benefit to myself and to society. So if I find that opportunity over here, I might stay here; if there's a better opportunity to fulfill that overseas, then that's what I should do."

Jamila seemed content with this answer, though she offered up the possibility that he "create his own opportunities" which he felt was basically the same as saying "be assertive in your quest to date my daughter, Mansour."

They all heard an announcement on the PA system that the lecture in the lecture hall would start in five minutes.

"Will you be attending the program next Sunday?"

This seemed to catch Nadia's interest. "We'll see."

He was about to excuse himself from the conversation and head off to prayer, then the special lecture, when a cry went up. Then several more cries of dismay.

He turned to Nadia to find her and her mother drifting toward one of the large televisions in the room, usually kept on silent so as not to disturb people. On the screen he saw columns of smoke drifting into the air from one, two, now three different sources. One was very clear: the familiar enormous statue of freedom had smoke rising up in front of it. The headline read Breaking: Bombs Detonated in Financial District and Capital.

Another explosion came on screen, this one very close to the Arlandican military stronghold. All was chaos, with no answers. All in the room stood staring at the screen, watching in shock as more and more columns of smoke appeared. A small airplane was shown falling from the sky near where the Arlandican stock market did its business. Then another twin-engine plane went down in the capital city, this one near the president's famous Blanche House.

"What . . ." someone said breathlessly. It was the only word spoken, as far as Mansour could tell.

Cries of alarm and horror kept up as the rain of explosions

fell, and the smoke rose. There was no Nadia, no Jamila, no Faisal, no future as a spy, no future of his own choosing. There was only the terror unfolding thousands of miles away on the East Coast. Someone turned the volume up, and the dreadful silence that had stolen over them intensified.

Reporters clambered over themselves to give out any information regarding the attack. It didn't make sense. People were flying planes into specific targets, all on the same morning, and the planes were filled with explosives. One explosion occurred on a small runway not far from the Seneca state capital; the news anchor guessed that either the terrorist loaded up the explosives wrong, or someone stopped the plane before it could get off the ground.

He had no recollection of breaking away from the group of watchers. After another hour, the explosions had stopped and the answers began to trickle in. Mansour wasn't there, though. Somehow he'd gotten back in his car, driven home, and sat on the couch with the television on. He stared at the world trying to make sense of what it was seeing.

Less than five minutes after the last explosion bloomed, his father called. "Mansour? My boy, are you all right?"

"Of course, Father." He wasn't all right mentally or emotionally, but physically he was thousands of miles away from any of the attacks—the coordinated and well-timed attacks. They could be nothing other than strikes from another country against Arlandica. A Middle Eastern country, no doubt.

"Listen to me. Terror groups from the region are claiming credit. You know what that means."

It meant violence against Muslims.

"Go home right away. Tell your friends to stay in for the next week, if possible. Keep your head down. Understand me? Whatever happens, don't upset anyone."

Mansour's stomach leaped into his throat. Why, of all the possible times, did it have to be the day he met a girl?

Chapter 18

Arlandica
Then

Mansour headed back to the Islamic Center and drove Fareed to his home. They'd had their moments of stunned silence in the aftermath of the explosions, while the newscasters reeled and attempted to get information to the people the moment anyone learned it. The attacks should've been at the forefront of his mind, but Nadia held pride of place, despite the horror and confusion.

They discussed what it meant, for Arlandica, for the Middle East, who might have perpetrated such a horrific crime, and what it would mean for Middle Easterners living here in Arlandica. Blowback would occur, but how bad would it be? Arlandicans had the capacity to be some of the most caring, compassionate people, but some were among the quickest to violence and the most destructive. Repercussions might fall on the Islamic Center . . . and surely individuals would face reprisals as well.

But West Beach traffic being what it was, they had time to get around to Nadia. And in all honesty, Mansour was no longer a secret agent in his own mind, and never had been a secret agent in training, so while he was definitely concerned with what had just happened three thousand miles away, what had happened in the Islamic Center felt much more pressing. He told Fareed the story of bumping into her—literally—the day of his mother's funeral and about how genuine she seemed. Following this, he went over the discussions and impressions of the day before the horrible explosions.

Fareed listened patiently. He was quickly nearing the best friend spot in Mansour's life. "That sounds interesting and maybe a sign from God that you should get to know her, of course with the intention of getting married."

Mansour felt the same. For all he liked about this country, it often seemed like people went through significant others the way some people went through socks.

"You are eligible to get married, and of course you know that Prophet Muhammad—peace be upon Him—said that as soon as someone is able to get married, they should get married. It is better for you. From what you know so far, do you see her as compatible with you?"

"She is well educated, from a good family, she seems a good Muslim, has a very pleasant personality, good company to be with, and she is also very good looking."

"This all sounds really good, but I don't want you to rush into something without thinking about it enough and considering all aspects of the situation. My recommendation is to take your time and study her well. From what you said, she seems to be a good prospect. You should also tell your dad and ask him what he thinks. He's smart and a very reasonable man."

In the heat of the moment he'd forgotten to tell his dad about Nadia! He kicked himself mentally for not taking the opportunity, though it felt as though the opportunity hadn't really been there to begin with. "Yes, I'll tell him, *in shaa Allah*. I'll try calling him tonight."

At night, when it was early morning in Terra Qurayshia, Mansour called his dad to ask him how he was doing and to tell him the entire story about Nadia from a couple of years ago up to that day's encounter with her at the Islamic Center. He had a lot to talk about, but most likely Faisal sensed something different about Mansour's tone and words. He deferred and let Mansour lay out everything: Nadia's demeanor, her course of study, her family, her looks. It all came out in an excitable rush, barely coherent and Mansour was eager to get feedback from his dad.

He laughed. "I know I have talked your ear off, Father. What do you say?"

Faisal paused. "Do you believe she will make a good mother for your children?"

This question surprised him, and left him quiet for a few moments. "I . . . Yes. Maybe. I would like to say yes, but I don't know."

"This is information you'll be looking to learn when you meet her again."

Yes. Of course!

"You said she was unsure about returning to the Islamic Center?"

"Yes," Mansour said.

"I should think that her return on Sunday would be a very positive sign." Mansour could hear the proud smile through the phone, and hoped he was right.

Afterward, the talk turned to the terror attacks on the East Coast. The terrorists had gone after government, military, and financial targets. They had nearly hit the president's mansion, had indeed hit the capitol building, though the damage happened while only a few legislators were assembled. They'd hit and done significant damage to the Monolith, a huge military complex where the leaders of the army, navy, and air force made the highest decisions. And while they'd attempted to bomb the financial markets in Seneca, there were too many buildings. They'd smashed into and blown up several other less important buildings instead. Still, hundreds were dead and hundreds more injured.

This wasn't on Faisal's lips though. He only warned Mansour to stay away from large packs of men, away from drinking establishments—which was easy enough—and to head home before sundown. Nighttime gave people a cloak of malignant courage.

"I'll have a series of cameras set up at the house," Faisal said.

Mansour agreed, but his mind had never strayed from Nadia.

The next few days moved slowly. Mansour couldn't wait until

Sunday to go to the Islamic Center, hoping to see Nadia there. If she was interested in him and her mom thought of him as a suitable potential husband, they would show up at the Islamic Center. He prayed the violence and the growing worry among the Islamic community wouldn't keep them from going.

On Sunday Mansour met Fareed at the Islamic Center. They arrived a half hour earlier than the Qur'an class and an hour and a half earlier than the start of the Sunday program. Even fewer people attended at that time. Mansour and Fareed prayed and stayed in the prayer hall, with Mansour reading the Qur'an facing the entrance to see if Nadia or her mom showed up.

Maybe twenty minutes later, Mansour saw Jamila coming in and Nadia immediately behind her. His heart started pounding from happiness, excitement, and worry that things weren't going to go as well as he hoped. He sprang up, placed the Qur'an on the shelf, and headed toward them. As soon as Nadia locked eyes with Mansour, her face beamed with sincere happiness. She blushed, looked down for a second, and then looked back at Mansour again as if to make sure it was really him.

Mansour greeted them with a slight bow. "Jamila, Nadia, such a pleasure to see you. I don't recall if you've met my friend Fareed. Fareed, this is Nadia and her mother, Jamila."

Nadia appeared nervous. She wore another beautiful headscarf—yellow, with green and blue highlights. The colors of her long dress matched her scarf, same as the week before. Jamila wore a long, dark blue dress with a nice blue headscarf.

They exchanged pleasantries before Mansour suggested they have tea together at the social hall. Nadia and her mom agreed to join Mansour, and they all headed there. It was still early so only a few people sat scattered about at different tables. A Keeryptian couple, husband and wife, and their two elementary school kids sat at one table. The kids seemed to be working on their homework while their parents had breakfast.

Mansour looked at the family and wondered if the husband

and wife ever got a moment of privacy away from the children. Here was another facet of the diamond of future married life he hadn't considered. Never mind whether Nadia could be a good mother, could he be a good father? He'd never begrudged his father the lifestyle of a constant traveler, but now he wondered if he hadn't seen enough of him, or they hadn't had enough quality time together.

Nadia smiled indulgently over at the family. Mansour understood her position on children and motherhood in a fraction of a second's expression. Not a word needed to be said to clearly illustrate the sort of person she was.

And then the spy question arose. If he accepted the call from his uncle, the king, what then? How long would he be away? He hoped it would all be wrapped up without his future wife ever having to know about the situation. It would mean lies, and lying was like building a tower in the desert.

At another table sat two Zamanistani ladies in their forties. A third table had two dark-skinned Black Arlandican guys in their fifties who spoke together in what seemed to be a serious conversation, perhaps business related. At a fourth table, two Isfarani brothers in their thirties sat and talked with an Algharibian guy, who was on the board of directors. Mansour knew them well.

He found an empty table and asked Nadia and Jamila to have a seat.

Jamila looked at the table with the two ladies. They waved their hands in greeting and asked her to join them. Jamila excused herself and, laughing, said, "I will join my friends over there. If you kids need anything, just yell out loud. Don't go anywhere else."

Mansour very much enjoyed Jamila's cheerful friendliness. The hesitance over his job and the possibility of frequent travel was gone. Mansour and Nadia laughed. This felt like a good icebreaker. He couldn't think of a better person to have as a mother-in-law. Such a cheerful and happy person.

Fareed joined them, but after a few minutes excused himself to chat with another friend.

Mansour and Nadia sat at the empty table by themselves. He noted people in the room looking at them briefly before looking away and getting back to what they were doing. Generally it was not acceptable in Islamic tradition for an unmarried man and woman to sit by themselves unless they were siblings. Since this was a public space and everyone could see them, it was all right. They still didn't feel totally comfortable, however.

"How was your week?"

"I had a lot of studying, a couple of quizzes, and homework. I had biology and chemistry quizzes, and I did well, thank God. I studied hard for them. I also go to the gym several times a week, depending on my schedule. Most of the time I go at least three times a week. How about you?"

"When I don't practice jiujitsu, I also go to the gym. We actually have a gym at home, so I exercise at least every other day if not every day."

"Jiujitsu?"

Mansour laughed and told the story of the fender bender in Keerypt and the road rage that had ended with him getting punched. "I want to be ready to defend myself if the situation ever goes bad quickly."

She seemed impressed by this idea. Dedication to perfecting the mind and body were important to the faith. "What kind of machines do you use?"

He launched into a lengthy overview of all the machines he used, including the elliptical every session for twenty to thirty minutes, the side lateral machine for the shoulders, the cable row for his back, the biceps curl, the leg extension machine, and lastly the pec fly. He also did pushups, sit ups, and pull ups. By the end of his descriptions of back day, leg day, chest day and bodyweight days, he expected her to have checked out, but that interested sparkle remained. She appraised his physique, which set off a rush of heat to his cheeks and ears.

"Sorry, I drifted off and got into too much detail."

"Not at all. Obviously you're doing a good job. I use different machines. I go to Curves gym, which is for women only. There's one close to my home and another one close to the university. It's convenient. How's your work going?"

"This week I was working nights again. We do most of our freeway work at night due to the heavy traffic during the day and not to add to the traffic congestion or inconvenience the drivers. We closed two lanes on the 210 freeway to replace damaged concrete slabs."

Surprised colored her expression. "Do you like working at night? Are you used to it?"

"It has advantages and disadvantages. The advantage is that I'm out in the field most, if not all, of the time. I only need to go to the office for submitting paperwork. I get to see the work and get experience, and time goes by very fast. The disadvantages are, of course, it's not easy to get used to switching your days—working at night and sleeping during the day—and sometimes it's dangerous working next to live traffic."

Mansour shared his experience with Nadia about his encounter a few months ago with the drunk driver during his night shift. The guy had nearly plowed into him, but luckily the Sunland Highway Patrol had come along before the man could do anything worse than swerve too close to Mansour.

The reaction, her concern and alarm, pleased him. He had a strong feeling she really cared about him.

"That's scary. You should be very careful and be safe out there. Perhaps you shouldn't be alone and stay either with the contractor or other SDOT inspectors."

"Yes, I agree. I think I made a mistake that night by being alone. I was lucky to have the SHP close-by."

"Yes, thank God for that. He is watching over you. Do you feel that? That God is watching over you?"

"I do, yes, definitely. I really believe that my mom's prayers are answered. She was a very good mother. She used to be worried about me, and shortly before passing away, I often heard her making supplications for me and my dad. She put her trust in God, and she raised me to do the same. I'm her only child; she wanted to have more kids, but she couldn't. Oh . . . I didn't mean to take the conversation in a depressing direction."

"Oh no, you're not. I'm enjoying listening to you, and I appreciate your candid discussion. You're a good communicator."

"How about you, Nadia? Do you feel that God is watching over you?"

"Yes, sometimes. Other times I'm not sure if God is pleased with me or not."

"Why do you say that?" he asked. "Do you have doubts?"

"Well, when bad things happen to me or my family, I'm not sure if they're a test or a punishment. Also, there're always more and better things I could do to please God, perhaps, that I'm not doing."

"Like what?"

"From the time I was young, when I saw less privileged kids, I'd feel very guilty. And now when I see so much pain and suffering in the world, I feel very guilty sometimes. I want to be able to take care of as many people as possible, but I can't. And now with what's happening all over the country . . . I want to head to Seneca and help people heal, but my mother says we should keep quiet, that there's a lot of anger against anyone with a headscarf, anyone with darker skin."

"That's a noble feeling, but it's unrealistic to expect so much of yourself. You also have responsibility to take care of yourself and build your foundation well. This is the time for you to focus on your education, and at the same time, if you have the ability to help, you should. There are different ways to help even from where we're sitting."

They brainstormed a list of possibilities together: donating money, writing an article to the local papers with her opinions and concerns, to spread awareness of Muslim sentiments, about how not all of them were terrorists or sympathizers. And closer to home, she could concentrate on being a good daughter, a good student, and a good neighbor. These were also required in Islam.

Mansour thought, despite his overwhelming pleasure at having her with him, that he'd better get going. They'd been sitting here by themselves for a long time.

Jamila sat close initially, but she'd stood up with her friends and joined two other Myrian friends farther away. More people had arrived in the social hall than when Mansour and Nadia had come in. Some people looked at them, which clearly made her uncomfortable. He wanted to place his hand over hers, and connect with her, but of course that wouldn't do.

"Nadia, I'm enjoying talking with you. I enjoy your company. I hope you feel the same way. I want to get to know you more, and be able to see you more, and talk with you more, and of course, I have the best intentions. I would like us to get engaged so it's more official, and we don't feel bad or guilty about it."

Her immediate reaction was as gratifying as it was adorable. He knew it was perhaps too fast but also felt surer of this than anything else he'd done. If only the tiny voice in the back of his mind wasn't protesting that he had a date with the Terra Qurayshian royalty as some kind of secret agent. He told himself, lied to himself really, that he could back away from Nadia. If he asked his father about the mission for his uncle, and it really was as important and harmless as his father had made it sound, he could politely excuse himself from deepening his relationship with this bright, perfect soul.

"I would like to ask your dad for us to get engaged. Are you okay with that?"

And yet, she didn't immediately leap to her feet and run to her mother. Instead, she hesitated. "Well, that's very nice. I enjoy your company as well, but I'm just concerned that we might be rushing into things that we're not ready for. Please don't get me wrong; I appreciate that you want to take this step. I really admire you for that. It's just that we're only starting to know each other. I just need to think about it and talk to my mom about it."

Of course, this was perfectly reasonable.

"Also, there's something I'll need to talk over with you. It's a bit . . . uncomfortable." She seemed embarrassed to bring it up, but nothing could stop him now.

He nodded quickly. "If it's all right with you, I can call you in a couple of days and ask you if you're ready for me to talk with your dad. In the meantime, shall we attend the lecture?"

The lecture was the first of a two-lecture series on Science and Qur'an by Dr. Gasser Hathout. The lecture hall filled quickly, and more chairs were added due to the high interest in this subject. They also had visitors from some local churches.

In the second of four segments, Dr. Hathout talked about the creation of Heaven and Earth with several verses from the Qur'an. He used the example in sura 55:37:

When the sky is rent asunder and becomes a flower-like painting.

When one looks at an image from the Hubble space telescope of the Cat's Eye Nebula, this verse of the Qur'an comes to life. Dr. Hathout then referred to another verse, which states that those who have knowledge revere God the most and have a great sense of awe of the majesty of the Creator.[5]

Mansour took a lot of notes. Nadia also radiated the joy and wonder of someone fascinated by science.

When Mansour left the lecture hall, Carmen appeared in front of him and gave him a hug. "Hi, Mansour, how are you?"

Mansour was taken by surprise and wanted to step back, but

---

[5] Qur'an 35:28.

there was no room. The place was jam-packed, and Carmen was too fast. Mansour immediately sought out Nadia and found her staring at him, her face reddening. Horror stole over him, and ice slithered into his guts.

"Carmen, it's good to see you," Mansour said quickly, and took her by the shoulders to put some distance between them. "Actually, I'm here with–"

She was saying something about her former mother-in-law, but he didn't hear. Nadia was gone.

Chapter 19

Arlandica
Now

Mansour started awake. He'd tried with all of his might to stay up and keep guard, but the rigors of the night had proven too difficult. He couldn't even remember nodding off. For shame. Too much was at stake for him to have made such a hideous mistake.

Luckily though, nothing seemed out of place. The sun's rays filtered through the trees at a slight angle, meaning that it was just a tad before noon, and they had plenty of daylight in which to get things done and get moving to safety. He peered into the shadows of his den. Nadia's eyes opened and met his own. She smiled.

"Mansour, is it time for breakfast? I feel like I could eat an entire restaurant."

He offered her a hand and she grabbed on, letting him assist her out of the shelter and back into the world.

"As horrifying as that sounds, I think I'm also hungry enough to chew on a few bricks and window glass."

She stuck out her tongue and made a face at him. "You know what I mean. We need a table filled with food. Something thick with calories for our growing boy."

His eyes went wide. "A boy? Are you sure? How do you know?"

She smirked. "He's got the appetite of his father. Never have I ever felt so famished! If it was a girl, she'd have petite sensibilities, like myself, and never ever be more than a proud princess."

Mansour beamed. "Well, I can't fault your logic. Have you thought of a name?"

Nadia stood and stretched. "Omar. Omar was your grandfather's name, right?"

Mansour nodded and turned his face to the sky. Surely his father was up there now, enjoying the just fruits of paradise as a reward for all of the thoughtful hard work he had put into making the world a better place for all who lived here.

"Yes, Omar it is. With such a strong name and such a strong mother, I doubt that anything will dare to stand between him and success."

She beamed. "So how do we find a restaurant out here?"

Mansour frowned. He wished he knew where "out here" was.

He'd have pulled the batteries and SIM cards out of their phones and ditched them, if he'd had time to grab either of them. He felt strangely naked without his rectangular answering device. The way the light came down suggested it was almost three in the afternoon before they finally came upon some vestige of civilization. Nadia's stomach growled and groaned along the way, but she didn't complain so much as grin at him, embarrassed. Mansour was impressed; he'd never realized that under the beauty and intelligence of his wife lay the inner strength of a soldier. Despite the circumstances, pride filled him. After all this time, she was still able to surprise him.

It was she, too, who'd spotted the thinning of the trees in the woods and an unnatural hill line that suggested development. Hungry as they were, they'd still had the presence of mind to sneak up and peer over rather than rush forward. From where they lay, they looked down over a rustic little Sunland town. A few farms dotted the outskirts, and central to the country homes sat a bank that also advertised itself as a general store. Nearby stretched a longhouse sided by shaven wooden planks. The sign on top of its flat roof proclaimed Steak and Potaters–A Diner's Delight. Their mouths immediately began to water.

Still, Mansour made sure to scan carefully before giving Nadia the signal to proceed. He noted the gas station, a sign for

Pork Chili–Only $1.99 taped up in its window and a few old trucks parked out back under a handwritten sign that read Car Dealership. In his head a plan started to come together. He still had his wallet, with surely enough cash for new clothes and the convenience store. Something quaint, if possible. Mansour was a suit man, so a pair of overalls might help throw off the scent. Plus there was magic to overalls, Mansour reflected. They caught the eye in a way that other clothes really didn't. You could ask someone who just saw a person in overalls what they looked like, and they never remembered.

He turned to Nadia and tried to picture her as a farm girl. What would she wear? Coveralls of her own? He wasn't sure, but it seemed like a safe bet. *An attractive one as well.*

"What? What are you thinking about, Mansour?" Her eyes held a coquettish glint, a shine that stated that she knew well what he was thinking about.

"I was thinking about disguises, if you must know, my dear. The problem with you and disguises is that anything I put on you will be unable to hide the glow of your beauty."

"Even a beard, a checkered lumberjack outfit, and an eyepatch?" she teased.

Mansour put up a finger, then lowered it. As usual, his clever wife was full of clever ideas. "Yes. Something like that might work." He laughed.

They clambered down the steep slope, stepping sideways for traction and bounding from stunted tree trunk to stunted tree trunk to keep purchase. Nadia slipped once and the little stones and scattered leaves that composed the carpet of the embankment went flying, but Mansour's strong hand found her arm and set her back on course.

Now at town level, the two of them strode across a short field of tall grass, passed a few blocks of small, sleepy houses, and went straight to the general store. The front was all glass and a sign that said Sale–Everything Here is For Sale. Nadia and

Mansour locked eyes and laughed. The sign might as well have said Beware: Dad Jokes Abound.

The door set off a symphonic chime as they entered. Behind the counter—a single slab of lacquered wood four inches thick—stood the shop owner. He looked at them and conducted the chime's tones for a full minute before they ended.

"Hi there. Name's Mark. What can I do you for?"

Mansour strode to his counter, his wife at his side. "I'm so sorry to ask this of you . . . We're—How do I put this? We're movie stars."

Mark eyed him, and arched an eyebrow as if trying to remember which movie he'd seen them in. Nadia definitely could pass as a movie star, which was part of the problem. She needed to be able to hide in plain sight.

Nadia picked up on this. "And the paparazzi are after us."

"We're just hoping you have something that would keep people from staring, if you know what I mean?"

Mark grabbed up a toothpick and rolled it between thumb and forefinger, as if considering either which movie he knew them from or how to deal with their request. He then stuck that toothpick in his mouth and rolled it back and forth from side to side again. "Yeah, I think I have something for ya. What would you think about some overalls? Nobody looks past the bib when you're wearing a pair of overalls."

"I know, right?" Mansour gushed. Nadia gave him a strange-eyed look, and he shrugged. "Yes, I'd love to have a pair of overalls. Plus whatever clothing goes underneath it. To be honest, if you hadn't suggested them, I'd have suggested them myself. But I tried to think up something for my wife here and, well, nothing came to mind."

"I know that's not true," Nadia said, grabbing and squeezing his hand.

"Well, yeah, ha ha. I, uh, I guess I don't know how to ask this—"

"You wanna make this pretty lady disappear from view, huh?"

"Exactly," he responded. "Honestly, all the attention she's getting is . . . It's a bit much."

"Can you make me look like a man?" Nadia blurted.

Mark's face went slack for a moment, then he yelled over his shoulder. "Hey, Charlene, you still got that Halloween costume from last year?"

"Who is it? Someone famous?" a voice yelled back.

"Definitely not." He turned and winked at Mansour. "Eh? You were in one of those Disney live-action remakes, weren't you?"

Mansour just smiled and squeezed Nadia's hand.

"Ha! Nailed it! Yeah, hey, let me get you the overalls and Charlene will get your lady set with the costume."

Mansour wondered just what they were getting at but didn't have to wonder long. The part of the costume they needed was a chest binder that Charlene had used to slim down. Over that they put a flannel shirt and three-quarter-length shorts, which made Nadia look more like a boy than a woman. The addition of sunglasses and a baseball hat meant she could pass—at a distance, anyhow—for a shorter man, perhaps Mansour's younger brother.

They left the shop holding hands, until they realized that some of the townsfolk were giving them the side eye. One old man grumbled about the kids these days as he ambled on past them.

Nadia's spirits lifted. "I can't believe that I'm undercover with you, a secret agent surrounded by enemies by day, in the arms of her lover by night." Then the realization seemed to dawn on her. "Did they shoot at us?"

He put out his hands. "What can I say? I'm an exciting guy." Then more quietly, he added, "I'll explain what I can, when I can."

That didn't stop her from asking. "Who were those people? And why?"

They walked down the street, checked both ways, and crossed

over to the gravel parking lot of Steak and Potaters–A Diner's Delight. From eye level he could see that the place had quite a bit of charm. A sign made of red and green neon tubing advertised The King of Beers, and a square of tagboard announced Karaoke on Fridays. They passed a few older cars and a rust-eaten pickup, opened the door, and were surprised to find another door, this one with no knob and a life-sized and scantily clad poster of Brenda Afina, Arlandica's most famous supermodel.

Nadia's eyes locked onto Mansour's face.

"A test of faith," Mansour replied, without looking back. "A test I pass easily and with no complaints."

Nadia relaxed. "A good answer, Omar's daddy," she said.

He grinned and pushed at the swinging door, which was like one you'd see in an old cowboy saloon, but full length top to bottom. An oddity that he quite enjoyed. Maybe when this was all over, he'd look into remodeling their home.

The two stepped in and saw a smattering of people, maybe a dozen, looking back with interest. The diner was divided into four sections: one filled with old arcade machines and a jukebox, the second with proper dining tables and a lunch counter, the third a long liquor bar crowded with brown spinning stools, and the last an empty dance floor with an old disco ball above it, and a small sound stage for DJ or karaoke events.

"I'll be right with you," a woman called from the bar. A plastic name tag announced that her name was Jan, the assistant manager. "I have to deal with a few early drunks first."

Two older men at the counter raised their hands into the air, pantomiming shooting guns, and laughed.

"Thank you. We've never been here before. Should we just wait here?"

"Nah, huns, go ahead and pick a stool, grab a game, or pick a table. Say, what are you here for?"

"Steak and potaters," Mansour said.

The drunks yelled their approval, and Mansour and Nadia made their way to a table.

The enormous menus surprised Mansour, given the size of the village. Unsurprisingly nothing was labeled as *halal*, however. Nadia's stomach grumbled, and he watched her with sympathy, knowing she'd have to skip over such luscious cuts of dripping beef—and, yes, even lamb—in order to properly honor her faith. She ended up choosing a salad with yogurt dressing and almonds. It looked both creamy and crisp, and something about its long name just spoke to him, so Mansour ordered the same. And both of them seized on the opportunity for some rich black coffee. They had two steaming mugs in front of them in no time.

"So . . . I haven't seen you two before. What brings you to these parts?"

Mansour suddenly realized that he hadn't seen a town sign and he had no idea what the name of these parts were. He channeled a few of his former coworkers and subordinates, and put on a slight drawl. "Well, ma'am, I'm sorry for my ignorance, but we don't rightly know what parts these are. The two of us decided to roll through the countryside and see what's where and who does what. One thing led to another, the pickup broke down, and we just left her. It was a cracked head gasket, and there ain't any fixing that."

Jan nodded, riveted.

Nadia appeared equally enthralled.

"So I says that maybe we should just walk ahead and get a tow, but that'll cost a lot of money."

Jan nodded. "It sure would, but if you got plates on that pickup, the DNR will find you and they'll fine you."

"Oh, no plates. Never even registered the sale."

"Smart man. Don't give those big government weasels nuthin' unless you absolutely positively need to."

"Damn straight, ma'am."

Nadia's eyes flashed, clearly surprised at him swearing.

"So I figure that's all taken care of," Mansour continued. "Everything, that is, except for getting another truck."

Jan beamed and waved for Nadia to scooch over. Then she sat next to her, lifting her apron and the hem of her serving dress a bit before sitting down. "That I can help you with. You seen the car dealership?"

Mansour nodded.

"Well, I just happen to have a 1992 Edison Pickup, flaking paint, rusted body, but well usable and a full tank of gas. Just put her up a few days ago."

Mansour eyed her with just the right amount of interest. Not just to play the part of the local yokel, but also to prepare for the inevitable bartering he figured was coming next.

But she surprised him. "The truck burns oil pretty good, so there's a smell, and you'll have to give her a new quart maybe every hundred miles or so. She leaks, too, so you gotta be careful about the DNR and the cops when you decide to drive off. Ol' Lawman Jimmy done pulled me over after he saw the puddle she left in this here parking lot. Haha. Let me tell you, he gave me about ten good reasons to junk that truck. But I decided to see if anyone else could get any use out of her first."

"Sounds to me like you didn't want to pay for a junkyard to take it in and scrap it."

Jan laughed. "Yeah, that too. Anyways, how much do you want to give me for it?"

Mansour thought about it. He had maybe a grand left in cash in his wallet, his spy's acumen for staying off the system as often as possible having stayed with him here in Arlandica. The truck could probably be gotten for two hundred if he bargained hard.

"Three hundred dollars. Plus I might want to grab a couple of dirt bikes or four wheelers from you if you got them. It'd be nice to avoid another hike if we break down again."

Jan nodded. "Sold. Let me go get your salads, and then when you finish, let's head on over and get everything sorted."

The salads came, and they were huge. But Mansour was ready to eat the table, so he had no difficulty wolfing it down. Especially since it contained a delicious blend of sour citrus and sweet vegetable goodness that he'd never tasted anywhere before.

Nadia did her part by eating heartily. She crunched and munched with great gusto, pausing only to slurp at her water, or partake of her coffee. And then they were set and off. Jan was straight and to the point, giving them two muddy dirt bikes for another $200, and helping to strap them down in the back of the truck. Then, after checking the oil and filling it, she bid them farewell.

The truck had a heady smell, but it wasn't bad after a while, especially not with both windows down. A few finished cigarettes in the ashtray added their own distinct odor to the mix, which Mansour didn't mind. It was the kind of atmosphere that people described as having character. All in all, the truck was charming in its own way.

As the sun set in the distance, Nadia bumped off to sleep, and Mansour turned on the old switch dial of the truck's stereo, rolling through stations before, quite accidentally, he heard mention of his name.

"I'm being told that the death count is now confirmed to be over two hundred people. The nation of Terra Qurayshia has sent its sympathies and vows that they will form a closer partnership with Arlandica to stop such extremists from even getting over to Arlandica in the first place."

The voice changed and Mansour heard the king speaking. "Mansour Al-Qurayshi and his wife are the children of zealots. Zealots that should never have been allowed to leave Terra Qurayshia in the first place. This act of vile terrorism could have been prevented, and my heart weeps for all of the brave Arlandican souls that have been prematurely released for their final voyage to Heaven."

This both infuriated and saddened him. Mansour knew the

king would release a statement of some sorts. He knew they were going to frame him. But to fabricate a terrorist attack and kill hundreds of Arlandicans just to have something to criminalize and demonize him? This was barbaric. Monstrous.

"The bombings occurred–" He clicked the radio off. He didn't want Nadia to hear it. In fact, he needed her not to hear it. The scope and magnitude, along with the speed of the attack told him what he needed to know: his cousin had been planning this for a long time, and the cooperation between the new king and the Arlandican president ran deeper than anyone had anticipated. He was being offered no chance to back out of this. The king had made that abundantly clear.

"I can fix this, my love," he whispered to himself. "I don't know how, but I'll get us to the state capitol, to Governor Adele Schwarzenvalder. And I won't let us be caught by the authorities. We will get through this."

Chapter 20

5 years ago
Arlandica

Mansour made his way home in a confused, disheartened daze. Carmen had disappeared just after saying something cryptic, and the look of utter horror on Nadia's face . . . Was it because of Carmen's forward hug, or something else? Surely she couldn't know about the plot to make him into a secret agent, but the suspicion that she'd somehow found out crept into his whirling thoughts.

He wandered about his empty house, wishing for his mother after so many years. His father had never been there for him like Fatima. She'd never been a source of conflict.

Nothing on the television took his mind off the strange events, nor anything on the internet. The gym beckoned, but he didn't feel up to pummeling the bag right now. Fareed might have good advice, but he didn't answer the phone.

Then he stared at Nadia's number on his phone. He debated calling for a few moments, then cleared his head. He'd been raised decisive, and Nadia was worth fighting for.

She picked up almost before it'd begun ringing, and before he could get in a word, asked, "Mansour, how do you know Carmen?"

Mansour was flabbergasted at this. He had no reason to lie. "She works with me at SDOT, and I was just going to ask you the same question."

Perhaps she'd fallen silent. No, she was crying. He was about to speak, when again she jumped in ahead of him. "Wait a moment."

It was more like three or four minutes. He wasn't sure what was happening but didn't want to lose his connection to Nadia again. He'd thought she was a conservative Muslim like he, and he knew they had a connection. The offer of engagement should've been something she jumped at. That way, they could meet without any of the guilt or uncomfortable glances.

His mind went into overdrive attempting to piece together what she'd give him next: some run-in with anti-Muslim people after she'd left, or some bad experience with another man who had proposed too early. That had to be it. She couldn't have zero experience—

She was back. "Remember that I wanted to tell you something, that I needed some time, and I was going to tell you everything next time we met? I guess I need to tell you now. Carmen's ex-husband is my brother."

Carmen's . . . ex-husband. The memory flashed quickly: the alcohol, the abuse, the threats.

"What? Oh my God!"

"Hiding such information from you didn't sit well with me . . . and I wanted to tell you, but it wasn't the right time. My brother, Marwan, went astray long time ago. My dad spoiled him; he used to give him a lot of money. He got married against our family's wishes. He stopped going to the *masjid*, left the house, and joined a bad group of people. We lost contact with him a long time ago. It's a horrible part of my life. I wanted to have a good brother to be close to and to rely on for so many things. I lost him. My parents lost him. I'm sorry I didn't tell you sooner."

This definitely complicated the situation. Mansour fell silent, and tried to contemplate how this would factor into his plans.

"I totally understand if you don't want to get yourself into such a situation. We don't have to see each other again."

"Oh no, please don't say that. I really like you, and it's not your fault what your brother did. I was quiet because it was a bit of a shock. I appreciate that you told me about it."

Silence stole over them again, a force that seemed to be trying to push him away from her. He didn't want to let it, but he had no idea what to say in this moment. It was like hearing his father shout at the future king that his only son would not become a spy.

She spoke softly, and he detected the raw hurt in her voice. She might still be crying. "I need to go now. Thank you for listening, and I would like to ask you to seriously consider if we should see each other again. I don't want you to make any promises right now or say anything. Please take care of yourself. Good night."

"Good night." It felt wrong to say it, but he wouldn't force her to talk with him if she didn't wish to.

Why did life have to be so complicated? Mansour was getting tired from thinking. He decided to get up and wash, to pray *Istikhara* and ask God for guidance, reading a special supplication for that. The *Istikhara* supplication was read after the non-obligatory prayer, asking God to help him decide on whether to follow a certain path or not. If the path he wanted to follow was good for him in this life and the next, then he asked God to help him follow this path. If it was not good for him, then he would ask God to help him avoid taking this path and make him content with what was destined for him.

After reading the supplication, Mansour called Fareed to chat with him and see any possibility of meeting up. Fareed realized that Mansour was not feeling well, and so he offered to meet Mansour at a coffee shop.

It took Mansour a good fifteen minutes to explain everything that had led to this. Fareed was also shocked and had never expected at all something like this would happen.

"Isn't it so weird that I told you to watch out and stay away from Carmen, and now what we were concerned about is even closer than we thought? It's such a small and ironic world."

"Yes, I thought the same thing, exactly. I am not sure what to do, my friend. I need your advice."

"I never knew any details about Carmen's ex-husband. I heard that he might be Middle Eastern but wasn't sure. She never talked much about him, other than that he was abusive and into drugs. That's about it. That's a difficult situation, my friend. Let us think about it from different angles.

"First of all, you and Nadia: other than her brother, you have a lot in common. She is from the same culture, from a good family—her brother is an aberration. She is well educated, she is a Muslim, and her hobbies are very similar to yours. From what I saw and what you told me, she has a really good character. She did tell you about her brother, although she did delay telling you. It's understandable . . . From what you've said, she was intending to lay everything out on the table before getting engaged. So ultimately she's honest."

Mansour had to give her credit for that intention and for the courage it must have taken to bring up something so painful. If Carmen hadn't become involved, she could've gone ahead with the engagement, married him, and then the secret could have come crashing in on them at any point as a total surprise.

Carmen's appearance, however alarming, had been an unexpected blessing.

"Let us relate that to the life of Prophet Muhammad (peace be upon Him). He had good support from his uncles Abu-Taleb and Hamza. However, his other uncle, Abu-Lahab, was a very bad man, and even God in the Qur'an said that Abu-Lahab would go to hell fire. That didn't diminish the status of the Prophet (peace be upon Him) one iota. You can't choose your relatives, they're forced upon you. You just have to deal with what you have.

"I strongly recommend that you do *Istikhara*."

Fareed laughed when he learned Mansour had just done that before calling him. "Well, so that's the answer to your prayer, my friend. This is a life-changing decision. I can't tell you for sure what to do. All I can do is to help you think and navigate through this difficult situation. You need, of course, to talk with your dad about that."

And really, Mansour chastised himself for not doing his due diligence regarding Nadia before he'd become so emotionally involved. More than that, he had a strange and possibly deal-breaking secret no one knew. He'd held it for close to ten years now, and at times it was possible to forget that the king of Terra Qurayshia had plans for him. But what would Nadia think if he told her? Would he tell her? Did he even have the right to demand all of her skeletons out of the closet if he wasn't ready to bring his out in the open? By now, he could barely contain the thought of not having Nadia as his wife. It had seemed destined when she reappeared . . . but destiny had laid its plans for him almost a decade ago.

"Mansour, don't be hard on yourself. No one could expect such an outcome, a bad person coming out of a really good family. Perhaps it was good that you talked to your dad before you knew about her brother, otherwise it would've been difficult."

"Do you feel sometimes that events are moving in a certain direction? Maybe destiny is pulling you toward something. You know, of course, when you pray *Istikhara* that you may not find the answer easily. However, events will unfold a certain way, and you will find certain things will be difficult and others will be easy."

Fareed recommended reading through more of the Qur'an and meditating on the dilemma he faced. Mansour thanked his friend deeply. Really, he considered Fareed more like a brother.

It was a good note on which to conclude their meeting. Fareed went home, and Mansour followed his friend's advice. He washed up, prayed *Maghrib* (the fourth prayer of the day) and then prayed another *Istikhara*. He then started reading Surat Yusuf (Chapter 12) and then skipped to read Surat al-Kahf (Chapter 18) and then Surat Maryam (Chapter 19) in the Qur'an. He loved these Suras. Surat Yusuf tells the story of Prophet Yusuf (peace be upon Him). Surat al-Kahf has different stories: one of them shows that certain events in life happen for a reason other than the one it appears to be. Surat Maryam has the story of the virgin Mary and her miraculous pregnancy and the birth of Jesus (peace be upon Him). The story of Prophet Abraham (peace be upon Him) and Moses (peace be upon Him) were also in this Sura. He then read Surat Yaseen (Chapter 36). It has been said that if, before reading this chapter, you asked God for something, then God would answer your supplication. The response may not be immediate, but it was a way of getting closer to God. He then prayed another *Istikhara.*

Mansour had dinner at home while watching *I Love Lucy* on TV. He found the show innocent and funny, and wished that contemporary shows would steer in this direction more, instead of the constant suspicion and violence. For dinner, he had rice with boiled chicken, zucchini, and carrots. He needed simple. It was time now to pray *Isha* (the fifth and last obligatory prayer of the day). He prayed two more non-obligatory prayers, called *Sunna*—these followed the practices of Prophet Muhammad (peace be upon Him).

Mansour made a lot of supplications to God, asking Him for guidance, wisdom, to increase his knowledge, to see the truth, and to protect him from all evil and from making bad decisions. He also prayed for his mother, whom he missed dearly.

Afterward, he felt some relief. The Qur'an gave him the sense of a much bigger purpose for life. Greater people faced greater challenges, and when they accepted the difficult tests and did the right thing, the reward just in this life was much greater than the struggle. The reward in the hereafter would be everlasting.

He continued with prayer the next morning, only to have his father call him unexpectedly. Faisal reacted with the same shock Mansour had felt upon learning the news of Nadia's brother. Ideally, of course, one wanted to join a new family full of peace and goodwill, not to start out with one member as an outcast.

Mansour had to get ready to go to work, so he couldn't talk a lot with his dad.

"Of course, my son. I shall take some time to consider this matter. Please don't leap to any conclusions just yet."

Mansour promised, then hung up. The day flew by with many issues to take care of at work. The contractor had filed several Notices of Potential Claims (NOPC) and it was time for Mansour to respond to them. He worked closely with his structure representative to finalize his responses to the structure-related claims for the seismic retrofitting of a bridge. And before he knew it, the workday was drawing to a close, and without a worry over Nadia or her brother.

On his way out, Mansour noticed Mike writing a change order. Also a resident engineer, Mike worked part-time as a reserve police officer, the same person who'd helped Carmen with her monster of an ex-husband, who Mansour had avoided thinking about all day.

"Mike, can I have a word?"

Mike flashed perfect teeth at him. "Go for it."

"Do you remember you helped Carmen place a restraining order on her ex-husband?"

The smile disappeared. "He bothering her again?"

"No . . . No, he's not. He is bothering me this time."

"What do you mean? What happened?" Mansour knew the shift in stance and expression; it meant Mike was now in cop mode. He rather welcomed it.

"It's a very strange situation. I met a lady who I liked a lot, and it turns out that Carmen's ex-husband is this lady's brother."

"What? That's crazy."

Mansour explained to Mike the story of how he had met Nadia and how he found out about Marwan, Nadia's brother. He concluded with, "I was hoping you could tell me if Marwan is a criminal. If he's committed any crimes."

Mike thought this over. "That's confidential information, but I can see you have a very legitimate concern. What I can do for you, buddy, is to find out and just give you a general answer. I can't tell you details."

"That's all I need, buddy. And coffee and donuts on me."

Mike smiled. "I'll just finish up this order and make a couple of calls, then call you."

Mansour thanked him and went home. He remained uncomfortable with digging into Nadia's past when his own future was already a lie by omission. But then, it was possible he could deny the Terra Qurayshian king's request. He could, in theory, say no to a king.

What a thought.

On the way home, he noted that, for the sixth or seventh time, volunteers were scrubbing away at anti-Muslim slurs spray-painted on the Islamic Center's walls. He sighed.

Forty-five minutes later, Mike called as promised.

"Good news or bad news?" Mansour tried to play it cool, but this information was potentially deal-breaking. He sat in his driveway and squeezed the steering wheel hard to keep from shaking.

"Good news! Well, Mansour, your girlfriend's brother is not a criminal. We only put a restraining order on him based on Carmen's reporting. He doesn't have a criminal record."

Mansour breathed a big sigh of relief. "Thanks a lot, my friend, I really appreciate your help. By the way, she's not my girlfriend. She's a potential fiancée."

"Okay, then hopefully congratulations, I guess? I'll see you at work on Monday, and by the way, I like Boston Cream and grande cappuccino." Mansour could practically hear him wink.

Relief washed over him, but the situation wasn't yet over. He dialed up Fareed again, who, like a brother, answered immediately.

"*Assalamu alaikum,* Fareed, how are you?"

"*Wa alaikum assalam,* Mansour. I am good, *Alhamdulillah.* How are you doing?"

"*Alhamdulillah,* are you available for dinner tonight?"

Fareed chuckled. "You must be celebrating something. What's the occasion?

"No occasion. I want to talk with you some more about the same situation. How about you come over to my house?" Mansour laughed. "Don't worry, I'm not cooking. I'll not torture you with my food. I'll order your favorite Farsian food, lamb kebab with rice and salad."

"Okay, thank God you're not cooking. In that case, I can't say no to the lamb kebab."

At 5 p.m. sharp, Fareed arrived at the door. Mansour welcomed him. He'd just gotten back with the broiled lamb kebab, basmati rice and salmon, and it was like smelling Heaven. They ended up sharing both plates. While enjoying the tasty dinner, Mansour updated Fareed on the information he'd gotten from Mike about Marwan.

Fareed took it as good news. "You were able to put speculation to rest–a lucky and highly beneficial thing."

Mansour had to admit this was true. "However, it's nagging at me. A happy and well-adjusted family of in-laws is a huge asset, but a bickering dysfunctional family can be nothing but a series of traps, like a minefield."

"You aren't wrong. Let's settle in and brainstorm all we can about positives and negatives. For instance, it might be possible to ignore this Marwan altogether if he lives over on the East Coast. He might avoid your future in-laws entirely."

They spent several hours doing just that: listing ideas on how Mansour could go about finding information in the least intrusive ways possible, making pros and cons lists about being with Nadia versus not doing so, and talking the problem out until the call for prayer for *Salat al-Maghrib*, the fourth prayer, came on from the special *Azan* clock. Afterward, they resumed the idea-making in the backyard. When it was all done, Mansour had some homework ahead of him. So many questions needed answering, but he was armed with a few good avenues.

And all throughout, he knew what he wanted the answer to these questions to be.

Chapter 21

5 years ago
Arlandica

Allah was making it easier for him to see how things really were. Of course, nothing in this world was perfect. Everything had positives and negatives. In a way, it was perhaps better to know the negatives ahead of time instead of getting surprised later on. So at least he knew what to expect and what to watch out for.

He read over the pros and cons list he'd made in private about Nadia for about the five hundredth time and saw no more changes he could make. Fareed had advised him to see if that made him lean one way or another, and it did. In the end, he'd scrawled down plenty of positives, and the only negative was her brother.

Mansour called his dad to update him on the news.

Faisal made reassuring sounds throughout his explanation. At last he said, "This Fareed is wise and a good friend. I feel much better about this situation. While not ideal, the situation might not be as bad as it first seemed."

"I agree."

"Nadia might have more information regarding her brother's problems and how they will or won't affect the two of you as a couple."

"Thank you, Father."

Mansour felt a lot more upbeat after his discussions with Fareed and his dad. He prayed *Isha*, the fifth and last prayer of the day, read some Qur'an and then went to bed to get ready for the next day.

Mike didn't have much time to talk with Mansour, but gave

him a couple of resources to peruse in the morning and on his work breaks.

At work, Mansour called Carmen to ask her if she could meet with him for lunch. She agreed right away. He then dropped off some paperwork in the downtown office and met with Carmen to go to lunch close-by.

She appeared puzzled, but he smiled and apologized.

"I don't wish you to get the wrong idea. This is about Nadia . . . I found out about her brother."

"Ah." If she was disappointed, she hid it well.

"I need to ask a few questions about Marwan. Anything that's too painful, you don't have to answer."

Her face scrunched down. "Ask me anything."

"I'd like to know as much as you're willing to tell."

He thoroughly enjoyed her Stivalian accent. "In the beginning everything seemed . . . great. Now that I think about it more, there were signs. Like, he had very good manners and it was obvious that he was from a good family. Unfortunately, his family didn't approve. Didn't attend our wedding. His dad was furious, and stopped communicating with him. The money from his family dried up."

They ordered Gallacian gyros, the ones Carmen claimed had the best tzatziki sauce in the city.

"That must have made things difficult," he said, and thought back to his cousin's problem in Keerypt. Money was a constant source of stress for many people.

"It was better that way. I know Marwan was too spoiled by having too much money. He was still very good to me and very kind. Then after a couple of years, he started to mix with the wrong people . . . and started taking drugs."

Mansour breathed out a low sigh. Drugs were on a similar level with alcohol in the faith: pollutants.

"And that's when he changed. He became a different person. I don't think I saw him happy after he started on drugs and alcohol. The abuse started. You know, just words at first. Then he'd grab me."

"I'm so sorry. A proper follower of Islam would never do these things."

She smiled sadly. "I know it now."

"You don't need to go on."

"No, you need to know everything. The gambling started after that. He dropped out of college, and ended up with job after job. They were all low paying and he'd get fired after a couple of months."

The food arrived, but Carmen didn't touch her wrap.

"I had to take matters into my own hands. I had to hide money from him, and I got ready to divorce him with the little savings I had. Then I finished my engineering degree and started working as an engineer. I survived. After the divorce, he basically disappeared. There was no money. I'm making enough to raise my daughter. I don't need anything from him."

"Do you know what he's doing now?"

"I stopped communicating with him. The last I heard, he was working as an auto mechanic. He seemed good at that."

"Well . . ." He let the statement hang while he let her get a bite in. "Hopefully he got off the drugs."

"I hope so, for his own sake. He's still my daughter's father, and I wish someday that she'll connect with him and get to know him when he's ready for that."

After a brief pause, Carmen asked Mansour, "Are you thinking of marrying Marwan's sister?"

"I met her a while ago, and I was interested, yes. Do you have any advice?"

"You deserve to marry a good woman. I wish you the best. I don't know her well enough. I've seen her a few times, briefly. She seems a very good person, very proper. I think she's very different from her brother."

"Thank you very much; that's very kind of you. I really appreciate your candid discussion, and I'm glad I talked with you."

Carmen grinned. "I owe you. At the time of my difficulty, you stood by me and that meant a lot to me. Not everyone would do that for someone they barely knew. That makes you a good person."

Mansour thanked Carmen again, and they both went back to work. Relief welled up in him. Marwan was more or less disconnected from the family. He had wondered if Carmen would paint a nasty picture of the family to make the prospect look bad for him. Mansour felt guilty of thinking that Carmen would do such a thing. She was really very kind indeed.

His next step was to talk with Nadia. He decided it was better to see her at the Islamic Center on Sunday, only three days from now.

Thankfully his work kept him very busy throughout the next few days—the seismic retrofitting project and two more minor projects besides. One of them was installing metal beam guardrails on a winding, scenic mountain route.

In the afternoon, Mansour split his time between reading the Qur'an, reading different books, and watching TV. He wanted to take a break from too much thinking and stressing out over which decision to take.

On Sunday morning, Mansour made sure to be there by half past ten. He prayed as usual and waited in the prayer hall, hoping to catch Nadia and possibly her mother too. He knew they'd be there before eleven and kept looking at the clock on the wall in the prayer area.

The eleventh hour came, however, and he'd seen neither one. Maybe he'd just missed them, somehow. He got up and headed to the bookstore, then the lecture hall, but didn't find them. He grew worried. Surely they'd be in the social hall.

Nothing.

Maybe they'll come in a few minutes.

Twenty minutes later and still no Nadia. He checked the lecture hall again, but nothing, again. They weren't going to come.

His spirits sank further. He should've called her to make sure. And, worst of all, he realized that she might've gotten the wrong impression by his days of silence. He might've come off as uninterested in her and ready to break off meeting with her.

He berated himself for that.

Though he attended the second lecture of the two-lecture series on Science and Qur'an, he didn't absorb any of it. He was making himself sick with worry. Afterward, he made his numb way home, sure that he'd ruined everything.

Maybe he could try calling her.

Jamila answered. "Mansour."

"I would–May I speak with Nadia please?"

"I'm afraid that won't be possible."

"I don't understand–"

"Your message the last few days has been very clear. Now if you'll excuse me–"

"That's not it . . . I needed some time to think."

Jamila said nothing, and the silence stretched out, which he took as an opening.

"It wasn't easy to find out about your son, especially so suddenly. It took some time to consider all this. I prayed for guidance, and sought my father's counsel. I had to step back and process it all, then consider the whole situation from all angles. I hope you can understand the need to do so."

"And you have come to a conclusion, then?"

"A relationship is built upon a firm foundation. And I've concluded that Marwan probably hasn't damaged that foundation."

Her silence was shorter this time. She sounded on the verge of tears. "Thank you for your honesty. Here is my daughter."

The further silence told him that the phone had been handed off to Nadia, and that she wasn't prepared to speak.

"Hello, Nadia. I missed you today at the center. How are you?"

"Hello, Mansour. Thank you. I am good, *Alhamdulillah.* How are you?"

"I am good, *Alhamdulillah.* I want you to know that I care a lot about you. I have a lot I want to talk with you about, and I'd like to meet you today. We could have late lunch at Shamshiri Grill; it's close to both of us."

"How about we go to a coffee shop? If that's okay with you."

"Yes, sure that's fine." He wanted her to be comfortable above all else. They agreed to meet at the coffee shop not far from her house in an hour.

Immense relief washed the trepidation and the worries away. An hour felt like a long time for him, but he saw a ray of light between what had started to look like a dark and gloomy day.

How had the week passed without seeing or talking with Nadia? He'd become quite attached to her and missed her a lot more than he realized. It was becoming clearer to him that she was the right woman for him. He lay on the couch for a few minutes to relax and clear his mind, then got up and got ready to go and see Nadia. The coffee shop was only ten minutes away, but he wanted to be there early.

Five minutes after Mansour arrived, Nadia showed up. On time, as promised. It was one of the things that Mansour liked about Nadia. She was good to her word. This was a characteristic of prophets, like Prophet Ismael (peace be upon Him) as described in the Qur'an.[6] Mansour was now even more observant of everything she did and said, and all of it spoke of a perfect match.

Her turquoise dress went well with her blue eyes, and interestingly she wasn't wearing a scarf. He'd not seen her without a scarf since he first met her. She wore a scarf only at the Islamic Center. He remembered how her beautiful hair looked: long and gleaming in the sun.

"*Assalamu alaikum*, Nadia, good to see you. You look really nice."

Nadia blushed and smiled, though she shut her expression

---

[6] Qur'an 19:54.

down soon after. She looked very pretty with her smile, and Mansour's heart beat faster than normal. Clearly she had her reservations about meeting him, and that was understandable. This proved all the more that he had to do this right.

"*Wa Alaikum Assalam,* Mansour, good to see you as well."

She tucked a lock of hair behind her ear and continued to glance up from her coffee. Every time she did so, he detected a hint of a smile. Her feelings about Mansour and interest in him showed clearly, and he felt it. She had worries and concerns—of course she did! She would've been a fool not to. He had similar worries.

All these melted away when they saw each other.

He leaned forward. "I really missed you, Nadia. I don't want you to ever think that my silence in the past week meant a change of heart or lack of interest. I was thinking a lot about the new information that hit me. I couldn't ignore it and offer a fake and flimsy support to you that would collapse at the very first hardship that we go through. Life is full of tests and we will have our own share, no doubt. It's important for me to be on a solid foundation, as I mentioned to your mom. I'm a civil engineer, and I like to use engineering terminology. To build a tall structure you need a good foundation." He chuckled, and again her smile peeked out. "Having said that, I have some questions for you."

She nodded.

"If you have any reservations about anything I ask—"

She shook her head. "No, no. Thank you for the sentiment, but the truth is important to me. Please, go ahead with your questions."

"What happened with Marwan?"

She deflated a little, and it was terrible to see. "I'll tell you from the beginning. Marwan is six years older than I am. He was a bit spoiled . . . or actually, more than just a bit. My parents couldn't say no to him. He was used to getting almost anything he asked for. My dad's thinking was to provide him with a lot of tools so he would become very successful. He didn't do very well at school even though my dad got him tutors."

Mansour sensed a "but" coming and wasn't disappointed.

"He wasn't interested in school. He barely graduated from high school and then started studying at community college for a year. He met Carmen at a disco club and started dating her, secretly. I was against it, and I told him to stop seeing her. My parents didn't know. Marwan never listened to me. He always told me I was too young. I met her a few times, and I couldn't say anything to my parents. I didn't want to betray my own brother. I cared about him and I loved him."

Who would put their younger sister into such a position?

"He eventually told my parents just before marrying Carmen, and they were furious. My dad didn't talk to him for a long time. I know my dad stopped giving him money . . . maybe at that moment." She heaved a sigh from a well of hurt that ran deep.

"He left the house and married Carmen, and they had a baby girl, Tamara. He started mixing with the wrong people, and I heard he used drugs and then later got divorced. He stopped communicating with us for a long time. It's very sad what happened. It breaks my heart. I don't–"

He held up his hands in the universal stop motion. "I'm very sorry; I don't mean to make you uncomfortable. Let me change the approach. Do you think he can have a negative effect on our relationship? Are you worried or afraid of him in any way?"

She considered this for a time, over a long sip of coffee. "No, I don't see that happening. He's not evil, just misguided. He cares about me. He wouldn't hurt me or anyone I care about."

"That's good. I'm sure you understand that it's something I need to know and it's important for us to discuss it."

"I understand. I have mixed feelings about it. I'm glad you know about it. I don't want to hide anything. And I am glad we discussed it. At the same time, I'm very sad that my brother is not in a much better situation. It is what it is."

"My hope is that we can put all the hurt and the misunderstandings behind us. It's very clear to me that I want to continue our relationship, and I want to meet your father so we can get engaged."

This time she didn't suppress her soft smile, which lent her even more beauty, if such a thing were possible. Mansour became aware of this and matched her smile with one of his own. His heart leaped with joy.

He knew then and there what he should've understood if he'd been honest with himself when she walked into the Islamic Center those weeks ago, that Nadia would be his future wife.

Chapter 22

Now

The truck rumbled on, over one-lane bridges, past gurgling brooks and even through a tunnel that had been carved into a giant redwood tree. He loved the way the trees dappled sunlight onto the road and the windshield, the way the air smelled, and the way the birds sang any time he stopped to stretch his legs. The scenery would have been impressive, if not for the fact that he knew that he and his wife were being hunted, accused of a crime they hadn't committed.

Mansour yawned. He wasn't going to avoid any of that if they caught him on the outs, too tired to stand or talk.

"Nadia?" he asked, gently shaking her shoulder.

She stirred and murmured something unintelligible.

"Nadia, I'm going to need you to take the wheel, my honey blossom."

"Dew," she murmured.

"My honey dew blossom," he corrected.

She smiled and he felt a thrill rise in his heart. She was everything to him. No corrupt president or power-hungry king would pull them apart. "Listen, Nadia, I need to get a few hours of sleep. Is there any way you can take the wheel?"

Her eyes opened fully and she nodded. "Of course I can, Mansour. Do you mind if I listen to the radio to help me stay awake?"

He pursed his lips, about to say no, but he was seconds from unconsciousness regardless of noise. But it was so unfair, especially if she was going to drive them around while he slept. She had to know now.

"Nadia, listen. I had the radio on for a while, and I heard some things that, well, I didn't want to tell you but that you need to know."

"What is it? What didn't you tell me?" Her eyes widened and her face tensed. She must have guessed the same things Mansour had. And now she knew without him even saying it that those things were much worse than she'd expected.

"They blew something up. I didn't listen long enough to know what, but there were a lot of people there. And they're saying that we did it. That we're religious zealots and terrorists."

Nadia's hand went to her overall-covered belly.

He settled his hand on top of hers. "No matter what happens to us, I'll make sure as well as I can, as soon as I can, that things are set up so that Omar can have a wonderful life. I swear this."

Her eyes glistened and she nodded. "Pull over up there, Mansour. I can drive. You need to sleep and be strong. I'll wake you up when you're needed."

Mansour pulled the truck over, popped the trunk, and added a quart of oil without even bothering to check the dipstick. Then he slammed it shut and climbed into the passenger seat. He fell asleep in moments.

♛

"No," he whined. His vision was tinged at the edges with the murky blurriness of dreamland. Normally he would've welcomed such a thing. Dreams are beautiful, the mind's filtering system. But today he knew this dream would be dark and violent. He gritted his teeth, turned sideways, and took up a defensive posture.

"Whatever you have for me, bring it. I want it now. No more waiting. No more hiding. Give it to me."

From the soft cloudiness of the dream world stepped Agent Pickering. In his hand he held two babies. They looked identical, but one emanated a feeling of pure good while the other radiated a dark and greasy sense of evil. The agent set them down on the white tiled floor beneath them.

"Congratulations, Mansour. You made a baby. A baby of the Al-Qurayshi line. A baby that will be our own." Pickering gestured to the evil baby and smiled triangular fangs at Mansour. "He will be our agent in preserving the traditions and culture of our people under the knowing gaze of our president."

A man stepped from the shadows. He wore the trademark deep-black suit with orange tie of the current Arlandican president. His black hair was slicked back and greased into place.

"It doesn't have to be this way, Mansour." The president picked up the good baby and started to rock him. The baby fidgeted and cried. "It's over; you're on the run. Stay running. Give up. Arlandica is mine. Terra Qurayshia is his. There is nothing you can do. Keep your truck. Go to the mountains. Build a cabin. Make a little life of your own somewhere. Forget about all of us."

"No!" Mansour yelled. "I will not run from this. You won't pervert the name of Allah and Muhammad while I still live. I profess that I will not stand down." Even so, terror and helplessness gripped his chest and squeezed until he sobbed once, loud, a hiccup that echoed eerily throughout the dream dimension. "Nadia is strong; I am strong. We will win."

Agent Pickering snorted. "Oh what a cute little agent Omar will be. I can already imagine the screams of pain that he will cause in service to his country." He strolled over to where Mansour still held his defensive martial position. "Would you like to hold him?"

The president laughed. "Mansour won't hold him. Didn't you hear what he said? His ideology and vendetta are more important than his wife or child. Don't hold your breath for this loser."

"No! I love them, and I love my country." Mansour found it hard to breathe, his chest constricted by his own fear. He sounded as if he'd just finished a marathon.

"You can't have both, Mansour. Choose." Agent Pickering commanded.

A platoon of mercenary soldiers arose from the dream fog and formed up behind him.

"We are legion," the president added. He walked over to Agent Pickering, and the two of them put the babies into identical cribs. "So what will it be, loser?" he asked.

Mansour screamed and awoke to the dappled light of dawn in a small country camping and recreational area. From the looks of things, Nadia was shaking him.

"Mansour! You're having a nightmare. Wake up!"

Mansour glanced all around, wild-eyed, his heart thumping in his chest. "Yeah, yes, thank you. What happened? How long have I slept?"

Nadia hugged him. "I was on the highway when you started murmuring and moaning. I thought it might be time for us to pull off and collect ourselves. Then I saw the sign for a camp area and rest stop."

"Oh, you beautiful woman," Mansour said. "Yes, this is perfect. Let's take a break here. I have some things I want to talk to you about, anyways."

The restroom area was rustic and quaint, all weathered wood and hardly any plumbing to speak of. It relied on a rusty pump to supply all of the water one might need into lightly warped buckets made of oaken slats. The smell was a heady mix of fertilizer and lime. It didn't smell as bad as it could have, but they weren't used to this sort of situation. Nadia turned pleading eyes on Mansour, who shrugged and stepped into the men's room, then almost retreated.

Enclosed within the oversized outhouse, the treacherous stink made him gag. Was this really how the people of Arlandica, so far away from its shining metropolises, lived? He couldn't understand it. But he did his business anyway before stripping off his top and washing himself thoroughly with cold water from his bucket.

He exited and found himself alone, the trees breezing softly overhead. Two benches had been constructed here by splitting a log in two and slapping the halves into the dirt, flat side up. He took a seat and looked up into the clouds.

What to do? What to do?

His dream might well have been a prophecy from above because it hadn't lied. If Mansour and his wife weren't around to raise him, Omar would become a puppet of either the crown or the presidency. Their Qurayshi family lines were too well interwoven for it to be otherwise. He looked around and took a deep breath. The air smelled wonderful, so clear and crisp, never any smog here. Just the world the way Allah had created it, meant for His servants, just a degree away from paradise. They could live in this, play in this, and Omar could grow up in this. No more agents. No more fighting. No more guns, broken bones, or bloody alleyways. Just living and loving in the arms of one another.

Nadia came out from the women's restroom and looked him over, but something about her expression had shifted.

He stared back at her. "Nadia, we can't do this. Little Omar is coming, and we have a responsibility to him. A responsibility that is not just holy, but familial as well. We can't let him grow up without our guidance and our teachings."

Nadia nodded. But her eyes were dark and troubled.

"We really can't. Nadia, if we go to Palmiento and meet with the governor, what then? Assuming she isn't some sort of trap for us, she's hardly strong enough on her own to fight the president! This is a suicide mission."

Nadia nodded, but her eyes bored into him.

"I'm saying that we can't! I'm your husband, and by the will of God, I'm the one who has the final say."

Nadia still said nothing. She turned her head away from him, instead, and gazed into the sky.

"You think I'm selfish," Mansour said.

"Yes. And silly," Nadia said. "I'll offer up a prayer for your forgiveness. It's all I can do."

"Offer as many prayers as you can, Nadia, because I will not waver. Omar deserves to grow up with his parents."

Nadia got up and walked to the truck, not looking back. Mansour muttered as close to a curse as he could muster, then stalked after her.

"Nadia, we don't have a choice!"

She got to the truck, cranked open its rusty door and pulled herself into her seat. "This is a test, Mansour. There is always a choice. Just, too often, we don't consider the hardest one because we're too interested in our own self-preservation." Nadia slammed the door shut and it sealed with an angry, rust-crunch clang.

Mansour stretched his arms to the sky and yelled, "Allah guide me, for I do not know the way!"

He did know the way, but deep in his heart he hoped it wasn't and that Allah would provide an easier out. He wanted clouds to part, for a ray of sunlight to shine down on him, for his parents to walk out of the woods, smiling at him, and invite them back to their cabin somewhere in the woods. And food would always appear in the cupboards, a *masjid* would be nearby, never troubled by people giving it dirty looks or threatening to burn it down. And all would be well.

Which didn't happen, of course.

The insects were the only sound out here, along with the far-off hum of a passing car. But from Allah, there was no answer. Mansour walked to the driver's side of the truck and got in, then started the truck and drove off.

Hours later, they stopped once for more oil and gas. The gas station attendant gave a puzzled frown when Mansour asked for a map of the area, but he helpfully pointed out a series of dusty atlases, both of the country and the state. Mansour drove off and down a dirt road that the map noted headed into a community of mountain cabins simply named Redwood Grove. He liked the name. It sounded family friendly to him. It also sounded quaint enough that neither police nor FBI would ever bother looking for them there. He imagined they might not even be the only fugitives living there once they settled in. But for some reason, that idea didn't settle him as he thought it might.

Nadia remained silent and gloomy the entire way, shrinking into herself as they rolled, bumped, and pounded over roots and through ruts in the dirt. The road became more like a trail, and Mansour thought more than once that they would have to stop the truck and proceed by way of the dirt bikes in their truck bed. But the old pickup pulled through, losing only its muffler to the bumpy dirt roads. They thundered and growled their way into the stomped-mud clearing of the village in full dark, just a spot before midnight.

"Well, Nadia, we're here. Are you going to talk to me now?" Mansour asked.

"My husband is a brave and principled man. You are neither. I will talk to him, should I see him again." Nadia didn't even bother to face him.

Mansour groaned and killed the lights.

In the pitch black that followed, he saw the beam of a flashlight bobbing from the right side. It flashed about, left to right, as though the man carrying it waddled. Sure enough, when he got close enough to make out in the backwash of the flashlight's rays, Mansour saw a rotund man whose short legs guaranteed him a distinct gait. Mansour rolled down his window.

"Hey there. I think you folks might have gotten turned around," the fat man said. "The rental cabins are a bit further up. It's an easy turn to miss. Heck, I'm surprised you all were able to make it all the way up here. Us Redwood Grove folk don't really bother with road maintenance, and most of you tourist folk get stuck on the way over."

"Oh, we aren't tourists," Mansour informed him. "We're people looking to get away from life and live off the grid. Is this a place for that?"

The fat man peered into the cab more intensely. "Who you got in there with you?" he asked.

Nadia finally turned. Mansour saw that she had discarded the hat, and sometime ago lost the chest wrap. "Hi, I'm Nadia, and I'm pregnant with our son."

The fat man nodded. "I think I get the way of things. All right, listen up, my name's Roger, but you can call me Mister Rogers if you want—most do and it makes me giggle, so don't ever think it don't. We've got a few empties. I can put the missus up in one for the night, and you and I, well, I reckon we've got a few things to talk about, don't we now?"

Mansour released a breath he hadn't even known that he'd been holding. "Yes. I agree."

"All right, then. Let's get things comfortable for you, miss. Need anything to eat or drink? The guest cabins are already stocked so feel free to dig in. If you have any problems, you come on over and let me know. Your husband and I'll be just next door, talking community and membership and the like."

Roger went over to her door and opened it, then helped her down and led her to the cabin. Mansour followed along like a scolded puppy. He watched helplessly as his wife ignored him even in the presence of company. When they got to the cabin, he waited outside until Roger had shown her where everything was, and then headed back out to join him.

Soon Mansour had nothing around him but darkness and the din of nature. He couldn't count the number of insects, and frogs croaked and peeped everywhere, along with the hoots of some type of owl. Possibly several. For all that, it smelled real out here, fresh and green. And he wasn't sure what was wrong with his ears until he realized he hadn't heard a car engine at all. Not close-by, not in the distance, nothing.

Roger pulled a pack of cigarettes from his breast pocket and slid one out. "Want one?" he asked.

"No, thank you. Though this would be the perfect time to have the habit," Mansour groused.

Roger raised the end of his cigarette to his lips and flicked a lighter, puffing a few times. The burning tip glowed orange in the darkness. "Nah, there's never a perfect time. Just a habit that doesn't really go away. Nasty stuff. It's gonna kill me someday." He took a long drag. "Smooth, though," he said, then laughed.

He started to amble back to his own cabin, and Mansour followed alongside.

"So what are these rules that we need to talk about?" Mansour asked.

Roger stayed quiet until they got to the porch. "Those can wait, mister . . ."

"Call me Mansour," he said.

"Those can wait, Mansour. Usually when folks come out here, it's because they're running from something. Especially people willing to drive over at this hour. And I don't really care about the who, what, where, if, and why, or any of that. But I do care about knowing what kind of people are going to be living in my community. And I especially care about whether they'll live a good life here with us. So what you're going to do is tell me whatever I need to hear to convince me that this is the place for you."

Something sparked in the night sky. A falling star! Mansour closed his eyes and left a wish upon the brief flare of its platinum tail.

"My wife and I've been through a lot, and now that she's pregnant, we're looking for a life that's easy and not so frantic."

Roger chuckled. "Rustic life ain't easy. It's not frantic, but it isn't easy. Try that again."

"We're looking for a life that isn't full of such fakery, such forgery, a life that isn't peopled and ruled by con artists and liars. I'm a man of faith, and I constantly find that I must break the tenets of my faith, just little parts here and there, to fulfill the obligations that've been put upon me. But here, living in a place that's much like that which God created for our first ancestors, I think this is where we're meant to be."

Roger nodded, dropped his cigarette and crushed it out with his boot. Then, to Mansour's wondering eyes, he picked it up and pocketed it. "If we don't take care of nature, then why should it take care of us?" he answered Mansour's unspoken question. "Let me look closer at you. At your face, Mansour."

Roger leaned in and the sharp stink of his tobacco drilled into Mansour's nose. He held his place, though, and allowed the mountain man to check him over for whatever he was looking for.

Roger leaned back and snorted. "That's a baby face, Mansour. You ain't no country man. Are you sure that faith is what brought you here? I ain't no religious man myself; I believe in God, and I believe He believes in me, so I don't need no rules or book or nothing, but you, Mansour, I think you might be fibbing to God, and maybe he might not take too kindly to such a thing. Why don't I have another cigarette and you . . . you can tell me your story, or you can stay quiet and do your debating internally. But you figure out whether you're telling the truth, so when you're ready, you can tell me the truth."

Roger smoked and Mansour opened his mouth to speak, then closed it again.

Instead of speaking, he thought. His dream played itself out in his mind once again, and Nadia's words on the road. He'd met the king of Terra Qurayshia once, and that meeting went through his thoughts. The president of Arlandica had his place in Mansour's ruminations as well, even though he'd only ever seen the man jabber on television. He recalled machine-gun fire and the fiery crash of a helicopter. Mostly though, he kept coming back to Nadia's eyes when he declared they were going to live in the mountains: the disappointment and how it grew into resentment. By the time Roger finished his cigarette, Mansour finally had the truth.

He woke Nadia a few minutes later.

"Your husband is back, Nadia. We have a mission to fulfill."

Chapter 23

5 years ago
Arlandica

The time and place Mansour arranged to meet Dr. Mustafa Al Tahan, Nadia's father, was Saturday at their home at 4 p.m. He'd never met the esteemed physician before but had spoken with him briefly over the phone. Nadia's father had a deep and intelligent voice, friendly but also serious. Mansour pictured Mustafa as a big, muscular man in his late fifties, dark complexion, dark hair, with a mustache and glasses.

He felt at once excited and nervous at meeting his future father-in-law. There was a chance the doctor would reject his proposal. After all, Mansour was employed at SDOT, which wasn't the height of prestige. He had to get this right and sent a prayer to God to help him say the right thing.

Almost instantly, Mansour felt a warm flush of confidence and serenity fill his very being. He was ready. In less than an hour, he'd ask the famous brain surgeon for his daughter's hand in marriage.

The maid opened the door. Jamila followed closely behind and welcomed Mansour to their home, then guided him to the guest living room. Jamila and Mansour exchanged some pleasant small talk about the weather and how nice the house appeared.

"I'm impressed with your house. It reminds me of where we stayed in Keerypt," he said. "Especially this furniture." The colorful Isfarani carpet looked thick and heavy and begged to have him run his hands through it. He breathed in the faint mixing scents of Middle Eastern cooking and a vanilla-scented candle.

Mustafa entered a few minutes later and threw most of

Mansour's preconceptions out the window. He was tall, not as dark as Mansour imagined, and thinner, with wavy brown hair and hazel eyes. He was also clean-shaven and dressed in an elegant professional style. Mansour never imagined such clothes when he thought of a doctor at home. He also wore a familiar cologne, something like what Uncle Muhammad wore, but Mansour couldn't place it.

Mustafa gave an inviting smile, but one tinged with something deeper. Not distrust, but perhaps regret. If Marwan caused it, Mansour could understand completely.

"Mansour." He extended his hand.

Mansour shook it and gave a half bow. "Sir, I'm glad to finally meet you."

"You're all anyone in this house talks about these days," he said, his indulgent smile now showing some mischief. He took a seat in an easy chair and motioned for Mansour to have a seat near him on the sofa. "How is your work at the SDOT?"

Mansour relaxed and fell into talking about guardrails, highway projects, night work, the design division, and accounts. All parts of the rotation were interesting and vital in different ways. He rather enjoyed the peace and quiet that came with being out in the field, in the truck, but also among the laughing, boisterous design team during the day shifts.

Mustafa was surprisingly easy to talk to, and Mansour gushed more than he meant to. He stopped in the midst of rambling and apologized.

"Not at all," Mustafa said. "Civil engineering is clearly a passion then, I take it."

Mansour nodded. "We're designing and building a safe, orderly, pleasant society. But I came here to offer your daughter my hand in marriage, sir, and it would please me greatly if you would accept."

"Of course I will!" Mustafa declared. "Royal blood is difficult to say no to."

He'd found out. He'd done his research and found Mansour online somehow.

"It's—I—" he stammered.

"Plus, I'm almost certain my daughter has found love. Your parentage, it's not a problem. But there are caveats. Conditions."

"Conditions?" Mansour clapped his mouth shut. Of course there would be conditions. Fareed and his father had both told him about various conditions that might exist.

"She's intending to go to medical school, and this is the place for it," Mustafa said. "You'd be hard-pressed to find a woman doctor in Terra Qurayshia."

Mansour nodded.

"That means supporting her through another six or eight years of schooling. This is nonnegotiable. Anyone who wishes to marry Nadia will agree, or no marriage."

"I'll be the only person marrying your daughter, thank you very much!" They shared a chuckle over this. "Of course I'll be happy to work beside her while she studies. I couldn't be more excited about marrying a brilliant and driven companion."

"That was the correct answer," Mustafa said, then nodded toward the kitchen. "And both the ladies and the cake have arrived."

Nadia appeared close-by, eyes brimming with excited, joyful tears. Mansour caught the serving tray before her trembling hands could drop it. Behind her, Jamila didn't look much different.

"Tea?" Nadia croaked.

They had cake and tea all together before Mansour excused himself and headed out. This was an auspicious first step, the first of many.

And yet, something wasn't right. Mansour couldn't put his finger on what it could possibly be. Right now he had everything he wanted: the girl, parties to celebrate their approaching union, a good job that paid well. His dad was even flying in the following day to help get guest lists together, work out invitations, head to the bank for the eventual transfer of dowry payments, and so on.

Yet there was a disquiet feeling inside Mansour.

Soon after tea, cake, and confirmation, Mansour and his dad went to visit Nadia's family to recite the first Sura, or chapter of the Qur'an, the opening *al-Fatiha*. This second step meant that officially Mansour and Nadia had the intentions of getting married. During that visit, they discussed the amount of *mahr*, or dowry, to be given to Nadia. This part of the Islamic tradition stipulated the groom pay a dowry to the bride, determined by an agreement between both families. Faisal had been in touch with Mustafa and Jamila and had proposed a generous dowry. Indeed, it was large enough that Mustafa, Jamila, and Nadia were pleased, and no negotiations were needed at all.

The third step was for them to actually get engaged in an engagement party to which they'd invite a close circle of family and friends. Nadia's parents handled this and would hold it at their home.

Both families came up with their own lists. It was nearly impossible to just keep it to a small circle of family and friends. Mansour tried, but between both families, they still ended up with over two hundred guests.

The engagement party, set in the large backyard of Nadia's family home, was very elegant, befitting a prince. They had twenty round tables with golden, decorative table covers, and white and red flowers adorned each table which sat ten people. They hired professional caterers to prepare and lay out the food: *Ossobuco Toscano*–Tuscan-style veal shank–chicken, salmon, white rice, brown rice, rice with nuts, different salads, a variety of vegetables, and desserts including *umm ali,* Mansour's favorite.

But some wrong feeling in his guts stopped him from eating a lot. Fortunately, or perhaps unfortunately, the guests made it easy to take his mind off whatever was bothering him.

Fareed attended with his family, Mike and his family, and

even his best friends from high school made their appearances. Nadia's side of the guest list was an international delight. The backyard filled near to bursting, and the party spilled out onto the driveway and into the front yard, where Mustafa's hired valets took the overflow of cars to a rented parking lot.

Shortly after lunch, the religious director of the Islamic Center spoke about the importance of marriage and family life as a building block in a healthy society. In a respectful and tasteful manner, he then recited a couple of verses from the Qur'an.[7] It seemed well received by the large number of non-Muslim guests, many of them Nadia's fellow university students and professors.

Everything should've been perfect. It was perfect. Mansour couldn't point to anything having gone wrong. The sound system wasn't too loud or too quiet, the guests hadn't gotten too lively and had the police called, the caterers had done a superb job of bringing enough delicious food for everyone, and he had the most beautiful woman in the place on his arm.

They were together all the time, and he worked hard to throw off the shadow of the unnamed stain trying to worm its way into his soul. People commented that they appeared like two birds flying high in the sky in harmony and matching each other in every way, their looks and moves. Mansour wore an elegant, expensive, dark blue Canali suit, a red tie, and black Canali shoes. Nadia wore a stunning red Giorgio Armani dress with black high heels, which made her almost Mansour's height. The party continued until late in the evening, and when people left, they gushed about how perfectly everything had gone.

Yes. Perfect.

The plan was that Nadia and Mansour's engagement would last for about six months, and they'd marry just after her graduation from university. She'd already been accepted into medical school in the same area.

After Faisal had flown out, and Mansour had settled back into

---

[7] Qur'an 30:21 and 49:13.

daily life—now engaged, with frequent calls to Nadia—Mansour realized what had been gnawing at him the day of the party: his secret.

The spy game assignment had faded to the back of his mind and over time had practically disappeared. With Nadia and the business regarding her brother, it had never made an appearance, not once. Life had enough drama and conflict without pressing a shadowy job he might never actually get sometime in the deep future. Instead he rolled through SDOT projects, rolled on the jiujitsu mat in the evenings, went out on dates with Nadia, and prayed when the *Azan* clock reminded him it was time.

No problems.

Except this was a problem, and a big one. He had kept a secret from his wife-to-be, and he had no idea how to breach the topic with her. She might take the situation in stride, as she seemed able to do with her brother and with the sudden appearance of Carmen, or not.

After only a few weeks, Nadia's family invited him over to have a conference call with Faisal about the wedding itself. Technology had progressed enough that they were able to project Faisal's face onto the family's large flatscreen television.

"It may seem far off, but I propose having a lavish wedding in the kingdom," Faisal said, referring to Terra Qurayshia. "The king and royal family will attend. It would be food and celebration such as you have never seen! All relatives living in Keerypt would be given visas and have their travel fees paid, of course." He finished with a delighted, toothy smile, a smile that said *of course you'll agree! How could you not?*

Mansour burned with embarrassment. Now that the secret agent job was again at the forefront of his mind, he felt guilt well up within him. Nadia didn't know.

And though his father had claimed the job might be optional, he felt a calling to act. After the terror attacks, sentiment had turned against anyone with darker skin, anyone wearing a headscarf, visiting Islamic places of worship, and in many cases people who weren't even Muslims. Several Sikhs had been threatened or beaten. The patriotic part of him wanted to make a difference, to represent his culture and, better, Terra Qurayshia, to show the world it wasn't a backward place full of terrorists. Another strong part of him only wished to have Nadia by his side, to build a life and help the people of Sunland, which he thought of as his home.

He leaned over to Nadia and whispered, "Would you rather have it here, or in Keerypt?"

"Honestly, here," she whispered back, and earned a beaming smile from him.

He peered down into the phone. "Dad, they're more comfortable here, and honestly, I am too." It had been years since he'd traveled to the kingdom.

"Agreed," Mustafa said. "So many of Nadia's friends are not of the faith, but she has told us she wants to have them attend."

To Faisal's credit, his smile faltered only slightly. "Completely understandable. I'll arrange for the Keeryptian side to fly over, and get them hotel rooms." This meant Muhammad, Teta, and all his aunts and cousins. In the coming weeks, he also arranged for the Qurayshian side of the family to visit for the wedding. It was turning into a massive event.

And the gnawing sense that he was getting away with murder continued to grow in him. The only relief seemed to be in avoiding it and staying busy with work, planning the wedding, and staring into Nadia's eyes whenever they went out to dinner or met at her folks' house.

The Keeryptian side of the family, namely Mansour's grandmother, uncle, aunts, Kareem, Nour, Nabil, Kamilia, and Dina, arrived in Sunland one week before the wedding, while the royal family's side arrived only a couple of days before the wedding. They'd changed a lot in the intervening years, but none more than Dina, who was now close to finishing high school, and

Kareem, who'd been to the gym even more than Mansour had. He was now a solid wall of muscle with a crushing grip, and he loved giving out bear hugs.

Mansour's Keeryptian cousins had never been to Arlandica before, so he took them to the regular tourist sites. Beaches, the movie studios, the tallest and most massive trees on Earth all filled his time and kept him at a low level of guilt over what he wasn't telling his future wife.

They all enjoyed the four-day condensed tour but were exhausted, especially from the long lines at the amusement parks. Dina especially enjoyed the large amusement parks.

Kareem and Kamilia noticed the abundance of parking spaces everywhere compared with Keerypt. The orderly movement of traffic in such a big city surprised them—no honking horns all the time as they did in Keerypt. Kareem spoke the language every civil engineer wanted to hear, commenting that with all these buildings and high-rise buildings, there was still parking available and sidewalks to walk on.

Mansour explained that any private development or even public development had to go through permits, and the city would not allow for adding traffic-generating facilities without providing adequate parking spaces for them. In some situations, he explained, for large developments, capacity improvements had to be made to the streets or freeways at the expense of the developer.

"It's unfortunate that none of these regulations are followed in Keerypt," Kareem said. "Whenever there's a development, we lose more parking, and traffic becomes more congested, and sidewalks turn into parking, instead of getting any improvement out of it."

"Yes, Kareem, you're correct," Mansour replied. "The laws are certainly on the books, but no one follows them. Also the development in Keerypt, unfortunately, isn't done with proper planning and infrastructure upgrades. Traffic and parking are among many problems. Power, water, storm drains, and sewers are another. There's no apparent calculation of the increased demand on these utilities to accommodate the growth."

Kamilia was very happy with this visit and shared her thoughts of how strange it was that Keerypt five thousand years ago had been on top of the world, while now it was so far behind.

"Those developers in Keerypt who break the law and mess up our traffic and parking only get the temporary enjoyment of making immoral profits," Kareem said, "but then they mess up the city for everyone else including themselves and their kids. They leave a terrible legacy behind them and leave this world worse than it was. They get a temporary win in this life and a permanent loss in the hereafter; what a terrible deal."

Nour and Nabil had a much better relationship after going to family counseling a few years ago, and they enjoyed their trip to Sunland a lot. They felt they owed a lot to Mansour's late mother, Fatima, and asked Mansour if he could take them to visit her grave. Initially only Amina, Muhammad, Samia, and Soraya were planning to visit Fatima's grave along with Faisal and Mansour, but in the end, all Mansour's cousins and Nour's husband joined them. They recited the *al-Fatiha* (the first sura of the Qur'an), which was customary when visiting the grave.

For the first time in years, Mansour found tears slipping down his cheeks. He desperately wanted them to be for his mother, the bittersweet joy of having so many interested in preserving her memory. But he had to admit to himself that some of his tears were the result of his own doing.

After that, he had a few days of rest before his wedding on Saturday night.

Chapter 24

5 years ago
Arlandica

The day had come. Mansour stood before her with one itching, black secret wedged in between them. He felt as if he touched her through a film of secrecy. It made him want to jerk away in disgust and go wash his hands.

After a while though, he commanded himself to go through with this, to enjoy it. He'd be fine. It was nothing more than a few months living and working in Terra Qurayshia, that was all, just under an assumed name. It was nothing more than acting! Nadia would understand. She might even be excited for him. And if it seemed dangerous, or Nadia had objections, he could bow politely and send his regrets to the king through his father.

Yes, he lied to himself. Everything was just fine! There'd be no problems.

They had selected the luxurious Biltmore Hotel in an upscale area of West Beach as the perfect place to hold the wedding. The hotel was known for the fresco-style murals, carved marble fountains and columns, crystal chandeliers, and embroidered tapestries. Everything about the hotel loudly proclaimed class.

In addition to the mayor, other celebrated folk were invited to the royal wedding. Mustafa and Faisal had many friends and business acquaintances who included film stars, singers, and famous athletes. Somewhere around seven hundred guests attended the affair, flush as it was with familiar faces, couture dresses, and sleek tuxedos. As a surprise to the bride, Faisal had arranged for Nadia's favorite Keeryptian band to fly halfway across the world to perform at their wedding.

In accordance with a long-standing tradition, most Keeryptian weddings included a belly dancer or two performing a sensual dance to some very loud music, but Mansour and Nadia didn't want that at their wedding. They decided instead to invite a local *dabke* dance troupe called Shamaz Dabke to perform for their wedding guests. Instead of hip shaking and skin, they were treated to a string of men leaping around with deft, coordinated movements. The lively *dabke* dance was far more regal and far more consistent with Mansour's and Nadia's conservative values and desire for a wholesome atmosphere. The powerful stomping rhythms and pulses of *dabke* were part of their souls and thoroughly enchanted their guests.

Mansour's concerns over the secret bled away with every smile and kind word from the guests. Eventually he convinced himself he was happy to have his close family and friends celebrating this special and joyous occasion with him. Almost all attendees commented on how beautiful, elegant, and pleasant it was to attend the wedding. The music level was just right, allowing them to socialize and talk with each other. And most of all, the radiance on his new bride's face as she recited the pledge to him while staring into his eyes chased away his concerns.

Nadia and Mansour spent five days at the hotel as a prelude to their honeymoon. They spent a lot of time in the room together and occasionally went for a walk down the street holding hands. They felt so close. They prayed together, thanked God for bringing them together, and made *duaa* for keeping them together for the rest of their lives.

Then they flew to Aragonia to spend the rest of their honeymoon. They stayed at the Ritz Hotel in Reciña by the sea for a couple of days. Even though Nadia came from an affluent family, she'd never stayed at a Ritz hotel before. For the first time, she saw curtains controlled electronically by switches next to their bed, something she found intriguing.

Nadia had a special swimsuit that covered her well, leaving

only her face and feet showing, so she swam in the outdoor swimming pool with Mansour and at the beach as well, something they both found relaxing.

While Nadia and Mansour were wandering around in the hotel, they saw a gleaming grand piano with no one playing. Their eyes spoke in a moment of eye contact. They sat down next to each other at the piano, opened the cover, and played the "Für Elise." They both enjoyed Beethoven's music and had practiced playing this music and other pieces together in West Beach. After "Für Elise" they moved to "Claire de Lune" by Debussy, then Bruce Hornsby's "The Way It Is," and ended with the recent music from the *Pirates of the Caribbean* soundtrack.

At that point an attractive lady in a short black dress appeared from nowhere with a violin and joined them in playing a selection from *Pirates of the Caribbean.* She had an expressive face and was definitely a talented violin player. They sounded great together and played for a while, having a wonderful time of it.

Many hotel guests surrounded them, listening and enjoying their playing. At the end people cheered and clapped for them. They talked with the violinist and discovered that she was a professional from Germany, same as Hans Zimmer, who scored *Pirates of the Caribbean.* She told them that she'd played a few times in Hans Zimmer's concerts. She was impressed with their piano playing, and they exchanged contact information.

Nadia and Mansour then went to Arronje and stayed at Hotel Gran Valajo Palacia Del Rojo. They visited the Arab wall erected under Muhammad I between 850 and 866, and in Alhambra, they visited the Omar Mosque in San Janar, the largest mosque in Hellea.

After four days visiting other touristic sites, they flew to Terra Qurayshia for a royal welcome. The agonizing itch of the undisclosed secret returned. Mansour was just lucky that Nadia hadn't been to Terra Qurayshia before, and she was too busy enjoying the experience to notice.

"This is amazing!" she gushed, first from the airplane in their executive seats while she stared out the window at the kingdom rising up to meet them, then later in the airport as they skipped out of the immigration line using Mansour's diplomatic passport. For the first time with her, he enjoyed the perks of being a prince.

Nadia next met Mansour's dad's side of the family, his uncle, aunts, and cousins. They were very kind to her, and she felt welcomed by the royal family.

"I met some of them before, but honestly," she whispered, "I don't remember most of their names."

He laughed.

She was introduced to the crown prince, who regarded the newly arrived married couple without a hint of emotion. A curtsy from her, a bow from Mansour, and a few words later, they moved on to meet the king. Unlike the crown prince, the king was open and frank with his joy over Mansour's life-changing event. Where the crown prince had been perfunctory, the king heaped praises on Mansour about the great luck he had in finding such an ambitious, brilliant, accomplished, well-spoken, devout, and beautiful wife.

The king's attention on him, and on Nadia, caused that dark itch to return. Mansour found it impossible to ignore now. It usually sat on his spine, begging him to wriggle in any chair in which he sat, and it bothered him any time she took him by the hand.

Mansour, well trained as a rider, took her horseback riding. At first, he sat her on the saddle with him, but afterward, when she felt more comfortable, she rode a horse by herself while he rode next to her to help her if needed. They rode miles away from anyone, but Mansour easily imagined a sniper with his sights trained on Nadia. He'd only hear the shot after she fell from the horse.

Ten days in the kingdom sped by, for Nadia at least. Mansour felt relieved to put Terra Qurayshia behind them, and they flew to Myria. There he met Nadia's extended family and did some sightseeing. During their short trip, Nadia took Mansour to her favorite places and explained their history. They visited her maternal grandparents, aunts, and uncles, and he found most of them delightful people. Not like Mansour, who steadily grew to despair for himself more every day.

He never strayed far from Nadia. In fact, for the first time in his life, he had no good way to excuse himself to pray for guidance without having to answer for what he was doing. This, he felt, was something like a spiritual blockage, like hardening arteries. He needed to banish this dark guilt, telling himself over and again that it was a small matter, that she would understand. It didn't work.

Next, they flew to Keerypt where Nadia met Mansour's mom's side of the family, and Mansour met Nadia's dad's side of the family. Mansour also took Nadia to the beach house his father often used, and they stayed there for a couple of days. The large living room had wide sliding glass doors overlooking the white sandy beach only a few hundred feet away. The ocean view was "like nothing she'd ever seen."

After a quick, but agonizing, ten further days in Keerypt, they returned to Sunland.

"I'm overjoyed to have seen all this," she told him, the morning of their departure. "To think your aunt Soraya only lives a few kilometers from my aunt."

He grinned at her and tried not to let her see that something had been eating at him for the better part of a month.

"It's like I've now seen all the corners of your life," she said. "The whole Mansour world has now been explored."

"Yes," he said. "The whole world."

She kissed him on the cheek. "I'm sure there's much more to learn."

"Of course," he muttered.

"And you got a tour of Nadia world!" She laughed, that

perfect musical laugh that reminded him of his mother. "Slightly less royal, but still–"

"Your family is wonderful."

"Of course they are," she said, but then her face clouded, and her mood soured. "Except that brother of mine."

He snapped out of his own issue, perversely thankful for an aspect of Nadia's life that wasn't absolutely perfect. Then he tried to shake this off and took her hand. "Don't talk like that. Your brother has decided upon his own path. And, by the way, he may surprise you one day. Perhaps he'll find himself."

She melted into his embrace. "Thank you, Mansour."

"It's nothing."

After all the traveling, Mansour and Nadia needed to take a couple of days to rest in Mansour's home in West Beach, which now became their home. Faisal and Mustafa had taken care of moving Nadia's things into the house. Their house was big enough and had two master suites, so they took Mansour's suite and Faisal kept the master suite, which he used to share with Fatima. Faisal spent most of his time between Keerypt, Terra Qurayshia and Hellea to follow up on his businesses and would visit Sunland only a few weeks per year.

While on their brief break, Nadia reminded Mansour of an earlier promise. "Remember, my dear, you promised me something a while ago while we were seeing each other at the Islamic Center?"

Mansour tried to remember, but he couldn't. Had he promised to tell her about the secret agent mission? It had taken up permanent residence in his head, and he wanted it gone.

"You promised to teach me something, but you never followed up on it."

Mansour was honestly puzzled. "It can't be piano, because you already know how to play piano very well. Maybe tennis?"

She laughed. "Oh, my dear, you forgot. You promised to teach me chess."

"Oh yes, sorry my love, I totally forgot. Let's start right now. I have my chess board in the library room. I'll get it right away."

The second day after their trip, Nadia sat down to some of his cooking, which consisted mostly of Arlandican fried food.

"I've made a decision on something I think is important," she said, "and I'd like to know your thoughts."

"Hm?" he asked, and poured her some orange juice.

"I'd like to wear the *hijab*." She stared at him, as if expecting a response.

"I . . . support your decision?" He stopped himself. "Of course I support your decision."

The atmosphere around Arlandica had cooled, but not by much, following the terror attacks on the East Coast.

"I hope to send the message that we're not bad people. We're not terrorists. It's a discussion starter, I suppose. I'd like people to ask me about it, so I can explain a little about the commandment in the Qur'an. I can also tell them it was my choice to wear it, and not by my husband's command."

He stopped in the midst of dealing with breakfast. "My dear, you consistently prove yourself the kindest, most thoughtful, most compassionate person I've ever met. I'm proud to have married you."

Chapter 25

Now

Driving back down the rough and unkempt trail was much easier than it had been driving in. The truck seemed to understand that Mansour was back. It leaped with urgency and gunned through the cracks and pits while rolling over the massive exposed roots of the Sunlandian wilderness. Nadia squeezed his knee and stared at him in rosy admiration. He was her Mansour, a hero willing to sacrifice it all for the greater good of all. He could read the love in her face, and he had no doubt now that he was doing the work of God. Mansour felt holy approval as he crested the next rise. Everything was clear.

What wasn't so clear, though, were the three deer jumping out in front of him just as he'd finally gotten off the trail and sped onto the highway. Mansour's pickup shrugged, shuddered, and then proceeded away from the hobbled buck it left behind.

And what was even less clear than that was the police cruiser that suddenly flipped on its lights, red and blue flashing and flickering to the beat of its siren.

"Mansour! The police!"

Mansour scowled. He loved Nadia to death, but yelling obvious things at him while he tried to figure out their escape was decidedly unhelpful.

Mansour took a corner, both sides of the highway opaque in this witching hour. Thick forest made it feel more like an underground tunnel than a proper tar and asphalt road. When the road straightened out, he stomped the accelerator and gunned it.

Behind him, the cruiser let out two harsh beeps. "State Police. Pull over now!"

The lights behind him sped forward impossibly fast and the car was on his tail in a second.

Nadia screeched. "Mansour, they are right behind us!"

Something inside him yelled out in rage, and he stomped the brake hard. The cruiser behind him smashed into the back of the truck and the entire truck frame shifted, one side jutting forward slightly even as the truck plunged off the road and into a ditch. The police squealed and spun, its front hood crumpled and smoking, before catching a jutting dip and flipping over onto the opposite side of the road.

Mansour coughed. There was a sour smell in his nose and a dazed feeling kept his thoughts scattered for a brief moment. The airbags. Thank God, somehow, this old truck had airbags. That lady must have had them installed after she bought it. A warm feeling filled him. It must've been expensive, but something in that warm heart of hers required that she keep herself and her passengers safe. He'd go back and pay her even more money. If they managed to survive it all, that was.

He reached out and his hand slapped into Nadia's, who had been doing the same thing. Their eyes met and they laughed. Neither of them was hurt. Mansour cast his eyes to the rearview mirror. The bikes had tipped over out of their mounts, but the straps had kept them safe as well. The twisted angle of the truck gave him doubts about its own condition. He turned the starter and it didn't even click. Yeah, that wasn't going to work.

"Nadia, we're going to have to take the bikes. Are you sure you're okay?"

Nadia nodded. "I am as good as I've ever been, Mansour. But maybe we should check on the police officer as well? He was just doing his job. I don't think he's one of the bad guys."

The two of them crept over to the flipped cruiser. It stank of fuel, and its blue police light had gone dead. Mansour held out a hand, gesturing Nadia to stay back. "There might be a fire soon. Think of Omar," he warned her. She nodded and held her ground.

The way the car was crushed between the slope of the ditch meant that he had to drop to his hands and knees to get a proper view of the officer. The man was alive and both of his eyes were swollen, while his nose sat at the wrong angle and streamed blood. The car's chassis must have hit at a strange angle because the man was all kinds of messed up, Mansour could see. He wrenched the door open as hard as he could. The man's right arm was obviously broken, as were his two legs, and the bottom of the car had crunched in and pinned him into his current position.

"Don't kill me," the police officer managed.

His police radio squawked. "Unit 78, you okay out there? Still in pursuit of the old blue pickup?"

Mansour put a hand on the police officer's shoulder. "You're going to be all right. I'm sorry you got caught up in all of this, but you'll be safe." He picked up the sender and clicked its button. "Um, hello. This is that pickup truck guy. Don't chase me. Trust me. There's a lot of bad stuff happening, and I'm the good guy. You'll hear all about it later on the news, assuming I succeed in my mission. But you, um, your Unit 78 is really hurt bad, and he needs medical assistance."

What was that they said in the movies again? He cleared his voice nervously. "Um, I mean officer down! Okay. So don't chase us. Save him." He shot a questioning look to Nadia, but she only shrugged. "So, bye!"

He hung up the sender, and the box squawked questions and demands. Mansour ignored those and put his hand back on the officer's shoulder. "You're going to be all right, really. We have to go now, but I want you to know that, after we're done with our mission, and after you understand that we're not the enemy, I'll come to find you and to ask your forgiveness for this altercation. Be safe, my friend."

Mansour walked away, and Nadia joined him as together they began to undo the straps that held in the bikes.

"That was really brave of you." She paused and pursed her lips, as if tasting her words. "It was more than that. It was right. It was very right of you." Mansour grabbed the unstrapped motorbikes and eased them down to the pavement of the road. "I'm proud of you, Mansour."

He turned to her, wrapped her up in his arms, and kissed her. "It was you. Your words and your beautiful mind that brought me to help him. I can't believe that I almost gave up!"

Nadia smiled. "You were going to make us into mountain people, like the cavemen of the old times when dinosaurs roamed the Earth."

"Dinosaurs and humans didn't live at the same time–hey." He laughed, seeing that she was teasing him. "All right, listen, follow behind me. There might be more deer, and you're carrying cargo more precious than I am. If I'm hit and I fall, leave me. Don't look back. I'll be all right. Just get to Palmiento! Get to the governor."

Mansour hesitated and considered telling her the secret place where all the documents were hidden. He winced. If she knew, they might drown it out of her with their barbaric waterboarding and other instruments of torture. Then again, they'd probably do that even if she didn't know.

"Nadia, just in case, you need to know. The documents have been stored away in the Islamic Cultural Center, hidden in the vent closest to where I first sat and talked with you."

Nadia put her hand to her mouth. "How clever. I'll tell Governor Schwarzenvalder if you can't." She put her hand on his hand. "But you will. There's no stopping you, Mansour. Not in this."

He narrowed his eyes and nodded. He would make it.

"Follow me, my dearest." Now to save Arlandica.

♛

The two motored down the highway, Mansour in front and Nadia in the rear, the grumbling of their engines thrumming powerfully through the chill night air. It felt very dangerous without a moon in the witching hour before natural light crept into the sky. In this rustic, tree-dense countryside, it felt to Mansour more like driving through a tunnel than through rural Sunland. His nerves ran high. Not only could he not see much with his single headlight, but also he knew that one mistake would cost them their freedom and little Omar's future.

But only once did they encounter any danger. The flashing lights of a police cruiser and an ambulance rushed past the two, presumably on their way to help their fellow officer, Unit 78. For some reason the officer had kept quiet about the motorbikes in the back of the truck before being trapped out of reach of his radio in the accident. Mansour sent thanks to Allah for this lucky oversight.

The sky began to lighten, and the world slowly came alive. First, the birds chittered, chirped, and chattered from the branches of the increasingly sparse woods bordering the highway. Then began the buzz of humans. A car passed. Then another. A rusty black pickup ran up to their rear and honked. Mansour and Nadia pulled off the road and let him pass. A window decal in his rear window read "My son can beat up your honors student." Mansour sighed.

Mansour pushed the stand down on his bike but left it idling and wandered over to his wife. "Nadia, judging by the time, I'd say we're about to hit the suburbs of Palmiento. I think we're going to have to make a plan. I expect that once we're in the city, being caught by the police might be a good thing, assuming Governor Schwarzenvalder isn't in with the enemy."

Nadia smiled. "It's good to be such a smart and paranoid man, Mansour. You'll be a good father. But the governor isn't going to betray us. I think we should get as close to the capitol building as we can, and turn ourselves in to the first police to tell us to."

"How can you be so sure?" Mansour asked.

"Woman's intuition." Nadia tapped her temple with the end of her pointer finger. "Plus, I voted for the woman for her morals and honesty. Tell me to my face that I'm a bad judge of character."

Mansour laughed. "Yes, okay then. But we still have to be careful. There might be crooked cops. In fact, I expect there to be crooked cops. And then there'll be FBI agents and some more of those black-van mercenaries. This is going to be tough, Nadia."

He thought of the cabins and shuddered. Had he made a mistake leaving them?

"Through trials and tribulations the Prophet was given vision, Mansour. We will suffer our trials boldly without fear, and we'll win."

"Yeah?" he asked.

"Yeah," she answered.

Mansour started his bike back up, and a moment later, the roar of Nadia's joined him. Then they were off. The tree line disappeared not far ahead, and the homes of the middle class with their deep-green manicured lawns and white picket fences replaced the woods of before. It didn't feel like the right kind of place for a motorbike. He slowed down to the speed limit and stopped at a red light. Nadia pulled up next to him.

"We're sticking out like a sore thumb," Nadia said.

"Yeah, I was just thinking about that. But what can we do? I'm pretty much out of cash, and I don't dare try my cards right now."

Nadia shrugged, the answer clear. They could do nothing. The light turned green, and they pushed forward again, passing a large park and entering onto a freeway. The road became crowded, not unlike a day long ago in Keerypt when Mansour had watched the country's people battle through their infuriating commutes. Cars honked and cut each other off. Drivers rolled down their windows and yelled at one another. Mansour and Nadia edged their way through on white lines and small gaps, picking their way through the mess.

And then they saw it. Up ahead, a checkpoint stopped and inspected every vehicle. And not just police officers, but also soldiers in black camo! The mercenaries were here in an official capacity. What was going on?

Mansour inspected his surroundings. The freeway was walled in on both sides, but he saw white and orange construction signs that blocked off an exit just before the checkpoint. A rising on-ramp that had yet to be finished rose to meet the sky and ended in emptiness. It looked dangerous.

Nadia pulled up alongside him.

"Nadia, I don't think there's any way around this. We're going to have to take that on-ramp."

Nadia followed the point of his finger. She turned to him, her face filled with horror.

"We can't do that, Mansour! That's death! That drop is way too high!"

"Listen, Nadia, I have a plan, but we're going to have to do it now before they notice us. Follow my lead."

Mansour kicked the bike into gear and pulled closer to the checkpoint. One of the mercenary soldiers, a man of some authority apparently, pointed at them and started yelling to his men. The soldiers grabbed up their weapons and held them at the ready as they began to wade through the mess of vehicles.

"Mansour!" Nadia yelled over the roar of the bike.

He nodded and yelled back. "Follow me."

He gunned his engine and slipped through the narrow spaces between vehicles. Nadia followed behind. The mercenaries shouted but didn't shoot. Mansour suspected they would've if there hadn't been so many witnesses.

When they reached the ramp, he paused and let Nadia pull up beside him.

"Now what do we do, Mansour?" she asked.

"Slowly, now, up to the top of the ramp and to the unfinished part." He quickly gave her the instructions she needed.

"We'll die!" she protested.

"No, trust me, Nadia. We can do this!"

She bit her lip, glanced behind at the soldiers drawing closer, then nodded.

They drove their motorbikes up to the unfinished top of the off-ramp and shifted to neutral. Behind them, the mercenary soldiers exited the mess of vehicles and jogged up after them.

Mansour winked at Nadia, turned the front of his motorbike to face the platoon, jumped off the bike, gunned it and dropped it into gear. The motorbike jolted forward, squealing, and sped into the mess of soldiers like a missile. They screamed and scattered. Nadia scooted back on her bike. Mansour jumped on and kicked it into gear. Then the two of them sped past the soldiers and, staying on the freeway side, tore through the empty checkpoint. Exulting, Nadia pumped her fist as they passed on through.

"That was amazing, Mansour! It makes me wonder what other tricks you have up your sleeve!"

"I expect that I might have to show you all of them before the day is over. Get out of the way, Palmiento!" Mansour yelled. "We're coming through!"

Chapter 26

Then

Arlandica

The next few years saw Mansour rise in the ranks at SDOT, and Nadia began and then nearly finished med school. The specter of the lie of omission slowly ground to dust. He'd cured that itch through focused prayers throughout each day and conversations with Fareed about the possibility of keeping a secret from his wife. When Fareed pushed, Mansour admitted it was a possible chance to work overseas in the kingdom, but he was certain he could refuse if Nadia objected strongly. As to why he had to keep the matter secret from Nadia, he just shrugged and apologized. This was the one thing he'd keep secret from everyone, he said.

The years passed by like an untethered kite on a windy afternoon. Nadia entered her second year of medical school at the University of Sunland at West Beach. She'd need another two years to finish her MD there and then a couple more to complete her residency. Mansour, by comparison, made assistant resident engineer, then resident engineer. All the experience he gained and the promotions he got came only because of his hard work and effort with nothing attributed to his family or father's status. He was—Nadia argued—right to be proud of himself.

A few years ago, the new division of program and project management had been created, a result of an effort initiated by the SDOT director's office. They'd solicited recommendations by the Arlandican Army Corps of Engineers, a major organization, then a task force reviewed the recommendations. The task force came up with an implementation plan to improve project management, which ended up being largely successful. The first few years saw some resistance by the work force and sarcasm toward the newly created position of project manager. However, after seeing the noticeable improvement in project delivery, no one remained skeptical.

When the position of senior engineer, project manager, opened up, Mansour had only fleeting thoughts of applying for it but later seriously considered it. As a project manager, Mansour would be able to manage the entire project delivery process from start to finish. He'd not merely work on the construction aspects of a project but oversee the entire project life cycle. What an opportunity!

Mansour knew he possessed all the necessary qualifications for this position. He already held full certification as a professional engineer in the state of Sunland. He could do the work; of that, he had no doubt. Nailing this position could greatly increase his salary, for one, and put a great big gold star atop his resume. In the long-term, it could open otherwise locked doors. Once inside, however, Mansour wanted to earn his own success—much the way his dad had done in the business world.

Mansour applied for the position and was told that the interviews would be in about a month—not enough time to study thoroughly for it. Nonetheless he did his best. Two days before the interview, he received a call saying it was postponed indefinitely. Though bad news, he thought that perhaps it was not meant to be.

An email was sent out about the project manager position encouraging people to apply. Mansour didn't like that because it meant an increase in the number of people in the pool, and therefore more competition. The email stated that those who had applied need not apply again; their previous applications were still valid. The storm cloud had a bit of a silver lining after all.

Mansour studied more and finally received a notification that they'd scheduled him for an interview, but the day before the interview, he received an email, then a phone call canceling the interview. Again.

He returned home, despondent, to find Nadia waiting for him. The cook had prepared his favorite dishes in preparation for an interview that would never happen. He sighed and told his lovely wife what had happened.

"I'm so sorry!"

"This is definitely not meant to be," Mansour said. "Perhaps it's a message for me that I need to stop here and just head to Terra Qurayshia and get a good job."

"I want the best for you, my dear husband. If you think it's best for you to go now then I'll support you. However, I would really prefer if you stayed a bit longer until I finish graduate school."

"That was the plan, but part of the plan was for me to get more experience at a higher level, and it seems that's not happening. I feel that my plan won't work, and it gets me really frustrated."

"I highly recommend you pray to God and ask Him for guidance."

Yes. For the first time in years, Mansour considered the job his father had mentioned. A hot pit of guilt welled up in his stomach. "I will, my love. Thank you for your understanding and your support. It means a lot to me."

Mansour followed his beloved wife's advice and knelt to open up his mind to what Allah might have to say regarding the matter. After several prayers offered up to God, he felt cleaner, absolved of much of the pressure on his shoulders.

He decided to seek his father's wisdom. He called early in the morning, but his father had already been up to pray *Fajr* at dawn.

"My son."

"Father. I'm glad to speak with you." Again, he told his story, while in the back of his mind, he wondered about the secret agent job. If he dropped the kingdom's need into Mansour's lap at this moment, Mansour wasn't at all sure what he'd say.

Faisal listened patiently and remained silent for several

moments longer than most would be comfortable handling. "You might wish to be patient and wait a bit longer. It may not be the best time to leave now before Nadia has finished her degree."

This was good advice, and Mansour decided to follow it. Patience was a virtue he needed to work on.

Eleven projects kept Mansour busy day to day, and he almost forgot about the position he'd applied for until he received an email. It explained that a grievance had been filed for the handling of the process of accepting the applications and the scheduling of the interviews. After resolving this issue, the process had started again, and the deadline for accepting applications was in ten days. They repeated the same statement regarding previous applicants not needing to apply again. Even more people would apply this time.

Mansour muttered, "*Que sera, sera*–whatever will be, will be." Worrying too much would help no one and accomplish nothing. Instead, he kept his faith in God.

A couple of weeks went by, and Mansour received a call to schedule an interview for the third time. He almost said, "No, I'm not interested anymore!" Instead, he controlled his anger and frustration and kept his cool. By now he'd studied very well for the project manager interview. He'd almost memorized *The Project Management Handbook*, which covered the project delivery process and its different phases, transportation programs, various types of organizations in managing projects, and tools used to support the management of project delivery.

Tensions were high the day of the interview; obviously he didn't want to blow it. It wasn't easy to reach this point, but he did his best to stay calm. When he entered the interview room, he recognized most of the interview panel, three men and one woman. As a resident engineer, he had coordinated project work with a couple on the panel. The rest looked very familiar, and it put him at ease.

They asked only a couple of questions about his current

work experience, and the rest of the questions were about how he would perform as a project manager. Mansour went through his answers smoothly, answered to their satisfaction, and then continued. He kept adding more information, speaking quickly as he'd memorized a lot from the handbook. Most of the panel were busy writing and barely had time to look at him. Then he realized he didn't want to overdo it, so he summarized and concluded quickly.

One of the panel members, with a slight chuckle said, "I think you got this covered pretty well." The rest of the panel looked at the man who spoke as if he was breaking some unspoken rule. The man's face turned a bit red, then he looked down at his notes.

At the end of the interview Mansour thanked them and shook hands with all of them. He teetered on the brink of wondering if he'd overdone it and thinking the panel member's comment meant he was definitely going to get the job.

Four days later they called, wanting to know if he'd accept the position of project manager. He would, and did.

They gave him a high profile project that needed a lot of attention, detailed work, and plenty of coordination with different divisions and agencies, all in the space of his first two days on the job. They were two projects combined into one.

This meant putting in more than the required forty hours per week, missing jiujitsu sessions, and seeing Nadia for a grand total of about an hour before bedtime. There was no overtime for the senior position, though. After he delivered this project, more projects arrived and the workload piled up. This was all good for Mansour because he was eager to gain the experience and do it in the shortest time possible. He had a lot to learn but had a wide-angle view compared to when he'd been in construction. Now in charge of the entire project, its funding, scope, schedule, and all the permits needed before getting the project to construction, the whole of it fell directly under his purview. He dealt with different people across the spectrum of administrative levels, in all departments.

Mansour understood that success didn't exist in a vacuum. It required excellent communication with the team, as well as respect and trust. No one had all the answers, but he knew how to get the answers by tapping into the collective knowledge of the organization. Eventually he managed to find a work-life balance that suited both him and his adorable wife.

The routine of it swallowed him up: making a difference from nine to five, and sometimes nine to seven, seeing eye to eye with his boss, the size of his new office, and most importantly the multimillion-dollar public-works projects he handled on a daily basis.

Another four years passed, during which time Mansour earned his Project Management Professional certificate (PMP) from the Project Management Institute (PMI), his Value Methodology Associate (VMA)–through SAVE International–and LEED Green Associate Certification from the Green Building Council. A lot of credentials and even more acronyms.

Nadia, in the meantime, finished up her medical schooling and worked through her residency. She looked forward to a position at a local hospital as a pediatrician.

Life, in other words, was good.

Around Nadia's sixth month practicing, Faisal returned to Arlandica, sat down with Mansour over tea, and said the words he hadn't known he didn't want to hear.

"It's time, my son."

His stomach froze. "It's time?"

Honestly, he shouldn't have let his emotions get out of control like this. He'd known this was coming, and he was getting to the point in the project manager position where he was getting restless again, like he needed a challenge. None of this was unexpected . . . He'd just forgotten about it.

"*Habibti?*" he called.

Nadia appeared with coffee and her mother's homemade baklava.

"When did you get that?" Mansour asked. "I could smell it in the kitchen but couldn't find it."

"That's because I hid it so well, *habibi*," Nadia teased.

Both Mansour and Faisal reached for a piece of the flaky confection. As if choreographed by some offstage director, they tasted the treat in precise unison. Both uttered an agreeable sound of satisfaction. Jamila's baking was legendary.

After finishing his baklava, Mansour drew in a deep breath. "Could you have a seat, my love?" he asked.

Clearly startled by the somber tone, she sat.

"I hope you can understand, and believe me when I say there was every chance this day wouldn't come. It was possible the kingdom would never call on me. But . . . in high school I overheard my father talking with the soon-to-be king about a plan, just a wild, speculative plan. My father was initially against it, but he soon saw the wisdom in my uncle's words, and after some convincing, he approved."

He leaned forward. "His Royal Highness, the king of Terra Qurayshia, has set up a committee to study and formulate a detailed, multistage hundred-year plan. This committee will carefully analyze our current situation with respect to the general economy, the business climate, the education system, and even the political system and introducing democracy in our kingdom."

Nadia took all this in quietly, with a sip of coffee and nothing else, while Faisal took a bite of the baklava and nodded slightly.

"Only the most influential members of the royal family are on the committee—my father included. The plan is to fully understand where to go in the future, and for that we must determine exactly where we are now."

"This sounds like a noble and ambitious plan," Nadia said. "It must be difficult for the king to plan to abdicate some of his power."

"You are truly insightful and compassionate," Faisal said quietly. "We plan to gather as much information as humanly possible, so with God's help, we might fully understand the present situation—the positives *and* the negatives—from as many angles as possible. The kingdom's most valuable resource must of course be its people. And indeed it has many trusted people—valued citizens who have studied and worked in western countries like Arlandica and several countries in Western Hellea. If some of these men and women were to return to Terra Qurayshia and share their knowledge with the rest of the kingdom—what a benefit to the country and its future."

Nadia fell silent, but Mansour knew this was one of her habits—a considering silence, one in which Nadia's hyper-competent mind processed and saw many facets of a situation faster than even he could.

Faisal turned to Mansour. "You don't know how important and valuable you are, my son. You are bright, honest, and loyal to the king. He knows this and has asked about you whenever we met."

Nadia appeared to like the sound of that.

"And you have practical work experience with a government agency." He turned his attention back to Nadia. "Now, what if a gifted, intelligent young man—like your husband, for instance—who had spent many years here in Arlandica, educated and experienced in a practical field, such as civil engineering, were to return and observe the current state of affairs from a different angle?"

"What sort of angle?" she asked slowly.

"Mansour has been away from the kingdom for a very long time. He can speak fluent Keeryptian dialect and could easily pass as a Keeryptian-Arlandican."

Nadia's serious expression deepened. "Please tell me more."

Faisal took a sip of his coffee and continued. "We, the committee that is, would very much like your husband to return to Terra Qurayshia—not as Prince Mansour, but as Mansour, a Keeryptian-Arlandican—with his mother's family name, of course."

"To what end?" she asked. "Why go through all that trouble?"

"If Mansour returned as a prince, he would be treated with the artificially protective airs afforded only to royalty. He would be coddled and pampered by every obsequious yes-man in the kingdom . . . but he would learn nothing. As a result, we would learn nothing."

Mansour was shocked by his father's frankness. His dad obviously felt very strongly about this subject.

"But if he returns as a Keeryptian-Arlandican, a commoner, albeit a very well educated and experienced one, he will be privy to the inner workings of society and commerce, and can be of great use to our people and our king. Mansour, posing as a foreigner of only average importance, will be able to see and observe the situation from a far more honest perspective."

Nadia returned to fact-digestion mode. Her eyes swirled over the dining room but took in and dealt with vast amounts of information all at once.

"It will be safe, but it will mean living and working in the kingdom for, we envision, around two years."

She let out a shaky breath. "Two years."

Mansour wanted to take her by the hand and comfort her but knew better. Instead he leaned forward, and in his gentlest tone said, "I'm a civil engineer, my love. I've been working toward bettering society my whole career. And the king has asked that I go undercover as a civil engineer, to help the royal family understand how to make the country better for everyone."

Nadia's shaking hand slowly set the coffee cup back on its saucer.

"I hope you can understand how sorry I am to have kept a secret like this," he said. "For years it has been a specter, a ghost following me around, but it never manifested, until now."

"And most importantly of all," Faisal added, "like any other job offer, you may turn it down."

Nadia sat, still and silent, for a short time. Then she stood, collected up their coffee cups and saucers onto a tray, and headed for the kitchen without a word.

Chapter 27

4 months ago
Arlandica

Nadia came to bed that night, wordless again. She'd been on the phone earlier, but he hadn't tried to eavesdrop. Those days were behind him . . . and perhaps ahead of him, but he wasn't about to spy on his own wife. Either she would come around, or she would not.

For a time, she sat beside him in silence and he kept his peace. But because he was Mansour and was the way he was, he couldn't simply stand by and watch.

"May I tell you a story, dear one? A true story."

She squeezed his hand.

"Before we were married, I headed to the beach, down Willow Boulevard. It wasn't long after I bumped into you . . . I remember I was listening to *The Wave*, 94.7, and thinking over what I'd learned from Dr. Hathout's latest lecture. He'd been talking about how the more responsibilities a person has, the more resources they have access to. Wealth, knowledge, time, health, whatever you have, you must give. If someone has all, they should give all. This is in the last part of sura 2:3—the pious people give from what they've been given.

"I parked in the parking structure and started walking to the beach. While waiting for the light on Coronado Avenue to cross Fernando Avenue, I saw a lady at the opposite side just starting to cross because she had her face buried in her phone. A speeding car was heading toward her, and the driver didn't slow down. Perhaps he wasn't paying close attention to the road. His traffic light was green, the pedestrian light was red. A large Black man abruptly lunged out, grabbed the lady, and pulled her back to the sidewalk. She screamed and dropped her handbag out of fright. It took her a couple of seconds to realize that he'd actually saved her life. She thanked the man and almost cried."

Nadia gasped at the story but held her silence.

"This shook me. The pedestrian light turned green, and I felt it was a message. See, the man could've just done nothing. He could've watched an accident happen in front of him. No one would blame him; he didn't cause it. But he chose in a split second to take action, not just be an observer. He chose to be an active participant in saving someone's life. The consequences of not taking an action would've been detrimental to the lady, her family, and to the driver of the vehicle and his family. He saved two people and prevented the pain and suffering their families would have had to bear."

He sighed. "This is something I've fought with for years. As a teenager I thought it might be great fun, and I threw myself into the job. I tried to fix all my family troubles in Keerypt for my spring break. Then I grew angry with my father about it, since I felt he didn't trust me enough to tell me about it. And then . . . the situation just fell off my radar. In truth, you came along, and you have been my everything since I saw you in the Islamic Center."

Nadia blinked several times in thought, and kept her face neutral. "This . . . is a serious matter. And sudden. We need to think about it logically without tangling our emotions up in it."

"I couldn't agree more, and I am thinking logically. I see a lot of good things coming out of this. In truth, I'd be thrilled to be the man on the sidewalk."

"You may mistake your work at SDOT for something less, Mansour, but it's possible that through your work, you've saved hundreds of lives."

The depth of her thinking caught Mansour by surprise. He'd been involved in dozens of projects throughout the years. Perhaps the guardrails, the highway maintenance, and the traffic through many projects had saved people's lives. It wasn't impossible.

"Do you mind if I ask my parents their opinion?"

"I don't mind, my dear. If they have any reservations, I'd like to discuss it with them as well."

Mansour wanted to give Nadia some space, so the following morning he went to his home office to take care of some bills and check on his investments of stocks and mutual funds. He then looked into employment opportunities in the kingdom. He could turn them down if she had a strong objection. Not long after, he heard Nadia call her parents, muffled as it was through the wall.

When she emerged, she was smiling. He arched a questioning eyebrow at her.

"My mother was worried we'd had a quarrel. I assured her it was not the case."

"Lovely!"

"Would you like to come? I'd rather you be there. And we haven't been over to my parents' house in a while."

As soon as they arrived at her parents' home, Mansour gave her free rein to explain the entire situation to Jamila and Mustafa, including her discussion with Mansour. Her parents had shown themselves to be wise and not rush to judgment.

"I notice you've been silent, Mansour."

"I didn't wish to attempt to sway you one way or another. I believed Nadia could present the facts impartially, and she did a perfect job."

Mustafa turned his attention to Nadia and gestured good-naturedly toward Mansour. "Nadia, *habibti,* please let us look at some facts. First, Mansour is a good husband, and he cares about you. Second, he did tell all of us that he was thinking to get into business in either Terra Qurayshia or Keerypt. Third, he told you from the very beginning that he was a Terra Qurayshian prince."

"I agree with you," Jamila said, "but this latest plan that he and his dad have will not be building up on his career. He will be sacrificing his time for something else. Two years is not nothing, and this . . . spy business feels . . ." She rose and brought in the tray of tea and that homemade baklava Mansour so loved. "It feels low, somehow."

"Yes, that's true," Mustafa admitted. "However, you and Nadia are assuming that these years will be a total waste of time. That may not be the case. I can see that perhaps this experience may raise him to a higher level in his career. If he is successful in his mission, which I hope he would be, he may establish a consultant business. It would not just be in Terra Qurayshia but international, given his connections and social status in Terra Qurayshia and in Keerypt."

Nadia leaned forward. "What about me? What will happen to my career?"

Jamila poured the tea, and set out a small plate of baklava for each of them. "Yes, I am concerned about Nadia's career. We don't know what will happen in the future. My daughter should not neglect her career."

"Mansour did say that they can get me a good job in Terra Qurayshia, but I'm sure they're not as advanced over there as we are here in Arlandica."

"That's not totally true. Some hospitals in Jumairah are at a very high level, and they are connected internationally with research and development happening elsewhere. The whole world now is more connected."

"Dad, you sound like you just want me to go there with my husband."

"I want you to be supportive of your good husband, and I don't see that doing that would hurt you. There is, of course, some sacrifice from your part, but that is totally fine. That's what a family should do. There have to be some sacrifices for the whole family to succeed in their relationship and in the outcome of the relationship. By that I mean benefits to you and your husband as one unit. And the ultimate success in the hereafter."

They all fell silent and looked at each other. Mustafa's wise grin became contagious. Jamila and Nadia smiled and took a deep breath at the same time.

"Okay, Dad, I think I'm convinced now. I'm just curious, did Mansour call you about this at all?"

Mansour smiled and raised his hands in defense but kept his silence.

"No, my dear daughter, he did not. I just can almost feel what he's feeling. As men, we always want to have support from our beloved wives. Sometimes, unfortunately, we get caught up in a selfish mode and we ask, 'What's in it for me?' In a good relationship between a husband and wife, that question should not be asked. Your mom made sacrifices for me to succeed in my work, and we are all reaping the reward."

"Yes, but not Marwan."

Mustafa's face became red and sullen. Jamila likewise found the tea tray especially fascinating, and silence invaded the room.

"It was my mistake that I spoiled Marwan and did not observe him carefully. Please don't confuse Marwan's outcome with what I'm talking about. You didn't turn out like your brother, so it's also a personal choice."

Nadia sighed. "Sorry, Dad; I'm not disagreeing with you. I just feel very bad about what happened to Marwan."

"We all do, and I pray for him every day," her mother said quietly.

"Me too," Mustafa and Nadia said at the same time. They turned, seeming to realize Mansour was in the room.

He gave his wife a bright smile before turning to her mother and father. "I thank you for your candor and wisdom." Then he returned his attention to Nadia and again arched that same questioning eyebrow.

"Of course, my dear husband, I will support you. I was just reaffirming my thinking."

Mansour gave Nadia a big, long hug.

He spent the next several months working, all the while looking for jobs in Terra Qurayshia through consulting firms and recruiters. The paperwork for his new identity was done and ready for Mansour just before he found some suitable positions and started applying to several of them using his new last name.

One of several applications he sent out was to AIPM, an international engineering company that specialized in construction and project management. They asked him to confirm that he was still interested in working in Terra Qurayshia and if so to provide some information about himself and his identity. The email looked authentic and Mansour replied back with the requested information. A couple of days later, he received a phone call from the same consultant asking him when he'd be available for a phone interview for the position for which he had applied. Mansour was pleasantly surprised with the interest shown and with the turnaround time of the response.

This was happening. He was going to be a secret agent.

On the specified date and time, Mansour's phone rang. Ayman, a manager from the engineering department overseas, was calling for the interview. Ayman had an obvious Middle Eastern accent and a strong, low-pitched and full-of-energy voice. He started speaking in English. "Hello, may I speak with Mansour please?"

"Yes, this is he."

Ayman broke the ice by asking whether Mansour wanted to have the interview in English or Arabic, and Mansour's only request was not to speak both at once. Part of the interview was in either language, but Mansour made sure to only speak Keeryptian dialect and not at all in Terra Qurayshian Arabic.

Ayman clucked his tongue. "Okay, *bash muhandes,* chief engineer, sounds good. Please go ahead and tell me briefly your background and professional development from graduating from college till today."

Mansour did his best to be brief while covering everything he'd done.

"That's great, really very good," Ayman said. "Let me ask you a personal question. Why do you want to come and work over here? Please don't get me wrong; I just want to understand your situation and know if you'd be able to adjust over here. It's a very different lifestyle than in Arlandica, I am sure you know."

"Yes, of course I understand your question, and it's very valid. However, as you know, I am originally from Keerypt, so I'm very familiar with the different cultures, and I've been to Terra Qurayshia a few times to visit with my parents. The main reason is that I want to be closer to Keerypt and also to improve my financial situation." Mansour almost choked, but he held himself—he didn't like to lie, but in this case, he had to, unfortunately.

"I totally understand, and that's almost always the case with all the expats over here. It's a financial reason. Do you plan on coming here by yourself or with your family?"

"I'd like to bring my wife along."

"You don't have kids, then."

"No, I don't yet. After this assignment, of course."

Ayman chuckled. "Do you have any questions for me?"

"Yes. How long will it take for me to know if I'll be going to Terra Qurayshia?"

"That's a good question. We have screened the applicants, and I just need to call twenty more people to interview them. Ha ha ha . . . I'm just kidding, *ya bash mohandes.* I actually have only one more person to interview. So you are a semifinalist. I expect you should find out within a week, at the most."

The interview lasted for about forty minutes. Overall, Mansour felt it went well.

Two days later, he received an email congratulating him for a successful interview, informing him that he had conditional approval, and asking him the earliest date he'd be ready to start work in Terra Qurayshia. The email came a lot sooner than he'd expected. His approval was conditioned upon successfully completing a medical exam, background check, obtaining a work visa in Terra Qurayshia, and the final salary agreement. Mansour wasn't worried about these conditions. He received a call a day later from AIPM Human Resources to discuss the salary and explain to him the onboarding process. It was all new to him and amusing at the same time. He never knew how much paperwork was involved in working in Terra Qurayshia as a foreigner.

One of the questions HR asked Mansour was whether he'd travel on a single status or family status. He told them he wanted his wife to accompany him, but they said that initially, in the first three months, he must be alone until he'd completed all his paperwork and probation in Terra Qurayshia.

The embarking process started, and Mansour went through it with a feeling that he was preparing for a play in a theater. It didn't feel real to him. It was just an adventure, a pretend game. It also felt very strange for him to need a work visa to go and work in his own country. It took a while for all this to appear real to Mansour.

At work, he spoke with Fareed and then his friend Ahmed about the kingdom. Ahmed had gone there for a similar work assignment but only had complaints about the backward and stubborn stance many of the office workers took in Terra Qurayshia.

"The mentality, attitude, and way of thinking is very different. The culture over there, unfortunately, is about finding someone to blame and spending more time and energy on who did what and when rather than focusing on how to fix a problem. And there are many problems because of the decision-making process."

"Well, I'm interested to go there and make a difference."

Ahmed smiled, but it wasn't a smile Mansour saw often. This one was full of dark bitterness. "That's what I thought too; I wanted to make a difference. Unfortunately, no one over there cared to learn about my experience or making a change in the system. Maybe because you're Terra Qurayshian, you can make a difference. But I doubt it as you must be really well connected to make an impact. I hope I'm wrong."

The night before his flight, Mansour felt a mixture of deep sadness at leaving his wife behind, but he also had a strange feeling of adventure and even excitement. As he packed his things, he thought of the challenges he'd face. He already missed his wife—even before the trip. When Nadia came home, Mansour rushed to her and embraced her in his strong arms. No words were spoken. Their eyes, full of love, met each other and spoke to each other in silence. They kissed. Mansour felt Nadia tremble and hold him tight as if to say "Please don't go, my *habibi*!"

Their lips parted and Mansour could taste Nadia's salty tears as he kissed his wife's soft cheeks.

He saw an angry, deep sadness in Nadia's eyes.

"My love, please."

She nodded. "I understand your mission, intellectually. Emotionally, it's more difficult to accept. I agreed with your reasoning. I consented to this trip. But that doesn't mean I have to like it. I don't like it at all."

He took her hand and placed his forehead against hers. "This will be for the better. A few months, and we'll be together. I love you so much, *habibti*," Mansour said to his dear wife. "I'll think of you every minute of every hour of every day until we are together again."

Nadia gave her husband a tight squeeze and smiled. They held each other for a long time, feeding off their love for each other.

The time came to gather his things and prepare for his long trip. Mansour knew that Nadia would be okay. He trusted that God would watch over her—and she'd be staying with her parents. Still, he didn't want to leave his young wife behind—not even for a short time.

Mansour could see Nadia's thoughts in her eyes. Despite the relatively short time they'd been together as husband and wife, she'd grown really close to her husband. Nadia could already read Mansour's moods and thoughts like the pages of an open book.

"Now, my husband, don't you worry about me. I'll be okay. I'll have my work and my parents to keep me occupied. We can call each other every day, and our hearts will be filled with each other . . ." Nadia's words came out choked by her strong feelings.

Mansour smiled a loving smile and held his wife close to his heart. "Nadia, *habibti,* what did I do to deserve such a wonderful and beautiful wife?"

On their drive to the airport, they tried to cheer each other up. Mansour gave Nadia a brief reminder of the importance of his mission to his homeland and how it would not only help his country but also help their future. The challenge wouldn't be easy, but the rewards were potentially great.

Mansour completed the boarding process and received a one-way airline ticket from Sunland to Jumairah, of course in economy class–he'd never flown economy before.

It's all real now, Mansour thought. He felt disconnected and depressed at leaving his beautiful young wife behind. Still, it wouldn't be long. And who knew how he'd be able to help the kingdom from his lowly position as *bash mohandes*?

Chapter 28

3 months ago
Terra Qurayshia

Anyone who'd driven for days or flown halfway across the world would understand the exhaustion that consumed Mansour over the course of the next twenty hours of cramped flight, layover, shuffling in line, and yet another cramped flight.

He dreamed of his childhood, of the first three years of elementary school in Zomorod. He'd been chauffeured to school in a large armored SUV and had his school bag carried for him to the class and from the class to the SUV. He'd played with a lot of kids, both friends and his many cousins, but he could only remember a few of their names now. He then moved to Keerypt for four years, where he completed his elementary school. He had a lot fewer cousins in Keerypt, but he enjoyed playing with them just as much, and spending time with his grandmother, especially during summer by the sea. After that, he moved to West Beach to start middle school there. He'd visited Terra Qurayshia and Keerypt several times since moving to Sunland. His life was like chapters in a book, and the dream like flipping through the pages.

Finally, Mansour landed in Jumairah. This time, no one waited for Mansour at the tarmac; no VIP or royal treatment. He had to take care of all the paperwork and details by himself—a new experience for him, but he felt up to the challenge. He picked up his carry-on bag and walked down the plane's stairs—there were no passenger boarding bridges in Jumairah.

He followed the signs to go to the passport service lines, not for citizens but for visitors with work permits. A series of very long lines, as it turned out. It didn't look good at all. He'd been through long lines in Sunland plenty of times, and these usually went fast, no more than ten to fifteen minutes of waiting. So he stood in line and got his Arlandican passport and documents ready.

In the back of his mind, he considered getting his cell phone ready to call his father or Abdulaziz, if he needed help. Then he crushed that thought. He couldn't chicken out so quickly. If he couldn't take standing in the airport, he definitely wouldn't be able to handle life in a foreign country. He turned off his cell phone and put it away.

Instead, he noted down the lines in his pocket notebook as one of the first aspects of life in Terra Qurayshia that could be improved—the first of what turned out to be many.

The process was clearly inefficient, and the passport officers were very slow and chatting with each other, laughing, and sometimes texting on their phones. Families stood staring, with young kids who were crying, clearly exhausted. This was the kingdom's first chance to make an impression on visitors, and it left a lot to be desired.

After nearly three hours, he ended up shouting in his Keeryptian-accented Arabic for the officers to get on with it, to do their jobs. What followed was pretty amazing: the men scrambled into positions, organized those waiting into several lines, and got people moving almost at once. He ended up waiting only fifteen minutes after his outburst.

From there he collected his baggage at the claim carousel, wondering how many dozens of times his bags had gone around in circles while he'd waited in the unbelievable lines.

He found a young Pradeshi man, fairly short, waiting for him outside the gate. Joseph had a sign with Mansour's name on it, along with the AIPM company name. Mansour was a very common name in these parts, and his Keeryptian last name, Abdel Ghany, was too. Luckily Joseph had a photo of Mansour so he identified him quickly.

Joseph kept himself well, with a carefully cropped mustache and a nice suit, and was cheerful during the drive to Mansour's company-provided residence. It was a fair drive, and despite Joseph's exuberant questioning, Mansour felt the exhaustion of travel blotting out his mind. After a few minutes, Joseph turned on the local news and allowed Mansour to drift in and out of consciousness.

He started awake when they reached the house.

"You'll want to get to bed soon." Joseph handed Mansour a key to the house, then began unloading Mansour's things and lugging them toward the small, somewhat dingy house. "Normally we start at seven sharp, but I'll be here to pick you up tomorrow at eight. You've had a long journey, yes?"

Mansour could barely respond but mumbled his thanks and stood wobbling on his feet. It felt good that someone cared for his comfort and convenience without knowing his true identity. He liked Joseph.

The work-provided house was meager by any standards. The quality of furniture, the finishings, the windows, and the old, loud window-type air conditioning units. Nonetheless, Mansour had no real complaints. Nadia wouldn't be here for months, and he could give it a good scrubbing in the meantime.

He had plenty to do: paperwork and procedures both. This all got moving when Joseph picked up Mansour in the morning. They had to go to the medical center for Mansour to get a health check on file. Mansour wrote some notes about all the tests that had to be repeated, as he saw no good reason for doing that other than lack of trust in the tests done overseas. Most of the foreigners came from other developing countries, and Mansour wondered if that had anything to do with the redundancy of medical exams.

He'd finished with most of the paperwork and some of the medical by morning's end. In the afternoon, he went to the office to meet his boss, Nadeem, known as Abou Youssef. In contrast with Keerypt, in Terra Qurayshia and that region, adults were called by their oldest son's name if they had a son, and if they didn't, by their oldest daughter's name. It was considered an insult if you called someone by their first name unless you were really very close to that person. So he was expected to use *Abou* (meaning father of) and then the kid's name, which meant he had to memorize the person's name and their son or daughter's name. Not a problem for Mansour, though he was much more used to calling Arlandicans by their first names.

A couple of weeks went by, with frequent calls to Nadia and his father, and Mansour started to get settled in. He first discovered that the building's elevator didn't work, and hadn't worked in the five years the front security guard had been there. He was also issued a computer but quickly found his internet didn't work except for a few hours each afternoon. He suspected, at first, that this was a prank pulled on him by some of the staff, but their laughter over his confusion was genuine; the internet didn't work, and wouldn't until just after lunch. Upon submitting a request for full-time internet access, he was flummoxed to hear his boss loudly announce to his assistant to remind him to submit the request the following week.

The following day, he got a phone on his desk. He didn't even ask for it, so he was impressed, even though it was a very simple phone—light beige in color with push buttons and nothing else. It only called local numbers and couldn't call any cell phone at all. He had to use the fax machine to call consultants on their cell phones. If they called him back, all they'd get was the non-harmonic music generated by the fax machine!

After a week at work, Mansour was told about the signing in policy at the office. Apparently, every employee had to sign in when they came in in the morning, sign out before lunch, sign in after lunch, and finally sign out when they left for the day. Mansour had never done this kind of thing before. All the sign-in sheets from the various units and departments were collected and faxed to the main office for the deputies of the executive president to go over. The surveillance level was mind-boggling, but he reminded himself to follow the policies without complaint. He had to overlook all these inconveniences and keep the bigger picture in mind.

Mansour kept adding to the list of improvements needed in his report to file with Abdulaziz and his father.

During that time, he reviewed his projects and got familiar with the work process. His boss, Nadeem (Abou Youssef), arranged for him to spend three days circulating through different departments, to meet people all over the company and to become familiar with the organization. Mansour found it very useful and beneficial. He took a lot of notes to learn about the work procedures and filled up his business card holder.

During this quick rotation, Mansour met some very nice people: Abdulrahman (Abou Mohammad) from the finance and budgeting department and Kamal in engineering, the same department as Mansour but from the technical support section, or TSS. He got along well with both of them and planned on meeting them after work, as they were both married, but their wives weren't in Jumairah. Kamal's wife was in Keerypt and Abdulrahman usually went home to his wife in Rayef, about a hundred miles east of Jumairah, on weekends. They both lived a single life in Jumairah. The same day they met at work, they met at night at Culture Café & Lounge by the sea. They talked for a couple of hours and enjoyed their time, as it was Thursday night, and the next day was the weekend. They got to know each other more and talked about their families, and eventually the conversation turned toward complaints about work, which was just what Mansour needed.

The next day Mansour prayed *Fajr* (the early and first prayer of the day between dawn and sunrise) at the *masjid*, which was close-by, only a few minutes' walk from Mansour's house. He stayed there, reading the Qur'an until about twenty minutes after sunrise, then prayed two *rakat,* and then went home. Apparently, by doing that, it counted as *Umrah* and *Hajj,* which surprised him.

"Abou Farris wants to see you," a tinny voice told him through his useless desk telephone the next morning at work. He ranked above Mansour's boss by an entire level, which made Mansour sweat for a moment. He wondered what Abou Farris wanted; surely he hadn't been identified, had he?

But the dark, smiling man with his glasses and thick beard smiled and waved Mansour in, dispelling his worries.

"I come back from vacation and find we have a new Arlandican on staff!"

Mansour bowed. "Keeryptian-Arlandican, but yes, Abou Farris."

"They must do things very differently overseas. I see here you worked with SDOT for a number of years."

"That's correct, sir."

"How about for the next three or four weeks, we give you an assignment? Have a look around the departments and see how things might be improved, could you?"

Mansour's heart leaped. It was exactly like his more secretive assignment. What a lovely surprise!

Farris went on: "Talk with anyone you feel you should. I'll send a memo around. Let's see what kind of improvements and suggestions you come up with."

Mansour thanked Abou Farris and explained that he was very keen to get on with this assignment.

These weeks practically flew by. As per his new assignment, Mansour arranged meetings with various employees and managers, beginning with the engineering department. He had decided to begin with his own department and subsequently set up meetings with other departments which worked closely with his, such as construction.

Some of the managers were skeptical and said that they'd done something similar before, only to have nothing come of it.

Mansour told them that this time was different, that the director was very interested in making changes and was committed to making it happen. He found out that other departments were very frustrated with the engineering department and had plenty of negative things to say.

A month later found him seated nervously outside Abou Farris's office. He'd tried to squash the homesickness by attending a barbecue with a fellow Arlandican from the company, and with frequent calls to Nadia, but his nervousness grew steadily as the day approached.

Abou Farris's assistant Shahid had scheduled him for 10–11 a.m. on Thursday, so at 10 a.m. sharp, Mansour was at the director's office, waiting for Shahid to let him in. Apparently, he had an important meeting full of people, as Mansour could hear many people talking. Whatever the conversation, it seemed like a hot issue, as the conversation was intense. Ten minutes passed. Mansour kept waiting in the reception area on the long red bench and decided to pick up and start reading one of the magazines on the table.

It was going to be a while.

He took a deep breath and sat back and relaxed on the bench with a project management magazine. Instead of reading, though, Mansour decided to organize his thoughts to have a good start as a practice for good communication. He usually tended to jump into the issue without proper introductions. It was now 10:20 a.m., and an anxious Mansour looked to the assistant.

"Sorry, sir, the meeting has taken longer than expected," Shahid said.

"Yes, I can see that. Is that common?" Mansour asked.

Shahid only had a blank stare in response.

"Do meetings usually run longer than expected?" Mansour asked.

"Sometimes, sir." Shahid seemed apologetic, but Mansour's

itchy nerves didn't care for apologies. Another ten minutes and then he'd reschedule.

At 10:28 exactly, the director's door opened and about twelve people came out, two at a time. At 10:30, Mansour finally entered Abou Farris's office. He had only half an hour remaining to go over all these important recommendations, and he was not in a great condition to get them across.

Should I go over an introduction or just skip to the issues as I usually do? Mansour thought to himself.

"*Assalamu alaikum,* Abou Farris, I know we have limited time so allow me to get into my findings with a brief overview." Mansour shook hands with Abou Farris and motioned for him to be seated.

"Yes, please go ahead," Abou Farris replied while walking to his desk chair to sit down.

Mansour sat on the chair facing the desk.

"There was a noticeable issue with delivering our projects over here in the engineering department as well as in the construction department. Most projects, about seventy percent, were not on time, within budget, or scope. At SDOT, we had a similar experience and found a solution." Mansour paused to gauge the director's reaction.

"Well, you have my attention, and I am curious to know what the solution was," Abou Farris said while staring at Mansour.

"In the early nineties the top management at SDOT, frustrated by project delivery issues statewide, launched a Project Management Peer Review conducted by the Arlandican Army Corps of Engineers, a major international organization, and the navy," Mansour said.

Abou Farris stood while looking at Mansour with keen interest. "What would you like to drink?" he asked and rang the bell for Shahid.

Shahid appeared in the office in a couple of seconds. "Yes, sir?" he asked.

Mansour hated to break stride but felt he must ask for something. He just hoped Abou Farris was interested and not bound by the limited time they had left.

"Water is fine, thank you," Mansour said quickly.

"You must drink something else beside water," Abou Farris said.

"Tea would be good," Mansour said to get Shahid out of the office and the focus back to the presentation.

"Please continue, you've got me in suspense," Abou Farris said.

"To make a long story short, the peer review findings and recommendations were reviewed by the SDOT task force, which resulted in revisions to project management practice in SDOT. Some of these, the applicable ones, are included in the list I've prepared." Mansour handed Abou Farris a copy of the two pages of recommendations he'd labored over.

"I met with many colleagues and managers from the engineering department, the construction department, and project management department. Their input is also included in the recommendations."

Abou Farris looked at the recommendations and started reading them.

"Your tea is ready, sir," Shahid said as he opened the door and brought in the tea and a bottle of cold water on a tray.

Mansour stood up to take the tea and water and placed them on the small table between his chair and the other chair facing the desk. Mansour sat down and picked up his copy of the recommendations to go over them with Abou Farris. Instead of reading each point word by word, Mansour wanted to summarize the main points.

He started explaining, "The project management style in general needs to be changed. Project managers should have a much stronger role and authority, which will need support from upper management."

Abou Farris looked up from the paper with a distinctly disappointed gaze.

Mansour hurried on. "Again, from my experience at SDOT, implementing the new project management system, even though it faced a lot of resistance initially, proved to be a great success." Mansour spoke confidently, trying to gain back the director's interest.

Abou Farris returned his attention to the recommendations, yet his expression remained full of doubt and dismay.

Mansour felt it was time to get into the meat of the recommendations. "In addition to implementing a strong matrix organization from a project management perspective, some functional units need to be moved from one department to another department. For example, the as-built section in the urban planning department needs to move to the construction department. The survey group needs to move from the urban planning department to the engineering department."

"What do you mean a strong matrix organization?"

"It means that each project manager, or PM, works across functional units and each PM reports to the principal in the project management department. Each functional unit in different departments reports to a functional manager. It also means that project managers would have a stronger role and more authority in controlling the schedule, cost, and scope of their projects."

Abou Farris turned the page, his face even more despondent.

Mansour continued, "We need to establish new sections in the construction department. For example, a constructability review section and estimates section. In the engineering department we need to establish right-of-way engineering, engineering services to include hydraulics, material investigations, and stormwater. Another section would be traffic management and roadway design. There are more points on the list, as you can see."

Abou Farris continued reading the list but soon put down the paper. "This is not what I am looking for. This goes against the newly adopted strategic plan of the organization."

No. He'd worked so hard on this and invested a lot of energy. Worse, he was right.

He could simply announce himself as a prince, fire the director and get him out of the way so these recommendations could be implemented. If Abou Farris had known Mansour was a prince, his reaction would've been totally different. He would've said, "These are all wonderful and brilliant suggestions, Your Highness," and they would've been implemented immediately.

Unfortunately, ideas were not measured on their own merits, but by who said them. Which was why Mansour was concealing his identity.

Mansour asked Abou Farris, "So what are you looking for? What kind of improvements are you thinking of?"

Abou Farris said, "I need recommendations that are within the strategic plan. Nothing major like what you have listed here."

Mansour hadn't had access to this strategic plan, by the way, and didn't know it existed. Fury rose in him, but he squashed it down. He tried to get more meaningful information out of Abou Farris, but the boss told him practically nothing. Still seething, he thanked Abou Farris for his time and excused himself, full of disappointment.

That day after work, Mansour headed directly home and began brainstorming issues with the corporate work culture of Terra Qurayshia to send up to the ladder in his report to his father and the king.

Problems began and stemmed from a high power distance index, or PDI—essentially the power of authority was magnified and subordinates would not dare to challenge the opinion or authority of the supervisor. What he didn't state in the report, and hoped he didn't have to, was that this was also not an Islamic value at all. Even Prophet Muhammad (peace be upon Him) did not force his authority on his companions. He allowed them to give their opinions in matters not related to religious obligations.

There was a significant difference between respect and just blindly following orders. Mansour had learned by living and working in Arlandica that you could respect someone and disagree at the same time. You may try to convince your boss of your position, and in the end, if your boss still insisted on maintaining their position, you should then concede and follow their decision as long as it was not illegal nor immoral. Here, managers didn't push back or give constructive criticism to their supervisors. Typically, they simply followed orders.

Other shortfalls Mansour had observed were managers being promoted too soon, a lack of proper training, an inability or unwillingness to listen to ideas and analyze the merits of given situations, viewing coworkers with suspicion, the culture of placing blame for mistakes, (and here he circled this and threw several warning exclamation points on top), and a general distrust of foreigners, or feeling they were inferior.

He fumed for a while before finally taking a few deep breaths and heading off to do some light grocery shopping. He couldn't wait to file this report and have Abdulaziz or his father look at it. He couldn't wait to have the king begin dismantling some of the worst aspects of the work culture he'd seen here in just his first month.

The next day at work, Mansour was reminded that it was about time to fill out the paper time sheet and turn it in. Nadeem's secretary, Ameen, showed Mansour how to fill it out. It wasn't simple and took twenty minutes to fill it out, and people who worked overtime had even more to fill out. If you made a mistake you had to start all over again. Mansour was used to doing it electronically at SDOT.

Over a couple of weekends in his eagerness to improve the system, Mansour developed a spreadsheet with macros that would take less than one minute to fill out and be done with it. He shared it with some of his colleagues. They loved it and encouraged him to submit it to HR to be adopted, and so he did, but they had no interest at all in adopting it or making any changes to the system. He was told privately by a sincere observer that being too efficient is not good for some people's job security. Mansour was sad to hear this but not surprised.

When doing his nightly reading of sura 56, he reflected on what happened at work:

Is it such a message that ye would hold in light esteem? And have ye made it your livelihood that ye should lie? (81–82)

Mansour thought on how deep these verses were. They applied to a million things, aside from clear criminal behavior and activities, they applied to inefficiencies or lies at work, to some politicians for legislating what's beneficial to them and not to the people they represent, and to some corporate practices whereby companies seek the most financially rewarding routes even at the detriment of people and society instead of following what best benefits the public.

Islam isn't against capitalism when implemented correctly, Mansour thought.

Chapter 29

Now

Black vans, armored Humvees with turrets, and even some sports cars with the decal of the Sagebrush Mercenary Company just kept appearing no matter where they went. Mansour and Nadia weaved through traffic, onto sidewalks, past distraught citizens and tourists alike as they tried to escape the mercenaries in their black camo uniforms, but it was no use. They might as well have been trying to navigate the bike through hardening concrete.

Nadia peered about frantically, trying to sight the next group of soldiers before they could sneak up on the pair. "What can we do?"

"Just keep trying," Mansour said. He shook his head and let out a frustrated sigh as a black van pulled into the intersection three blocks in front of them and swung left, heading straight for them. He revved the bike, popped over the curb onto the sidewalk and gunned it through a gas station past dismayed squawks and frightened hollers.

They were now on Nolan Avenue West, no closer to the capital than they'd been previously. Mansour looked down at the gas gauge. He was just a few spurts short from chugging on fumes.

"Nadia," he said, his voice quavering for the first time. "We aren't going to make it."

"Trust in God, Mansour."

Mansour gave a brief prayer and then felt his jaw drop as a Humvee tore into the intersection directly ahead. He shot a glance over his shoulder at the van. Nadia tightened her hold on him, and he stopped the bike for a moment. Rows of clothing stores interspersed with more practical places for tools, machinery, and electronics lined both sides of the road. Probably he could head into one of them and whip together something to help them out. If only he had time.

He noticed a side road that led past the electronics store, a big warehouse-looking building, all brick and mortar, that proclaimed itself to be the All Stop Shop. He figured there was a loading dock back there and probably a side road leading to a different block.

"Pull the bike over, Mansour. You're under arrest!" a clipped, authoritative voice boomed. It caused a flash in his mind of his wife's face as they tore a bag off her head, his unborn child kicking in her womb.

"Nadia, this is going to get crazy." Mansour angled the bike over and gunned it, almost hitting a white-haired old woman with a walker as he sped by.

"Watch it," Nadia warned.

Mansour nodded. It would take all he had to get out of this loading area before the mercenaries could cover the other exits.

The dirt bike groaned and stuttered as it shot forward and sped past the white, pull-down door that signified the store's loading dock. Yes, there was a wide one-vehicle road that intersected this one. Perfect! He leaned to the side and the bike drifted, its tires squealing and screeching their protest. Nadia's arms tightened about Mansour's waist.

The bike stuttered again. It was running on fumes. *Not good.* Mansour gave the bike all he could to just get them out of that alley. He soared ahead, but a black van and a Humvee appeared and blocked the exit. He braked and swung sideways, sending them both into a tumble to the side of the alley. Mansour lay on the ground, his breath knocked out of him. He was dimly aware of a similar group of mercenaries pulling in front of the other end of the alley, and he was sure there were soldiers coming down by way of the loading dock as well. This was it. It wasn't how he'd thought things were going to end.

Nadia stood up, holding her side. Mansour wondered if she'd cracked a rib on their drop. It hadn't been a gentle fall.

"Freeze! Hands in the hair!" A group of black-camo goons piled out of the back of the van and advanced on the pair with their weapons leveled.

"You can't shoot us. That'd bring up questions, wouldn't it?" Mansour yelled. He got off the ground. "You, all of you, are evil, and you'll get your just desserts in hell."

The man laughed. His soldiers fanned out on both sides of him into an arc. "I don't think any of us was ever expecting to go anywhere else."

Suddenly the sound of sirens came from outside the alley. Above, the rotors of an approaching chopper filtered into the closed corridor of the alley.

"This is the Palmiento Police Department," a bullhorn yelled down from above. "You are under arrest. Good job, Sagebrush, but this is our jurisdiction. We'll take it from here."

Mansour blinked as squad cars slid into position opposite the mercenary groups on both sides of the alley. No doubt others had gone to intercept the mercs at the landing dock. This was perfect. The governor was coming to save them.

He looked at Nadia and she nodded and smiled. "Told you she was the perfect candidate."

The mercenary commander growled and turned around. "Someone get Bigfoot up on the comms. We need someone with higher security clearance immediately. Spread out and take positions. Weapons ready. Don't shoot anybody unless I say so."

One of the soldiers gestured his M-16 at Mansour and Nadia.

The commander pointed at all of the exits. "We've still got him. We just need to talk the police away, Rodriguez."

The soldier nodded and joined the others in setting up a staggered defensive line against the Palmiento police. Mansour could hear more police arriving and, he assumed, more Sagebrush soldiers as well. A news chopper joined the Palmiento police chopper overhead. The merc commander saw it as well and swore.

"Bigfoot on the line, sir," a mercenary soldier yelled.

The merc commander grabbed the plastic phone from his comms pack and yelled into it. "We've got them cornered, sir. But the police are here. In force." He paused and listened. "Yes Abdul has been taken care of. Yes. Yes." The commander shook his head, his face pale. "Yes, sir, to the last man. Make the nation wonderful again, sir. Big Daddy out."

Mansour's eyes widened, and he grabbed Nadia's hand. "Run!" he screamed.

The commander swore and dropped the phone, leveling his M-16 and firing bursts of fire in their direction. "Bigfoot says kill them!" he screeched.

A few of the soldiers turned and fired at the pair, and a crescendo of shots rang as the police officers began to fire their weapons at the mercenaries. The heavy *rat-tat-tat* of fifty caliber machine-gun fire blasted from the tops of Humvees, and something exploded around the corner.

Mansour and Nadia ran to the loading dock. They could see officers and mercenaries engaged in a brutal firefight at the mouth of the alley. The two of them sprinted to a set of stairs and ran up to the door next to the loading gate. But it was locked.

"Mansour," Nadia screamed, "look out!"

Mansour dropped to the floor just in time. A three-shot burst blasted where he'd been standing, tearing holes into the door. He looked over the battlefield. The shots had come from the mercenary commander, a grizzled man with a salt-and-pepper mustache. Curiously his uniform had no insignias or rank of any kind.

"Oh, Mansour," he said, dropping the magazine and grabbing another from his ammo pouch. "Today you've done a hell of a thing. You've made me shoot police officers! Defenders of our great nation!"

Mansour stared. "That was you. You did this, all of this, when you and your mercenaries sold out to that traitor of a president."

"Please, call me Jemmings. I'm going to die here anyways, just like you, so you might as well know my real name."

Mansour grabbed the door handle and it popped off the door under his weight. Undaunted, he pushed himself back up and stood defiantly upon the dock. Another explosion tore up the alleyway and a police cruiser went up in flames. "Why have you sold out our country, Jemmings?" Mansour asked.

Nadia clung to his shoulder and watched the mercenary silently.

"Our country?" Jemmings snarled, rage clouding his face. "This is Christian land. The constitution says so. The question is why did my country sell me out, all of us Christians out? You don't belong here, Mansour. And I'm going to die a patriot for a man who's going to make this a Christian nation again."

Mansour pushed Nadia off himself, and Jemmings leveled his rifle. Mansour threw the door handle, dodged out of the way of a new three-round burst, and leaped off the dock just in time to see Jemmings stumble backward as the handle hit him in his firing eye.

"Why won't you just die!" Jemmings shouted. He fired blindly, bursts spraying across brick and mortar. Nadia screamed and headed for better cover. Mansour charged and tackled the man.

"We are Arlandicans too!" Mansour panted, putting the man in an arm bar with his legs draped across his chest. Soon he heard Jemmings scream and felt the give of the man's shoulder as it came out of the socket. He didn't stop like he'd been trained to do in jiujitsu; instead, he broke the mercenary's elbow. Only then did he roll away and get to his feet.

More dull thuds announced a series of explosions from the main road, and an APC burst through the mercenary defenders, skidding to a halt at the dock. The back ramp dropped.

"Mansour? Nadia? Get in!" a SWAT officer yelled, while

others laid down suppressive fire at the dazed and cracked line of Sagebrush soldiers up the alleyway.

Nadia got to her feet and ran to Mansour. She grabbed Jemmings' rifle from the ground and leveled it at his chest. Mansour slowly raised his hands and started to edge toward his distraught wife.

"You–you . . . monster!" Nadia cried, tears now flowing freely down her beautiful face.

Mansour grabbed her shoulder. "We must go, now, Nadia. Leave him. The courts will take care of him."

They jogged away to the SWAT team, and behind them came the anguished scream of a broken man. "Nooooo!" the mercenary commander's cracked voice bellowed.

Mansour turned and saw the man stand, helmetless, and pull a 9mm pistol from a hidden holster. Before the SWAT officers could react, he put the pistol to his temple and pulled the trigger. Mansour tried to keep from looking, and clutched Nadia to himself.

"We have to go, now!" the SWAT officer screamed.

Mansour and Nadia ran up the ramp and watched as it closed. It seemed like the battle was dropping off now. Soldiers dropped their weapons and raised their hands in surrender.

"It's over," Nadia said, and she found comfort in his arms.

"Soon," Mansour amended. He nodded thanks to the officers about him, and the two shakily headed for the protection of the governor.

♛

An alarm beeped overhead in the white-tiled kitchen and Mansour frantically swept his kitchen towel to and fro to get it to stop. Smoke billowed from a pot on the stovetop. He swore he'd only left it for a second.

From the living room, Nadia laughed even as a buzzer sounded and a flashing light appeared on their soundboard.

Mansour clicked it.

"Is everything all right up there? We're showing that the fire alarm tripped."

"False alarm," Mansour answered, then killed the connection. He looked over the stove and the charred remains of his omelet. It had looked so easy online.

"I take it that breakfast might take a while this morning?" Nadia asked, her voice high and flighty with the comedy of the situation.

Mansour surveyed the mess and groaned. "That depends. Do you like your eggs crunchy?" he asked.

She tittered and came to join him. "Oh, tsk, tsk, Mansour. You never were a good hand in the kitchen. Why don't you go relax in the living room so I can clean this all up and maybe make something edible?"

He smiled and gave her a soft, embarrassed kiss. "That's a wonderful idea from a wonderful mind."

"Better yet . . . we do have a cook on staff."

"An even better idea."

He went to the sofa and lay down, and she joined him a few minutes later. He did this a lot these days, now that they were in hiding. It'd been a month since they'd been pulled out of that firefight, an incident now being referred to as the Battle of the Palmiento PD by the media. They still showed clips of the fight, captured live via Eye in the Sky journalist turned Pulitzer Prize winner Gerald Reynolds. From the footage he'd seen, there had been heavy casualties on both sides and fighting had gone on over many blocks. There'd been shock across the world. But that had been at the beginning.

After the battle, he and Nadia had given Governor Schwarzenvalder the location of the documents as well as a rundown on everything they knew. He learned later from the news that mercenary forces had attacked the state capitol building itself, though he didn't see much of it at the time. They, along with the governor and other important statesmen, had been evacuated by helicopter over a city stretched through with flame and violence. Riots and looting had broken out as well, and the city had fallen into utter chaos.

In the aftermath they lived here, in a nice little villa, one of several on this island in the middle of who-knew-where. An elite special forces contingent guarded the place, and a wonderful support staff took care of all of the residents' needs. They enjoyed a life of splendor, here in the middle of nowhere. But they were cut off from communicating with the world and only able to glimpse it via a limited search engine online and the large-screen TV in their living room. It felt strange to be so far removed from Arlandica. Especially after they'd done so much to save it.

According to the news, things had snowballed after that day. The president had tried to change the constitution, using his own loyalist forces—the national guard and some militias scattered throughout the country—and threatening to kill the members of Congress if they didn't vote as he wished. None had listened, apart from those already party to his conspiracy.

Evidence of the president and multiple congressmen's treacherous dealings with the king of Terra Qurayshia hadn't just been presented to the senate, but had also been given freely to every news outlet in Arlandica and abroad. The king of Terra Qurayshia, on a diplomatic visit, found himself surrounded and captured by the FBI as he tried to flee the country.

Facing criminal charges, the president had taken desperate measures. He and his men seized a handful of members of Congress and locked themselves in the Capitol, all pledging to fight to the last man in a meaningless last stand with federal forces.

According to the news Mansour and Nadia watched on TV now, the armed forces and national guard, having refused to turn to the president's side, were trying to take back the building while attempting to do as little damage as possible. Snipers popped shots from every conceivable angle. It was only a matter of time before the building, and the president, fell.

Nadia got up, located the remote, and turned the TV off. "What are you thinking?" She lay across his lap and poked at the whiskers on his chin. "Don't tell me nothing, because you're always thinking something."

"Yeah. I was just thinking that if the president hadn't tried to make Arlandica into a dictatorship, he really could've been a dictator. He didn't think things through. Remember Jemmings? That man was a patriot, a misguided patriot anyhow, and he thought he was fighting for his country. A lot of the people who put the president into power thought that. And they were willing to go all the way to give him what he wanted."

Nadia frowned. "That's sad. That's true, but it's depressing. Do we live in such a horrible world? Is this not the magical place that Allah created for us? Did we ruin it so much?"

Mansour rubbed his chin, then rubbed his hand over Nadia's belly. "Some, of course, are corrupt, but there's so much more good in the world. The sort of people who live quiet lives and make their neighborhoods better one day at a time. Even the corrupt think they're doing the right thing, my uncle first and foremost. Sin will rise always, and we must be vigilant against it, and so we shall be."

"And when you're gone, Mansour? What happens when all of the good men are gone?"

"When I'm gone there will be Omar. And if he's gone there'll be others. There will always be others. It's the way of our world. Good will always defeat evil where it hides."

Nadia stood back up and walked to the kitchen, but she paused at its threshold. "I love you, Mansour."

He looked at her, his shining beacon, the real hero of his amazing story, and he smiled. "I love you too."

Glossary of Muslim Terminology

Alhamdulillah – All praise is to Allah.

Allah – God. Muslims, Christians, and Jews call God Allah in Arabic.

Assalamu alaikum – Peace be onto you; used as a salutation, like hello.

Awqaf – Foundation or endowment fund established by well-wishing people for a certain good cause, usually by wealthy people.

Duaa – Supplication to God.

Fajr – The early morning daily prayer, before sunrise.

Falafel – Vegetable burger made of garbanzo beans.

Habibi – my beloved for a man.

Habibti – my beloved for a woman.

Hadith – Sayings of Prophet Muhammad (PBUH)

Hajj – Pilgrimage to Mecca during the eighth to the twelfth of the month of *Thul-Hija* (the twelfth month of the Islamic calendar.)

Haram – Forbidden in Islam.

Hijab – Covering of a woman's hair, similar to a nun's habit.

Ibrik – *A* container with a spout used for storing and pouring liquid, mainly coffee.

In shaa Allah – God willing.

Jihad – To struggle for a cause. The greatest *Jihad* is to struggle with one's own self to make correct moral decisions instead of following one's own whims and desires.

Kabsa – Saudi food made mainly of rice and beef.

Mahr – Dowry.

Mandi – Saudi food made mainly of rice and beef.

Maqluba – Saudi food made mainly of rice and beef.

Masjid – Mosque, any place where people do *Sujood* (prostration to God).

Molokhia – Green Egyptian soup: leaves of *Corchorus olitorius.* It is used as a vegetable, mainly in Middle East, East African and North African countries.

PBUH – Peace be upon him.

Raka'ah – The act of bending and bowing down during prayer; the upper body would be parallel to the floor.

Rakat – Plural of *raka'ah.*

Sura – Chapter in the Qur'an; it contains 114 Suras.

Thikr – Remembering God by saying special praises to God as Prophet Muhammad (PBUH) did.

Umm Ali – A delicious Egyptian dessert equivalent to North America's bread pudding.

Umrah – An Islamic pilgrimage to Mecca. Unlike *Hajj* it can be performed at any time of the year and takes only two to four hours to perform.

About the Author

Ashraf Habbak was born and raised in Egypt. He has studied, lived, and worked in England, the United States, Saudi Arabia and now resides in the United States with his wife.

Acknowledgments

I would like to thank my friend Timothy Davis for his encouragement, Tahlia Newland for her guidance and editing, Brent Meske for his writing assistance, and Katherine Kirk for her proofreading.